THE MOST REMARKABLE MOM

THE MOST REMARKABLE MOM

From the Editors
Of *True Story* And
True Confessions

Published by True Renditions, LLC

True Renditions, LLC
105 E. 34th Street, Suite 141
New York, NY 10016

ISBN: 978-1-938877-83-4

Visit us on the web at www.truerenditionsllc.com.

Contents

HOW TO BE
A GREAT MOMMY
Life lessons from our littlest future reader!

". . . and we're having pizza for lunch, and chocolate ice cream, and Tiffany says her daddy is even gonna dress up like a clown!"

Smiling, I made a left at the light and headed down Spruce Street. "That sounds like fun, Sadie."

"And we're gonna play games, and win prizes!"

I cast a sideways glance at my daughter, smiling again. Sadie looked positively adorable, her dark, chestnut curls brushed back neatly from her face, momentarily tamed into submission by her colorful, knit cap. She looked like a regular little lady in her brand-new corduroy skirt and vest that I'd purchased specially for the occasion. This was a significant event in her life—her very first birthday party invite! Though I'd shot half a roll of film before we left the house, I was tempted to reach into my bag for my camera right then and there and snap one more picture for the family album.

Curbing the impulse, I went over the rules again, just to make sure she had them straight. "Don't forget the magic words while you're there, Sadie—please and thank you, right? And be sure to wait your turn at the games."

"I know, Mommy. You already told me that."

I made another left-hand turn. After driving two more blocks, I glanced down nervously at the invitation in my hand. Is this right? I wondered. I'd left our home on Barbara Avenue fifteen minutes earlier feeling happy and excited, but as my neatly printed directions took me deeper and deeper into a rundown section of the city, I started to feel uneasy. Surely, I thought, I must've made a wrong turn somewhere. . . .

Finally I came upon our destination—a narrow, one-way alley called Linden Place. The alley was so shabby looking that I had to drive past it twice before I could find the nerve to pull in. I drove slowly as I checked the house numbers and I wanted to cry when the number listed on the invitation in my hand matched up with a deteriorating, old apartment house where three grubby-looking men and a scantily clad girl lounged out front on the rickety porch.

Oh, Lord—it can't be! I thought with despair. This is not at all what I had in mind! I can't possibly take my daughter in there!

I slowed the car and was seriously considering crawling right on past when Sadie pointed at the crazily tilting structure. "Here it is, Mommy!" she exclaimed. "This is Tiffany's house!"

"Oh, I don't think so, Sadie, honey," I said, inching the car forward.

"Yes, it is! Look in the window!"

I glanced at the grimy, finger-smudged picture window, where a red-and-blue banner was hung, crookedly announcing: It's A Party! Then I glanced back at my daughter. Seeing the eager anticipation on her face, my heart and my head engaged in an out-and-out tug-of-war. We're not rich by any means and I've never actually considered myself a snob, but that is certainly no place for a sweet, innocent little girl! I thought with dismay. I shot another glance at the front porch and thought darkly, and those people don't exactly look like pillars of the community!

Sadie had yet to learn about the status quo and there I was, completely unprepared to give her a lesson. As it was, she'd been looking forward to the birthday party for two weeks and I wondered frantically, What possible reason can I give her for not going now, at the last minute? What am I supposed to do now?

There are days when it's really tough to be a mommy and believe me—that day was one of them.

I started planning for my baby when I got married, at age twenty-three. When I got pregnant right on schedule at the age of twenty-five, I thought I was going to be the perfect mother. I read all of the latest parenting books and decorated my nursery with all of the colors and shapes that are supposed to be intellectually stimulating for infants. Heck, I thought at the time, childrearing is really nothing more than common sense!

Back then, walking through the mall with my husband, Rob, I would see a toddler throwing a tantrum and smugly pat my belly. No child of mine will ever act like that, I thought. We'd go to visit our friends and I'd regard the toys and kid-clutter that had taken over their houses and think, Never in a million years. My house will always be neat and orderly—a happy, healthy environment.

Indeed, the first few years of Sadie's babyhood were relatively easy and I stuck to my plan. My house and my child were, if not always squeaky clean, at least presentable. I was a strict disciplinarian and I did not stand for tantrums; I adored my little girl and she worshipped the gray-flecked, Berber carpet I walked on.

When Sadie started kindergarten, though, things started to get harder. All at once I wasn't the brightest star in her heaven anymore and I had to begin the long, hard process of letting go. She would come home from school filled with stories about her pretty, new teacher and I'll admit to feeling those small, irrational pinpricks of jealousy. It's only natural, Erin, I consoled myself. And anyway, it's good for her to experience other people. I wanted my daughter to have lots of friends and I think I was every bit as excited as Sadie was the day she brought home the party invitation.

She stepped off the school bus that afternoon and raced into the house. Before I even had a chance to ask her about her day, she thrust a red envelope into my hand.

"Mommy, I got invited to a party!"

"Oh! Let me see, sweetie." I eagerly opened the envelope and pulled out the red-checkered party invitation, on which Dora the Explorer announced: It's a celebration! I smiled. "Cool beans! But who's Tiffany?"

"She's my new best friend."

I didn't recognize Tiffany's name as being one of the kids from playgroup, but as I scanned the invitation, which promised a day of games, pizza, and chocolate cake, I was proud and happy that Sadie was invited. My daughter's first birthday party, I thought. What fun!

I can still remember attending my first birthday party at about the same age—a candied-apple-and-pink-lace affair that my mother enjoyed just as much as I did. She sat in the kitchen with the other moms that day, trading recipes and childcare tips while we "party animals" ate strawberry cake and played Pin the Tail on the Donkey in the next room.

It will be good for both of us, I thought, penciling the date on the calendar in my kitchen.

I told my husband about the party that night over supper. "So we'll have to run out to the mall as soon as the dishes are done," I finished.

Rob gave me a look that plainly told me that I was going overboard—again. "Can't we just find her something at Wal-Mart?"

"Well, we could, normally, but I want this gift to be really special. And besides, Sadie will need a new outfit to wear to the party."

"It's a bunch of five-year-olds, Erin," Rob said, looking grumpy. "It's not like she needs a little black dress, for cripe's sake."

"You just don't get it, Rob. This is a milestone!"

"All right," he said with a sigh. "Whatever you say."

We went to nearly every store in the mall that evening in search of "the perfect gift." Finally we decided on a Harry Potter T-shirt and a CD featuring a collection of Disney favorites. "Look, Sadie," I said, "it even comes with a book so she can follow along with the songs!"

We took the gifts home and wrapped them in glittery, Happy Birthday paper, topped them off with shiny, red bows, and then set them on the coffee table in the living room to await the grand celebration.

And now the big day had arrived. But staring up at Tiffany's

3

apartment house, I felt my earlier joy melting away just like birthday party ice cream in the sun.

"Mommy, stop! You're going past it!"

With a sigh, I pulled into the rutted parking lot across from the house. I took my daughter by the hand and navigated the littered yard. The three men nodded pleasantly as we stepped up onto the front porch.

"You must be here for the party!" one of them said in a big, jolly voice.

"That's right." I forced a smile and pushed open the screen door.

Inside, the house was decked out with multicolored crepe paper streamers and bright, colorful helium balloons. Though she'd decorated the room to make it look as cheerful as a carnival, it obviously hadn't occurred to Tiffany's mother to tidy up. Cobwebs hung from the ceilings; the furniture was dusty and the carpets, dirty and stained. On a rickety card table in the corner, eight little goody bags were neatly lined up like happy little soldiers.

A shy, young girl, not much more than a child herself, greeted us and introduced herself as Tiffany's mother. "I'm Janelle Hendricks," she said.

"I'm Sadie," my daughter proclaimed proudly.

"Thank you so much for coming," Tiffany's mom said to me, and then, over her shoulder, "Tiffany, look who's here, honey!"

Tiffany was the dirtiest little girl I have ever seen. Her face and clothes were smudged with dirt and her hair stuck up wildly all over her head. But when she gave Sadie a wide smile, I could see how overjoyed she was that my daughter had come to her party and I felt a twinge of guilt for having even contemplated driving past.

Well, I thought with a sigh, this is obviously not going to be an opportunity for me to make new friends, but there's no reason why Sadie can't have a good time. I scanned the tiny, cramped apartment, looking for a place to plant myself, deciding, I'll just sit quietly in a corner where I can keep an eye on things.

When I suggested as much, though, Janelle looked embarrassed. "Um, I wasn't really planning on having the parents stay," she said shyly. "I mean, we don't have a lot of room here, and I didn't order that much food. You can just come back and pick her up at three o'clock, if you don't mind. . . ."

Well, what could I say to that? "Oh, well—okay, then," I stammered. "I mean, if you're sure."

I gave my daughter a kiss and then Sadie raced off to collect her goody bag and I reluctantly returned to my car. My feelings of worry were followed closely by ones of irritation as I wondered, What on earth was Janelle Hendricks thinking?

4

For Sadie's fifth birthday party that summer, I went all out. I took the day off from work to clean the house from top to bottom and I baked an enormous cake in the shape of a ballerina and I ordered enough pizza and chicken fingers to feed a small village. I hired a professional magician for the kids and I made all of the parents feel warmly welcomed with margaritas and assorted hors d'oeuvres. For my daughter's party, I thought, everything was just perfect. Couldn't Janelle have at least cleaned her house?

I thought again of the shabby neighborhood. It looked like the sort of place where bad things happen. Janelle won't let the children play outside, will she? Please, Lord, I fretted, please be with my baby in that horrid place!

I drove around aimlessly, surreptitiously circling the block for two hours. When I couldn't stand it another minute, I went back to retrieve my daughter. I pushed open the screen door and saw that a raucous game of Twister was in progress. Relief washed over me; Sadie looked perfectly safe. In fact, she looked downright happy, full of good times and chocolate cake. When she noticed me hovering in the doorway, though, she actually looked disappointed.

"Have a good time, babe?" I asked.

"Yeah! And look at all the great stuff I got!" she cried, dumping her bag of dollar-store prizes onto the filthy carpet for my inspection. I tactfully and purposely averted my gaze from the six goody bags that still sat on the card table, unopened.

Did the parents of those children follow my first instinct and simply drive on by? I wondered.

Janelle thanked me warmly for Tiffany's gifts and for letting Sadie come. As she stood before me with her hands resting on her daughter's shoulders, I felt another pang of guilt. She's not really so different from me, I realized. Whatever else Janelle Hendricks is, she's a mother doing the best she can to see that her daughter has a good time on her special day.

In the car, I quizzed Sadie about the party—who else attended, what she had to eat, and what games they played.

"It was mostly just me and Tiffany's family," she said, adding, "They're pretty nice."

"Did Tiffany like her gifts?"

"Yeah, she liked them, but she doesn't have a CD player."

"Why didn't her mother say something?" I asked. "We could've taken the CD back and gotten Tiffany something she can actually use."

"She is using it, Mom."

"But how is she using it if she doesn't have a CD player?"

"She's gonna keep it on the table beside her bed. She says she's just gonna look at the pictures until she gets a CD player. Her mom says they're saving up to buy one."

I hesitated, and then, curious about my daughter's take on the situation, I said, "Tiffany doesn't have much, does she?"

"She's got a lot on the inside, Mom."

The gentle rebuke stopped me cold. It shamed me, somehow.

I was still thinking about the comment later, as I got ready for bed. She's got a lot on the inside. . . .

I got the distinct feeling that somewhere in the experience God was trying to teach me something.

A clean, healthy home is important, there's no doubt about it, I thought. But somewhere in between Tiffany's mother and me, there has to be a balance.

I'm not the type of person who could ever live with filthy carpets and grimy windows, but sometimes, I realize, I get so caught up in cleaning and in organizing our lives that I forget that life is a celebration. In my pursuit of perfection, I sometimes lose sight of the simple fact that each day of a child's life is a gift, an invitation to enjoy the experience of parenthood—not an agenda to be rigidly followed. I've taught Sadie some very important lessons, like the value of good manners and politeness, and of playing by the rules. But Tiffany taught my daughter a couple of lessons I overlooked—lessons about friendship, and about human worth.

Maybe, just maybe, I realized, I should rethink my priorities.

And then I wondered, guiltily, How many good people have I shied away from inviting to playgroup, just because they come from the wrong side of town? How many warm, sunny days have I put off taking Sadie to the park while I cleaned out my closets? How many opportunities for bonding have been lost while I folded laundry or waited for the kitchen floor to dry?

Ironically, it took a child to teach me the true meaning of successful parenting. The truth is: Sometimes life gets messy. Sometimes, try as you might, there are cobwebs you just can't reach. Sometimes, you have to give yourself a break—you have to say, Hey, it's okay.

And hang your streamers, anyway.

THE END

Mother's Day Surprise
POEMS OF LOVE

I always imagined I'd have children some day. When I was a little girl, I played with dolls. Tommy Preston, the little boy next door, always groaned when he saw me coming because he knew I'd try to talk him into being the daddy. When I got tired of pretending to be a mommy, I turned my play area into a classroom and "taught" my dolls and stuffed animals with them all lined up against the wall.

My mother was wonderful. She was the best role model a girl could have. Not only did she hold down a full-time job after I started school, she spent time with me when I needed her. And she rarely ever lost her temper. When I misbehaved, I knew she'd handle me fairly and that the punishment would fit the "crime." She also got creative when she needed to, which is probably why I'm so successful at what I do.

Fortunately, I was a pretty good kid through high school and college. I majored in elementary education, but after I got out I decided that there were already enough dedicated people teaching the lower grades. The schools were all crying out for junior high and high school teachers. That was where they had the most attrition of teachers.

So I went back to school and became certified to teach several subjects on the secondary level. It was quite different, but I knew I could handle it. This only took me a couple years, but all the classes I took were at night since I needed to continue working.

The minute I walked through the doors of the suburban high school, I knew I'd found my calling. The kids were like sponges. At my first school, most of the children came from families of educated parents, so most of them were college-bound. In fact, there was no question that their parents had made arrangements for them to continue their education, which made things much easier for me. Those kids were there to learn.

"Miss Christiansen," one sophomore boy said. "I've learned more from you in one year than I learned the first nine years of school."

Another kid chimed in. "Yeah, it makes sense the way you teach English. I always wondered what Shakespeare had to do with me, but now I see the beauty and fun of learning literature." He added, "Shakespeare was pretty cool for his time."

Beaming, I nodded, thanked them, and then insisted they get back to their lesson. The comments from those children motivated me even more to continue working on my teaching skills. They were all very smart, and they needed someone to challenge them.

Within three years, I'd received several awards for my teaching. The principal of this school recommended me for a performance-based bonus, which I received. The next year I won "Teacher of the Year" in our county, and that was followed by a state recognition award. All this for doing my job.

I'd made friends with other teachers who spent quite a bit of time in the teachers' lounge complaining about their jobs, their pay, their students, and anything else they could think of. I hated gripe sessions, so I never hung around long enough to get involved. Negative thinking had no place in my life.

I was still single, so there was no one at home when I got back to my apartment at night. That was fine for a while because I could concentrate on grading papers and preparing my lessons. I figured that it would take me a few years to develop a good enough lesson plan to consider it the template for the rest of my teaching career.

Each day was a blessing for me in the classroom. All the eager students begged for more. And the school administration was in awe of how I'd accomplished such a feat.

"It wasn't hard," I said when I was called into the superintendent's office. "I just share my thoughts with them and encourage them to voice their opinions."

"There's more to it than that," he said. "Which is why we've decided to videotape your classes." He cleared his throat. "With your permission, of course."

"I don't know," I said slowly. "I don't want anything to threaten the integrity of the lessons."

Holding his hands out to the sides, he smiled. "We'll get everyone's permission, and everything will be above board."

After arguing with him for a few minutes, I eventually gave in. I came away agreeing that if other teachers saw the way I taught, it might help them with their own students. Wasn't that what teaching was all about? Helping children develop a love for learning? All the algebraic equations in the world and a steady diet of sentence diagrams couldn't hold a candle to a person's desire for more knowledge.

The videotaping sessions went fine. To my surprise, the students were totally uninhibited while they were being watched by the cameras. Tapes were sent home with the rest of the teachers in the school, and soon, several of them were using my techniques. The results were fabulous.

I loved the fact that everyone was benefiting, but I didn't like all the attention I was getting personally. That wasn't my purpose. All

I wanted was to turn out scholarly people. I'd always thought that a passion for learning would prevent people from falling into the traps of bad influence.

Personal fame and recognition were a distraction as far as I was concerned. I hated that everyone was focusing on me.

When I expressed my concern to the principal of the school where I taught, he told me I should speak to the superintendent. "You're the one who's been affected, so it would be more appropriate if you told him, not me."

"Do you think he'll take the time to discuss this with me?" I asked.

"Are you kidding?" he said with a loud chuckle. "He'd stop the earth from rotating if you wanted him to."

Laughing nervously as I backed out of his office, I replied, "I seriously doubt I carry that much clout."

To my surprise, the superintendent of schools in our area agreed to see me at my earliest convenience. It was that easy. One quick phone call did it.

When I walked into his office, he grinned and leaned back in his chair as he gestured toward a soft leather chair across from him. "What can I do for you, Miss Christiansen?"

As nervous as I was, I had to clear my throat to speak. "Uh, I'd really like all this publicity to stop."

He leaned forward. "The celebrity status is getting to you?"

I nodded. "That's not why I'm teaching. I'd much rather my students go out there and make names for themselves. I don't want people looking at me as anything other than a good teacher."

With a kind smile and a nod of understanding, he said, "I think you're the best thing that has ever happened to this school system, Miss Christiansen."

"Thank you," I said shyly as I glanced down at my shoes.

"What are your ultimate goals as a teacher?" he continued.

"My ultimate goals?" I said as my mind ticked ahead. "I think I'd really like to work with students who don't have as many learning opportunities as the ones I'm currently teaching."

He frowned. "You're not happy in your school?"

"I'm very happy there, but I'm not sure it's the best place for me."

I let out a heavy sigh. I didn't want my principal's boss to get the wrong idea, but I did feel compelled now to be honest and let him know what I really wanted out of teaching.

"Where, then, do you see yourself?"

I shrugged. "Maybe at a school in an underprivileged area? Somewhere that students think school is a punishment rather than a place they want to be."

Squinting, he tapped the eraser of his pencil on the desk. "Do you realize how many risks there are in schools like that?"

"Yes, I do, but that's where I think I can make the biggest difference."

Since I didn't have a family who depended on me, and I didn't see my dream of being a mom in the near future, I wasn't as concerned about the risk as someone who had small children at home. And I knew about a school on the other side of town where most of the children dropped out before they got to their last year of high school.

"Let me think about this," he said as he stood to dismiss me. "Have you discussed this with your principal yet?"

"No, not yet," I admitted. "But I will. First thing tomorrow."

"Good. I'll give you time to do that, and I'll talk to him about it. You need to stay right where you are for the remainder of the school year, though."

"Yes, of course," I said as I backed out of the office.

When I told my principal the next morning, he didn't like the idea at all. "You belong here, Miss Christiansen," he told me. "Some of those kids in the other schools would eat you alive."

"I hate to tell you this," I said with conviction and hesitation. "I feel like they need me more than the kids here. All my students have parents who expect big things from them. They have support at home. I want a challenge."

It took me a long time, but eventually, he gave me his blessing to apply for a transfer. "Just remember that if you ever want to come back, don't let pride stand in your way."

I assured him I wouldn't. And I got in touch with the superintendent of schools, who'd already discussed it with the principal.

"If you're absolutely positive this is what you want," he told me, "I can put you in a very needy school next fall."

"That's what I want," I told him. "I have no doubt."

I finished out the school year with more than half my class mastering Shakespeare and other fine literature. The rest of the kids, although not totally sure of themselves, had a pretty good understanding, which was all I could hope for. They'd all learned what I was about to do, so they threw me a surprise going-away party on the last day of school. I felt honored that they cared enough about me to do that.

Summer went by quickly. I was anxious to blaze new trails, although many people were worried about me. At the superintendent's advice, I took a course during the summer on how to deal with difficult children who had major problems. I learned quite a bit.

Teachers always go in a couple weeks before the children to get started on lesson plans and for meetings with the rest of the faculty. I found myself in the midst of a hodgepodge of teachers, mostly people who'd accepted whatever they could get, just to get their foot in the door of the school system. They couldn't believe I'd actually chosen to leave the cushy school to come here.

"You must be nuts," one woman remarked. "I'd give anything to have your old job."

Another person agreed with her. "Have you thought about what you're giving up?"

There was one other teacher, though, who watched me react to those comments. Later on during the workshops, she came up to me and patted me on the back.

"I think that what you're doing is wonderful," she said. "I love teaching these kids."

"Did you do the same thing?" I asked. "I mean, did you come from another school?"

"No," she slowly replied, "this was my first teaching job, and that was eight years ago. But you have to be aware that this won't be easy."

I laughed nervously. "I realize that. I just hope I'm up to the task."

"Make sure they know who's in charge immediately. Once you establish that, you can start teaching. If you don't, they'll run all over you."

"Okay, thanks," I told her. I'd already learned to do that in my class.

"I'll give you some helpful hints before school starts for the kids," she offered.

"I appreciate that." And I really did. I could tell I'd need all the help I could get, based on some of the stories I was hearing.

My classroom was in dire need of paint, but there wasn't time to get it done before the kids started school. I added things to my list as they came up so I could start requesting supplies from the school administration office. There also weren't enough erasers and a few other things I considered essential to being able to teach.

When I called in my requests, the woman in the administration supplies office just laughed at me. "We can't keep sending you all those things when they'll disappear in a few days."

"What do you mean?" I asked her.

"In that school, supplies have a very short life span. If they're not kept under lock and key, they somehow manage to walk out the door."

I told her I understood, then left the school and headed straight for the teaching supply store. I bought the things I needed with my own money and vowed to keep trying to get them from the district.

When the first student walked into the classroom, I was pleasantly surprised. It was a boy who actually smiled at me as he took a seat on the front row.

"Hi," I told him. "I'm Miss Christiansen."

He just kept on smiling at me. He'd gotten into a very uncomfortable-looking position that I wondered how he maintained. He was slouched down in the chair, his legs sticking out into the aisle.

"Why don't you sit up?" I asked. "You'll be a whole lot more comfortable."

His smile faded. "You don't know nothin', do ya?" he said, his voice sounding much more ominous than he looked.

I was stunned. "We can talk later," I told him. Several of the other students had begun filing into the classroom.

As the desks filled with students, I noticed that they all seemed to know each other. And they were very social. In fact, they were so social their voices nearly deafened me.

Putting my hands over my ears, I cleared my throat. A few kids on the front row turned to look at me, but they quickly turned back to what they were doing.

The bell rang, and they kept right on talking as if I wasn't there. Although I'd asked for that class, I still hadn't been prepared for this. What in the world was a teacher supposed to do when her students ignored her?

It became obvious that I had to get their attention somehow. I glanced around for an idea then it came to me.

Going around behind my desk, I pulled out my chair. Then I put it in front of my desk, making sure it was sturdy enough to hold me. A few kids had turned to watch what I was about to do. Good, I thought. This should get their attention.

I was glad I'd worn slacks, something I rarely did before. But I knew I'd have a lot of physical kids, so I decided to dress like this just in case.

As soon as I was certain the chair would hold me, I jumped up on it and started waving my arms. Everyone grew quiet and looked at me—some with wide eyes and others with a lack of interest. When one boy turned to make a comment to the girl behind him, I put my hands behind my ears.

"Would you care to share that with everyone?"

All eyes turned to him, and he started to squirm. The girl began to giggle.

I cleared my throat. "I'd really like to hear what you have to say."

He shifted his feet beneath the desk in front of him, but he didn't make eye contact with me. I let out a long sigh.

"If anyone has something to say in my classroom, that's fine, as long as you say it to all of us."

"Uh, you the new teacher?" one guy asked. "The one from the other side of town?"

"Yeah," a girl in the back said. "The one who taught those rich kids last year?"

I shrugged. "It all depends on what you consider rich." Then I

12

hopped down off the chair. "My definition of rich is a person who uses their potential to the maximum and contributes to society in a positive way."

"What's that supposed to mean?" the first boy asked. "We don't speak your language."

"What's your name?" the outspoken girl asked.

"Miss Christiansen," I replied.

"What's your first name?" she said, staring at me in defiance.

I sucked in a breath and slowly let it out. "That doesn't matter. You may call me Miss Christiansen."

A few people started snickering, but she didn't say anything. I wasn't sure if I'd made my point, but I could hope.

The first day was pretty much like that all the way through. I got absolutely nothing accomplished with the exception of telling them my name and establishing the fact that I would stand on a chair to get their attention.

After the last bell rang, I was exhausted. The teacher who'd spoken to me during the workshops magically appeared at my door, leaning against the frame, her arms folded over her chest, smiling at me.

"Well?" she said. "How'd it go?"

I shrugged. "Okay, I guess."

"I heard you stood tall today."

With a chuckle, I replied, "Yeah, I didn't know what else to do to get their attention. This is much harder than I thought."

"Yes, but I think that once you hit your stride, you'll do fine. Your heart's in the right place."

She pulled away from the doorway and came on inside, her hand extended. "I never formally introduced myself. I'm Gail Peters."

"Hi, Gail. I'm Lori Christiansen."

"Well, Lori, looks like we're in for a particularly rough year."

I scrunched my forehead. "Why do you say that?"

"The monster is back."

"The monster?"

"Yeah," she said as she sat down in a student's desk. "Jimmy Bryant."

That name rang a bell, so I figured he must be in one of my classes. I couldn't place him, though. "What does he look like?" I asked.

After she described him, I realized he was the one I'd reprimanded for turning around and talking to the girl behind him. I told Gail.

She widened her eyes and said, "Oh."

"Oh?" I repeated as I sat down across from her. "What do you mean by oh?"

"Jimmy is one boy who doesn't let anyone get the best of him. Watch your back."

My palms began to sweat as I laughed nervously. "He can't be too bad. What kind of things does he do?"

"Well," she began. "For starters, last year he set the cafeteria on fire when they wouldn't give him an extra dessert."

"Can't he be prosecuted for that?" I asked. "Arson is pretty serious."

"Oh, yes, but that doesn't stop him. He's done many things that are just as bad."

I sat and listened to one story after another of how Jimmy had stuffed students in lockers and not let them out, how he'd set off firecrackers in the chemistry lab making everyone flee for their life, and how he'd stolen from almost every teacher at the school. This kid was a serious repeat offender.

"Why do they keep letting him back in school?" I asked.

"The system," she stated flatly. "He'll be here until he's twenty-one, then he'll wind up in prison somewhere."

I rubbed my eyes. "What do you think he'll do to me?" I finally asked.

"Who knows? Jimmy operates on the element of surprise."

"Oh, that's just great," I said. "Any suggestions?"

Gail stood up and motioned for me to follow. "Let's go to the office where all the student records are kept. Bring your class rosters."

She looked at all the names in my classes and told me which ones I needed to get control over. "If you can get them to cooperate, the rest of them will fall into place."

"They're the ring leaders, huh?" I asked.

"You might say that."

I looked up all those students and made notes by their names. Then I went home and began to think about what to do. I had no idea it would be this tough. All the movies and television shows about problem students didn't even come close to what I was dealing with. For the first time, I questioned my sanity in having transferred here. At least I knew I could always go back since the principal had told me he'd make a spot for me if I wanted it.

The next day I went to my classroom feeling a little nervous about what Jimmy might do. I let out a sigh of relief when he didn't show up by the time the bell rang. That was my first mistake.

Halfway into the class, the fire alarm in the hall went off. Thinking it was a fire drill, I instructed the children to line up and leave the school in an orderly fashion. They ignored me and stormed out of the classroom, almost knocking me down in the process. I was just about to leave when a hand came out from behind the door and pulled me back in.

I gasped as I turned around. It was Jimmy. He grinned at me with an evil look in his eyes. My heart hammered in my chest.

"You don't mess with me," he said through clenched teeth. "Anyone who makes a fool of me will pay."

I swallowed hard and willed my brain to work. After a long pause, I licked my lips and said, "Jimmy, I had no intention of making a fool of you."

"But you did, and that's what matters."

He wasn't letting go of my arm but was looking me in the eye. That would've been good if I hadn't been so frightened. I tried my best to keep the fear from showing, but I wasn't sure it was working.

"All I want to do," I told him, "is teach high school English."

"That's too bad, isn't it?" He shook me so hard my teeth rattled.

I closed my eyes, then looked him in the eye again. "What are you going to do, Jimmy?" I bravely asked.

He loosened his grip. "I haven't decided yet."

I chose that moment to yank myself free. To my surprise he didn't try to stop me.

"Look," I said, taking a chance and hoping he might listen. "If I give you a chance to save your pride, will you cooperate with me?"

Jimmy gave me a strange look. "Cooperate with a teacher? Me? I don't think so."

"Then tell me what I can do to get you off my case."

"You can leave me alone." He took a step back and began to look over his shoulder nervously.

"Are you expecting someone?" I asked.

Jimmy spun around and glared at me again. "I'm always expecting someone. People in this school are out to get me. I don't trust anyone."

"That's a shame," I told him. "I think trust is something people have to earn. If you haven't earned it, maybe I can show you how."

"You can't show me nothin', lady," he said before he turned and ran out the door.

Within seconds, a couple of policemen walked through my classroom door. One of them walked around the classroom, looking under desks and behind shelves, while the other came up to me. I was still shaking from being held hostage by Jimmy.

"Where'd he go?" the cop asked.

I pointed to the door, my hand shaking. "He left right before you got here. I'm surprised you didn't see him."

He placed his hands on his hips and shook his head. "Jimmy Bryant is one slippery dude. We can't seem to get through to him."

"Why is he still here?" I asked.

The cop studied me for a moment before he said, "You're new here, aren't you?"

I nodded. "I transferred from another school in the district."

"You might want to consider going back. This school is filled with problem children. Most of these kids only have one parent, and they're rarely home. Some of them live on the streets, and the only meal they get is lunch at school."

"Really?" I asked. I hadn't realized it was that bad. "What about Jimmy?"

"He lives in his car, a beat up old wreck he wound up with when his father split."

"Where's his mother?"

"Who knows?" the officer asked. "Probably in a crack house somewhere."

This was all information that wasn't in Jimmy's records. In spite of what he'd done to me, my heart went out to him. The poor kid didn't have any guidance. That was the saddest thing I'd ever seen. He was obviously a born leader, but with what was going on in his life, he'd wind up leading a lot of people to destruction.

I went home that night with a mission in mind. At first I had no idea what I'd do to accomplish my goal, but it wasn't too long before a plan began to formulate in my mind.

The next morning, I made an announcement to my first class to get a feel for how they'd respond. "Next week, we're having a pizza party after school. Whoever participates during classroom discussions is invited."

One girl in the front row looked at me like she didn't trust me. "How do we know you'll come through for us? Teachers love to tell us one thing and do another."

"You'll just have to trust me," I told her.

Another kid piped up, "I don't trust nobody."

I could tell this wasn't going over very well. I held my hands up to quiet them down. "Okay, tell you what. We'll start with something else, and then work up to a pizza party."

"Like what?" the first girl asked. She was obviously the spokesperson for the class.

I thought for a few second before I replied. "How about candy?"

"All depends on what kind," the girl said.

Taking a step toward her, I said, "What kind do you want?"

"I like chocolate bars with caramel."

Someone else yelled out, "I can't eat those. They get stuck in my teeth."

Then a few more kids got into the discussion, and before I had a chance to control them, they were arguing over what kind of candy I should bring. I had to stand up on the chair to get their attention again.

"I'll bring a variety, okay?"

All the kids looked around at each other then nodded. "Okay, but if

16

you don't bring the candy, we won't be in your discussion. You'll have to show it to us before we talk."

I smiled at the boy who said that. "It's a deal."

When I told Gail my plan, she shook her head. "Bribing them? You should be ashamed of yourself."

"I couldn't think of anything else to do," I told her. "When the police officer told me about Jimmy living in the car and that the only meal he got was here, I figured that this would be the best way to get their attention."

"Smart thinking," she finally said. "Let me know if it works."

On my way home, I stopped at a discount store and bought enough bags of candy for all my classes. I made sure there were three different kinds, just in case someone didn't like something.

"Don't pull it all out at once," Gail said when she came in to make sure I'd remembered my promise to the kids. "If you do, it'll be gone by the end of the first period."

I found an old coffee can and poured candy from each bag into it. All of it was individually wrapped, so I figured it would be okay.

The students all came into the classroom and sat down a little more quickly than usual. When the bell rang, the outspoken girl said, "Where's the candy?"

I lifted the coffee can. "Right here."

She folded her arms, smiled, and stuck her legs out in front of her, something they all seemed to do a lot. I realized early on that this was their way of making a statement of defiance.

The class discussion left much to be desired, but I gave them each a couple pieces of candy if they at least tried. Everyone got some. By the end of the day, I didn't have to say anything to the class. They were all eager to talk. They'd heard about it from the other students.

Although my plan had worked, I quickly realized that these students expected something from now on. I had to come up with something else—something I could afford, since the school didn't reimburse me for anything I did to bribe the students.

I tried rewarding them with certificates for not having to redo their homework, but since they rarely did homework assignments anyway, this plan didn't work. This was turning out to be more challenging now that I had their attention. I had to keep it.

Gail had a suggestion. "Why don't you talk to some of the local merchants? Maybe the bakery has some day-old cookies they can donate. Or get a hold of one of the candy companies?"

"Great idea," I said. "I'll try that."

It took me more than a dozen calls to get three companies to donate goodies for the kids. And none of them were willing to do it on a regular basis.

With the same general concept in mind, I also approached a couple of the civic groups in the nicer sections of town, and I got donations for my cause. I didn't want to only buy candy, so I made a list of several things I could do.

"You're brilliant," Gail said. "These kids need a few basic things, like food and treats that they don't often get at home, and you're dangling it in front of them to make them perform."

"You make it sound bad," I told her. "Almost like I'm an animal trainer."

"In a way, you are," she said. "Even Jimmy is participating from what I've heard. That's a major accomplishment for him."

The students knew that when they came to my class they'd get something. They were never sure what it was, which made it all the more interesting. I began to enjoy the element of surprise, so I spent a lot of my classroom planning time coming up with unusual things.

"Bubble gum?" one girl said. "They never let us chew gum in school."

"I had to beg the principal to allow this," I admitted. "But the first time someone drops it on the floor or sticks it under a desk, that's the end of the gum. I'll let you chew it in class, but you have to spit it out in the garbage can on your way out of the class."

I didn't really expect them to cooperate, but they surprised me. No one disobeyed the rule of not being allowed to take the gum past the classroom door.

Several of the kids started coming up to me after class, asking if I'd help them understand what we were studying. Since I didn't have anyone to go home to, I stayed late and helped them until I thought they had a decent understanding. And for asking, I had rewards for them, too.

By the end of the first semester, I had a full classroom for at least an hour after school let out. The principal and all the other teachers were amazed at the transformation in these students. They started talking about it at one of the teachers' meetings.

"These kids are not only doing their assignments for you," one of the math teachers said. "They're doing homework from my class, too."

Gail laughed out loud. "Yeah, but some of them ask me when I'm going to start giving out candy. I can't afford it. I'm a single mom with two kids to feed."

I smiled back at her. "I have plenty of stuff for your students," I told her when she and I were alone. "I couldn't say anything in front of the other teachers, but since you've helped me so much, I want to help you."

Word got out to the superintendent that I had been successful in my first semester. He sent me a letter commending me for a job well done. In fact, he'd admitted he didn't think I'd last the whole year, and he was pleasantly surprised.

But I was still not totally happy with the results. I knew that most of the students responded well to rewards, but I thought I should be getting more from Jimmy. He was still closed off, and I got the feeling he only spoke during our class discussions to get the treats.

"What does Jimmy do after school?" I asked Gail. "I kept hoping he'd join the others who come in for help, but he never does."

She shrugged. "Who knows what Jimmy does? I suspect he just walks the streets and terrorizes children and little old ladies."

"I have to do something."

Gail placed her hand on my arm and looked me in the eye. "Lori," she said. "Don't take the whole world on your shoulders. You've already worked miracles around here. You can't be everything to these kids. Face it, honey; some of them won't survive the system."

Shaking my head, I replied, "I just can't accept that. I can't let Jimmy continue to self-destruct. He's too smart for me to let that happen."

"Don't say I didn't warn you," she said as she walked away.

I meant what I told her, but no matter how hard I thought about it, nothing came to mind. So I decided to just wing it with Jimmy. And I'd try playing it straight without any psychology involved.

As his class was leaving one day, I called him to the side. He hesitated before he held back.

"Whaddya want?" he asked.

"Is it possible for you to hang around after school for a few minutes this afternoon?" I asked.

He looked at me then shuffled his feet. "For what?"

My mind went into overdrive. I now knew I had to think of something that would appeal to him. My thoughts of not using psychology on him flew out the window.

"I have to move my desk, and I need a big, strong guy to help me do it."

A guarded expression was still on his face, but I could tell he was thinking about it. Finally, he nodded. "Just me? Or would you like for me to get one of my friends to help us?"

I grinned. "If you know someone who can help, that would be great."

"See ya later," he said as he walked out of the classroom. His step seemed a little lighter, although I thought that could've been my imagination.

I'd stuck a couple of individually wrapped pastries in my locked file cabinet. They'd come in handy after Jimmy and his friend moved my desk. Then I realized I didn't have any idea where I wanted them to move it, since that was a spur of the moment thought that had just popped into my mind.

I had to think of something by the end of the day. I got an idea to totally rearrange the classroom, so by the time they got there, I was excited.

It took them about half an hour, but when they were finished, I took out the pastries and handed them to the boys. Jimmy started to open it right there, but then he stop and he thought about it then he tried to hand it back to me.

"You don't have to do this," he said.

I pushed his hand back and said, "But I want to. You were really a big help to me today, Jimmy. I've always wanted to have a horseshoe configuration in the classroom. I thought it might be fun for a change."

Jimmy took a quick look around the classroom and shook his head. "This is weird, but then so are you."

Slowly, I nodded. "Thanks, Jimmy. I consider that a compliment coming from you."

He walked out of the room, scratching his head with one hand and stuffing the pastry in his mouth with the other. For the first time, I felt like I'd really gotten through to him.

The students all seemed to like their desks in a horseshoe around my desk. It really made it easy to have discussion about the literature we were studying. And Jimmy was proud of the fact that he'd been the one to help me. He began to open up more and more.

By April, several students had come to me to ask for personal advice. Most of it was pretty basic, involving moral issues that were pretty cut and dry. I always told them to do the right thing, even if that was the hardest thing to do. "That way you won't have to worry later," I told them.

There were some things I needed to refer them to someone else about, like when I was informed of a student's eating disorder. This was something I wasn't equipped to deal with.

Although I hadn't covered even half the material I normally did, I knew I'd made major progress with these children. They were developing a love for literature because they now understood it. Even Jimmy was caught reading when he thought no one was looking.

"You're amazing," Gail told me at the April teachers' workshop. "You've been here less than a year, and you have those kids eating out of the palm of your hand."

I tilted my head back and laughed. "Yes, literally."

Mother's Day was fast approaching, and I wanted to do something I'd done before. At my other school, I had the students all write poetry for their moms. I was in awe of their talent, and I had no doubt these kids would do just as well. But nearly half of them didn't have moms at home.

Not one to be too discouraged, I came up with another idea. I told the students that for Mother's Day we were going to write poetry to the women in our lives who made the biggest difference. I told them that my own mother had died several years ago, so I was writing my poem for a friend from college.

At first, they all grumbled about having to write poetry. "That's for girls," one of the toughest boys in my second period class said.

"Do you like rap music?" I asked. I knew he did because he came in rapping almost every day.

"Sure I do," he told me as he bobbed his head.

"Rap is poetry set to a rhythm. In fact, all music with words is poetry. If you look at the lyrics without the musical notes, you'll see what I mean."

"So I can write rap?" he asked.

I nodded. "Yes, as long as it's for a woman who's made a difference in your life and is appropriate for the classroom."

He snapped his fingers and said, "Man, I can do that."

All the kids were talking about it as they filed out of the classroom. One girl lingered behind. I smiled at her.

"Hi, Tanya. Can I help you with something?" I asked.

"I write poetry," she said shyly.

This was the last girl I ever thought would do something like write poetry. She dressed provocatively, and she never seemed to understand what was going on. Her attention always seemed to be on the guy she sat behind.

"That's wonderful, Tanya," I said. "Then you should enjoy this assignment."

She nodded. "I will." Then she left the room.

It was still a couple of weeks before Mother's Day, but some of them told me they'd already started on their poems. I was pleasantly surprised to hear this, since I expected them to wait until the last minute.

The Monday before Mother's Day, I noticed several of the kids in my second period class whispering, then glancing up at me. Sometimes they laughed but other times they just nodded. I knew they were up to something, but I had no idea what.

On Friday morning before school started, Gail told me, "Something's up with your kids, Lori. I don't know what it is, but I've heard your name mentioned several times this week."

"I know," I admitted, "and it's starting to make me a little nervous."

"It would make me nervous, too," she said as she ducked out of the classroom. "Good luck."

I didn't have much planned for that day. The students knew that their Mother's Day assignment was due, so I figured I'd get a few of them to read their poems to the class. There were enough of them who thrived on the attention that I knew the time would be filled.

When the first period students arrived, I noticed a certain amount of tension in the air. Whatever was going on, I knew I'd find out soon.

As soon as I closed the door, everyone exchanged a glance, then they stood up and said in unison, "Happy Mother's Day, Miss Christiansen!"

Then they all stormed my desk with their poems. "I wanna read mine first," one of the girls said.

"No, me first," another girl said, edging her out of the way.

"You may all read your poems, but please sit down first."

The all nodded and did as they were told—a little too quickly for my comfort. Something is definitely not right with them today, I thought.

The minute the first girl read her poem, it dawned on me what was going on. They'd all written their poems to me.

Tears quickly formed in my eyes as they said sweet words about their feelings toward me. When I heard the words "shining star," "beautiful angel," and "magical lady," all of them referring to me as a teacher, I openly wept. I didn't hold back, and they all got quiet.

Unexpectedly, the first girl turned and said, "I told you she was the crying type."

Everyone laughed, including me. Then I stood up, thanked them, and told them that they were my shining stars, beautiful angels, and magical students. "You've made this year one of the best ever for me," I told them.

All my classes did the exact same thing, and each one was just as wonderful as the first. Even Jimmy had a poem for me, although his was only four lines long. But it meant the world to me.

At the end of the day, several students hung around and helped me clean the classroom. Tanya, the girl who'd told me she wrote poetry, informed me she was the brains behind the plan. Somehow I had the feeling she might be.

"I believe in expressing my feelings through poetry," she said. "And since you've been like a mother to so many of us, I thought this would be a good thing to do."

Once again, I started crying. Tanya just stood there with an eraser in her hand and laughed at me. I cracked a smile and started laughing right along with her.

I'm now in my second year at that school. From what I've heard, all the incoming juniors have requested me for their English teacher, although there's not enough room for all of them in my classes. The principal has asked me to give a workshop on how to appeal to these children. I agreed to do it because I sincerely love children.

As the years passed by, I realized that motherhood meant so much more than having my own children. It meant being a good example and mentor to young people who need me. Although no one has ever called me "Mom" or "Mother," I have hundreds of children I'd do anything for.

THE END

I DON'T WANT TO BE
A MOMMY, AGAIN

A sob caught in my throat as I looked down at the little strip with the pink line, lying on the counter. Blinking back the tears, I wanted to try again. But I knew another test would show the same results as the last three had: I was pregnant!

I loved my sons, but I didn't want another baby. Not now!

"Why, dear Lord?" I cried. "Why did this have to happen? This is my time—my chance."

With my stomach churning, I hurried to the kitchen for a cracker, then sat down at the table and took a bite of the cracker. I looked through the window at the trees, so beautifully clothed in the warm colors of fall.

I glanced over at my rose garden. Next spring, the pink and red roses would make a beautiful bouquet for Mother's Day . . . and I'd have three children.

Yet, with this morning sickness, how could I finish my fall classes at the university and pretend that things were all right when they weren't?

My husband, Gavin, had been overjoyed when I told him about my possible pregnancy. "Maybe we'll have a girl this time, Em," he said, brushing my lips with a kiss. "A baby girl that looks exactly like her mother."

By evening, I felt exhausted and unable to think any further. I slipped into my nightgown, fell into bed, and looked down at my stomach—imaging how it would look in four months' time.

Tears caught in my eyelashes and streamed down my face. This problem hung like an albatross around my neck, threatening to choke me.

I closed my eyes, hoping against hope that Gavin would think I was asleep. I felt too tired to argue.

Gavin slipped into bed and gathered me close. "Emily, everything will work out. You'll see."

"Stop it, Gavin," I begged.

He kissed my shoulder and lowered his face. "I love you. I want this baby. Don't do anything foolish."

I bit my lip, trying to hold back the tears. I reached up and patted his cheek. "Go to sleep, please. We'll talk about it tomorrow."

I lay awake for hours. I looked over at the moonlight streaming through the bedroom window. Thoughts of this unwanted pregnancy drowned any thoughts of sleep. Could I bring myself to have an abortion?

Gavin and I had talked about the issue of abortion more than once. Having been brought up to attend church faithfully and to believe in God, he was firmly against abortion.

I doubled up the pillow and poked it under my head. I'd always believed that a woman had a right to say what happened to her body. But I never thought I'd have to make a decision like that, though.

The next afternoon, I sat at the snack bar in the student union with Colleen, my classmate and closest friend. I bit at my fingernail, then winced as the nail broke.

"Okay, what's bothering you?" she asked, sipping the soda she'd ordered. "What's wrong?"

I twisted a napkin, torn it into little pieces, then threw the wad of paper on the table. "Oh, Colleen, it's just awful!"

"You worry about your grades," Colleen told me, "but you always do well."

"This isn't about grades."

"What else could it be?"

"I don't know what I'm going to do!"

Colleen smiled. "Well, let's see. A wonderful husband. Two super boys." She leaned across the table. "In the spring semester, you'll be in student teaching, then graduation."

"I've struggled so hard to get back into college," I cried.

Colleen handed me a tissue. "Well, are you going to tell me what's going on?"

My head throbbed. Bile from the morning sickness filled my mouth, threatening to send me to the bathroom. It felt like a death sentence.

"I'm pregnant," I told her. "And I don't want to be!"

"I'm sorry. Really sorry."

I bit my lip. "I dropped out of college, worked, and helped Gavin finish school. Now, it's my turn to graduate. He promised me." I leaned across the table. "I've made a decision," I told her. "Lots of women have done this." I looked at Colleen and gathering every ounce of courage I possessed and announced, "I'm having an abortion."

"What did Gavin say about that?"

"He doesn't want me to do it, but it's my life," I told her. "Mark and James are both in school, and I don't want to be pregnant."

"I know how much you wanted to teach," she soothed. "But maybe a baby to love, a little girl. . . ."

I shook my head furiously. "Don't, Colleen—please. I can't fight both you and Gavin. I haven't told the boys. It's best if they don't know."

Colleen glanced at her watch. "I've got a class, but I'll stay if you need help getting home."

I pushed myself to my feet. "I'm going to skip my last class," I told her. "I've got to leave."

"Call if you need me. Promise?"

I nodded. Somehow I managed to drive home and get into bed. But I fell into a troubled sleep. Sometime in the night, I awakened to feel Gavin wrap his arms around me. Restless, I gently moved his hand, tiptoed out to the kitchen, and started a pot of coffee.

As I poured the water, I glanced over at the peanut butter and jelly on the counter and the breakfast dishes in the sink.

"Can't anyone pick up after themselves?" As I reached for a cup in the cabinet, I noticed the family album open on the dining room table. My heart caught in my throat. Mark and James's baby pictures were lying on the table.

As I poured a cup of coffee, I remembered my first Mother's Day. Mark was seven months old. What a proud mommy I had been. Gavin went out and bought three red corsages. I laughed remembering how I tried to keep Mark from eating the petals as we drove to Sunday morning services at church.

Now, I dabbed at my nose and thought about the baby. I loved my boys, and deep in my heart, I always wanted a girl, but not now. At times, I was very angry with Gavin . . . why couldn't he understand?

How many times in the last few weeks had I tried to explain to him how I felt? We always ended up arguing. Then came the moments of guilt and the overwhelming feelings of being alone.

The next morning after Gavin and the boys left, I made a telephone call. "Colleen, I need you today."

"What is it? What can I do?"

"This afternoon I'm going to have the abortion." I held my breath as a long pause came over the telephone.

After what seemed like an eternity, Colleen spoke. "Are you sure you've thought this over? I wish you'd give yourself more time."

I squeezed my eyes closed as a wave of nausea swept over me. "I've run out of time," I told her, firmly. "Will you go with me?"

"Of course, I will. I don't want you to be alone."

I leaned against the wall for support. "We'll leave after our 12:30 class, okay?"

"Okay," came the quiet answer.

Although I went to my class, I couldn't keep my mind on the instructor's words. Could I really go through with the abortion? What would Gavin say? And what if the baby turned out to be a girl? Finally, I left the classroom, went to my car, and waited for Colleen.

"Want me to drive?"

"No, I can do this," I said, with the confidence I didn't feel. I slid behind the wheel, took a deep breath and pulled into the traffic.

We never reached the hospital. A pickup truck filled with teenagers on their school lunch hour zoomed out of an alley and smashed into my side of the car. Colleen screamed. Thrown against the steering wheel, I hit my head and lost consciousness. I don't remember the drive to the hospital.

When I opened my eyes, my chest hurt as if someone were standing on it. I could feel someone lifting me onto a gurney. "Oh, oh," I screamed.

"It's all right," the nurse said, patting my arm. "Who would you like us to contact?"

Pains shot through my stomach. I could barely speak. "Gavin, my husband," I managed to say.

I closed my eyes, trying to block out the pain as the nurse cut off my clothes. "How is Colleen?"

"Your friend was treated for minor injuries," the male voice told me. The oxygen mask came over my mouth. "And the teenagers escaped with only cuts and bruises."

The pain stabbed through my stomach again, nearly doubling me over, but I willed myself to open my eyes. "Where's my husband? Why isn't he here?"

"He's been called," the doctor said. He put his stethoscope to my chest. "You have multiple injuries and possible internal bleeding. Let's take you over to X-ray and see what we have."

I tried to lie still while the doctor worked on me, but I hurt all over. Tears slipped down my cheeks. Where was Gavin?

"We'll give you something for the pain," the doctor assured me.

Even though my chest and stomach hurt beyond words, alarm shot through me. "I'm pregnant," I blurted out. "Will the medication hurt my baby?"

I couldn't believe what I had just asked. Although I'd planned on an abortion, the motherly instinct was coming through. Deep in my heart, perhaps I wanted this baby as much as my husband did.

After a short a short nap I awakened, and Gavin was waiting for me. He brushed my lips with a kiss. "Hi, sweetheart," he whispered, placing my hand in his. "I'm here."

Tears caught in my eyelashes as I held his hand, afraid he might disappear any minute. "Oh, Gavin," I whispered. "Thank God you've come."

"We think you may have some internal bleeding," the doctor told my husband. "We're moving her into ICU."

I gripped Gavin's hand. "Don't leave me," I begged.

My husband leaned closer. "Not a chance on it. I'm with you."

They moved me to the intensive care unit, hooked me to the heart monitor, and started IVs. The nurse was taking my vital signs when the doctor stepped into the room. "We believe your internal organs are bruised and your spleen is enlarged."

"Am I losing the baby?"

"You're not hemorrhaging," he said, "and that's a good sign. We should have the results from the other tests in the morning."

Gavin held my hand. I blinked back the tears. "I'm sorry I ruined the car."

"That doesn't matter," he whispered. "Colleen filled me in. What I want to know is why you tried to go to the clinic without me?"

"Because you wouldn't listen to me," I cried. "You didn't care how I felt."

"I do care," he muttered, touching my lips with a kiss. "I love you."

"Just five minutes," the nurse cautioned.

An hour later, Gavin sat by my bed again. "I'm sorry I was gruff," he said in a hushed voice.

I caught my breath and tried not to move. It hurt too much. "I wanted you to go to the clinic with me. I needed you beside me."

"You didn't tell me what you were planning, though," he said. "You didn't give me a chance."

Tears trickled down my cheek, and I turned my head toward the wall.

"We believe your liver was lacerated," the doctor told me, after he examined me the next morning. "But we're trying to avoid X-rays because of the fetus."

He turned to face Gavin. "She's not out of danger yet. If the internal bleeding continues, we'll still need to take her to surgery."

"And the baby?" I breathed.

The doctor leaned against the wall. "The more time that passes, the better chance you have for the pregnancy to continue and for the liver to heal itself."

As the doctor turned away, Gavin leaned over the bed. "I've done this to you," he whispered. "You begged me to understand, but I couldn't—wasn't willing to let go of my conviction. If only I could turn back the clock. If only I could have another chance with you. Please."

I wanted to tell Gavin he had been right, but I was afraid. I couldn't stand to feel rejected—abandoned and all alone—again.

After surviving three days in ICU, they moved me to a private room. I gave Gavin my best smile when he entered the room with a huge bouquet of roses.

"Hi, Em." He grinned, setting the roses on the table next to the bed. He took my hand. "Baby, I love you so much! I was so scared of losing you. If you still want this abortion . . . it's your decision."

I reached over and patted his hand. How long had I waited to hear those words? But, was this what I really wanted? I tried to pull Gavin's arm closer. "I've needed your love, your understanding, and your support for these months. I needed to know you were with me no matter what."

Despite the IV, Gavin gently put his arms around me and whispered, "I love you. Without you, Emily Rose Fielding, life has no meaning."

I placed a kiss on his cheek. "I've never loved you more than I do now at this minute," I told him. "But, with you by my side, we can face whatever comes to us—together."

Gavin helped Mark and James pick a bouquet of roses from my garden on the next Mother's Day. Callie has wound her daddy around her little fingers. Her brothers treat her like a doll, spoiling her shamelessly.

I stayed home during the spring semester and rocked my baby, then finished my college education. I plan to teach first grade at a neighborhood elementary school.

Now I know how fragile, but very precious, life really is. Callie is such a special gift. I've learned the true meaning of Mother's Day.

THE END

WILL HE EVER HAVE
A MOTHER'S LOVE?

I pressed the phone to my ear, then slumped down in the kitchen chair. I could hear my sister crying on the other end.

"It's Ryan. He has leukemia."

It was about her son—and it was horrible news.

My nephew.

Only, he wasn't just my nephew—he was also my son. Only a handful of people knew the real truth, and my husband and three children weren't included in that handful of people.

The sobbing on the other end of the line continued. I swallowed hard and searched for the comforting words that I knew Justine was waiting to hear from me. Despite the age difference—I was twenty-six and she was thirty-five—we were close.

But we rarely see one another. I live in San Diego, and she lives in Miami, just about as far away from each other as two sisters can get.

That had been a stipulation on the day that I'd given birth to Ryan. No one was to know, and Justine and her husband were to take Ryan and move away. I'd only been fourteen at the time. We'd see each other on holidays, or when necessary, such as a funeral or a family reunion.

We talked on the phone once a week, however, and kept in touch daily through email. I knew everything about Ryan, just as she knew everything about my three children.

Most of the time, I could forget that I, not Justine, had given birth to him. But there were times when I couldn't.

Such as now.

"Justine, I'm so sorry." The words sounded cheap, but what else was I supposed to say? What would she say if our situations were reversed? I heard Justine catch her breath in a sob.

"Why is God doing this to us, Gwen? He knows I can't have any children of my own! But you . . . you get pregnant at the drop of a hat!" She sucked in a sharp breath. "I didn't mean that, Gwen! Please, forgive me; I don't know what I'm saying!"

"It's all right, honey. I know you didn't mean it." I suspected she had, but I knew that she hadn't meant it maliciously. She spoke the truth. I'd had four children without any problem—one that I hadn't wanted—while she and her husband, Brent, had spent tons of money trying to find out why they couldn't have kids. It didn't seem fair. Especially since I was two months pregnant again. I was glad I hadn't told her.

"God!" She sobbed, and my heart clenched in sympathy at the sheer agony in the sound.

I was crying silently, not wanting to add to her pain. I had to be strong for her. "I'm getting on the next plane, sis. I can be there in twelve hours."

"Okay." There was a long moment as Justine tried to control her sobs. She only halfway succeeded. "Do—do you need me to send you some money?"

Swiftly, I calculated the amount in our savings account, winced, then said, "I think I have enough to get there."

When I was certain Justine would be okay, I gently told her to try and be strong for Ryan and Brent before I hung up. I called my husband, Doug, at work. He works at a computer outlet store that remanufactures computers. Doug was brilliant, but not overly ambitious. We could just scrape by in calling ourselves a middle-class family. I managed a few business websites that brought in a little extra cash, but our daughters kept me so busy with school activities that I could only work part-time.

Our house was mortgaged to the hilt, our checking account was frequently overdrawn, and our savings account was something to laugh about. Yet, we were happy, for the most part.

I was lucky, and a pang of guilt struck me again as I thought of my sweet sister and the hardships that she'd endured. Not only was she unable to have children, but she'd also been diagnosed with multiple sclerosis the previous year. Thankfully, she appeared to have the milder kind, but she had to have costly injections twice weekly.

"Doug Cunningham."

I jumped at the sound of my husband's absent, clipped voice, my thoughts elsewhere. "Honey? I have some bad news." Quickly, I explained the situation and told him I was going to Miami.

He sighed impatiently. "That's terrible news, and I don't mean to sound callous, but how are we going to manage the trip? What are you going to do with the girls, and how are we going to pay for it?"

I took a deep breath, thinking quickly. "You have a few sick days coming. Can't you take them?"

After a pause, he said, "I guess I can. What about the—"

"We've got enough for a one-way ticket. Justine said she'd reimburse me and get me back home." She actually hadn't said that, but I knew that she would. "Honey, she needs me." And Ryan's my son. I thought the words, wanting to say them just to get the secret off of my chest, but I knew that was not the time. I didn't think there would ever be a time, because too much time had passed. Doug and I had been married for eight years. Our daughters, Rachel, Christina, and Gina, were all two years apart, with Rachel being seven years old.

Obviously, they weren't old enough to stay home alone by themselves, and I knew that as much as Doug loved his daughters, he wasn't looking forward to playing "Mr. Mom." Our youngest, Gina, seemed to be stretching her terrible twos into the terrible threes.

Gina suddenly appeared at my side, thumb in mouth, favorite teddy bear in hand. She still looked sleepy from her nap. She opened her mouth long enough to say, "I'm hungry," in a pouty, demanding voice.

Doug heard her. "You've never been away from her," he reminded me.

I could hear the panic in his voice.

I quickly counted to five. I loved Doug, but I knew he could use the time with his daughters. "You're her father, Doug. She'd be better off with you than with the baby-sitter." We couldn't afford a baby-sitter, and I was banking on Doug knowing that.

"All right. Do you know how long you'll be gone for?"

I bit my lip and told a little fib. I knew exactly how many sick days Doug had coming. "Two—three, at the most." Five, if necessary, I thought to myself. I'd probably come back home to a wrecked house and a family who would never touch hot dogs or the microwave again, but my sister—and my son—needed me.

Now, I decided wisely, was not a good time to tell Doug that he was going to be a father again. I knew that he wanted a son, despite his reluctance to add to our brood because of our financial situation.

"Aunt Gwen!"

I knew the moment I heard Ryan's cheerful voice and saw his smiling face, that they hadn't told him the news. I stood in the doorway with my small suitcase in hand and swallowed hard, fighting tears that were partly due to fatigue. My sister would never know how close I came to turning around and going right back out that door. I was angry that she'd waited, angry and panicked. How did one tell a twelve-year-old that he had cancer and might possibly die?

How did a mother tell her own son?

But I was Aunt Gwen—not his mother—at least, not legally. Unfortunately, that knowledge didn't make my heart any less vulnerable to losing him. In my heart, Ryan was my baby and always would be. I don't regret giving him to my sister and wonderful brother-in-law, but I also couldn't forget that I had carried him for nine months, given birth to him, held him in my arms when he'd first opened his eyes. I was his mother, and nothing would change that fact.

"What are you doing here?" Ryan asked, taking my bag from my cramped fingers like the gentleman he was. "I mean, it's cool and all, but did someone die?"

I watched his smile slowly fade as apprehension took its place.

Soothing words would have been appropriate, but I found that I couldn't speak.

"Did—did something happen to—"

"Gwen! Ryan, stop gabbing and take her suitcase to the spare room. Can't you see she's about to fall down on her feet?"

Mutely, I met my sister's false smile, once again fighting the terrible urge to burst into tears. I couldn't resist shooting her an accusing look. Her guilty reaction told me that she hadn't missed it, either.

The moment Ryan was out of earshot, the smile dropped from her face. Her eyes misted and her bottom lip began to tremble. Justine had always been a pretty crier. "Please, don't be mad. I just—we just couldn't tell him until you got here."

"I wished you had," I said woodenly. Our embrace wasn't as warm as it should have been, and I immediately felt awful. My disapproval was the last thing Justine needed right now. With an inward sigh, I tightened my arms around her and gave her a hard, comforting squeeze. "We'll do this together," I whispered encouragingly in her ear. "Just let me get a quick nap. I feel like a zombie."

My sister drew back, her thick black lashes spiky with tears. She mustered a faltering smile. "You look like one, too," she teased.

I made a face at her. "Thanks a lot. Where's Brent?"

"He's at work." She lowered her voice, glancing at the hallway.

The hallway walls were covered with impressive black-and-white pictures of Ryan at various stages in his life. More graced the foyer, and I knew beautiful photographs of my sister and her son adorned the living room. Brent was a very successful photographer.

"We didn't want to make Ryan suspicious. You know how bright he is."

Yes, I did know. And my heart was breaking.

Watching the hallway, I kept my voice low as I said, "Surely he's curious about the trips to the doctor and all the tests?"

Justine flushed. "I told him we thought he might have mono."

I closed my eyes, reminding myself that Justine was a wonderful sister, a devoted mother, and a great person—she just wasn't a strong person. Nobody was perfect. "He's not going to be happy with you when he finds out you lied to him." I didn't mean to sound harsh, but with Justine, sometimes I had to be. She was older, but I was stronger in many ways. She fainted at the sight of blood; I didn't even flinch. We were different.

"I know, I know. Brent agrees with you." She twisted her fingers and stood there, looking miserable. "I just couldn't do . . . it . . . without you."

Love bloomed in my heart. I had given my sister a child, and she

33

never let me forget how grateful she was for that fact, and she never tried to shut me out. She didn't have a jealous bone in her body, for which I was grateful.

"Have you told Mom and Dad yet?" I asked.

She shook her head, her face still flushed. "No, no. I'm sorry, Gwen. I'm a coward, I know, but I wanted you with me when I told them."

Sometimes I hated being the stronger one. Our parents were crazy about their grandkids, and I knew this would be a harsh blow to them.

She pushed me toward the hall. "Go on, have a nap—regain your strength. I've a feeling we're going to need it." She swallowed a sob and took off in the direction of the kitchen.

My nose twitched. I smelled cookies and knew that my sister had been baking. She always baked when she was upset or nervous. She said it was good therapy. Since she was a great cook, most people didn't mind it.

I ran into Ryan coming out of the guestroom. His, smiling face made my heart do a fearful somersault. He looked exactly like my eldest daughter, Rachel.

"I turned your bed down for you and fluffed up your pillow," he informed me. He rolled onto the balls of his feet and mimicked a hook shot. "Mom tell you I made the team?"

The smile that came to my mouth felt stiff and obviously fake. "Yes, she did. Congratulations, and thanks for turning down the bed covers. You're a true gentleman."

I'd made him blush. Impulsively, I reached out and hugged him to me. My heartfelt ready to explode as I thought of the future he might not have—of the basketball games he might not get to play. Of the children he might never see.

"Aunt Gwen?" There was fearful curiosity in the freckled face that stared at me. He was nearly as tall as I was. "Are you sure there's nothing wrong? Why didn't you bring Doug and the sea monkeys?" He'd taken to calling the girls a variety of names. Sea monkeys was a new one.

I ruffled his hair. "The sea monkeys stayed behind with their gorilla dad because we couldn't afford to fly everyone."

"So why are you here?"

Persistent devil, I thought, searching for a suitable excuse. Doug and I didn't believe in lying to our kids, but Ryan belonged to Gwen, so I reluctantly followed her rules. For now, anyway. I gave my shoulders a casual shrug as I said, "I missed you and my sis, nosey. Isn't that a good enough reason?"

"I guess." But he didn't sound convinced, and as Ryan turned to skip down the hall, he called back over his shoulder: "I guess whatever it is, you guys will eventually let me know."

Justine isn't exaggerating when she says he's a bright kid, I mused as I went into the guestroom and shut the door. I fell onto the bed and let the tears flow. I felt so incredibly sad and helpless. Why, God? I asked silently. Why Ryan? Why this good, loveable, bright child? Do you need him that badly—more than we do? Our preacher said that we shouldn't question God's motives, but how could I not?

When I awakened two hours later, my bones felt like mush and my head was pounding. I opened my eyes, stifling a gasp when I saw Justine sitting on the edge of the bed.

She was holding a glass of water and three aspirin. She held out the aspirin to me. "I remember how you get when you fly. Headache?"

I nodded, then winced as I took the aspirin and washed them down with the water. "Brent home?"

"Yeah. I've got supper ready. I fixed your favorite—lasagna and garlic bread."

Justine hopped from the bed and began to pace, betraying her agitation. "I wished I knew how he was going to take it. Oh, God," she wailed, covering her mouth and speaking between her fingers. "How can we tell him? He's just a kid!"

I swung my legs from the bed, gave them a moment to become solid, and then stood. My head continued to pound. I was hungry, jet-lagged, and dreading the coming meeting. "Let's eat and get this over with," I said, stumbling to the door.

My sister followed reluctantly, attempting to ignore the obvious. "I also made your favorite dessert."

Because I knew that she needed the distraction to give her time to get hold of herself, I went along with her. "Let me guess. Banana Split cake?"

"You're good."

I stopped at the door and took her hand. "No. You are, and you don't deserve this heartache, sis. I wish that I could take your pain away. I wish that I could change this moment, make it go away."

"I know you do," she whispered, blinking rapidly. This wasn't a time to get emotional, not when we were about to share a meal with my shrewd nephew, and we both knew it.

Ryan unwittingly continued to make it nearly impossible to act normal as he went on and on about making the basketball team. The coach had been very impressed with his hook shot, he informed us.

I tried not to look at my sister or Brent, who both looked as fragile as I felt. The lasagna was good, but Ryan was the only one doing it justice. He had three helpings. Apparently his illness hadn't affected his appetite yet, or his energy level. But I knew enough about the disease to know that it would only be a matter of time before both his appetite and his activities would be limited. For an energetic twelve-year-old, it would be devastating.

When I realized that Justine was drawing out the dinner, I took the liberty of hurrying her along. I didn't think my stomach could stand another moment of the nail-biting, nerve-wrecking tension. "I'm ready for dessert. Shall I help you get it?" I asked brightly, staring pointedly at my sister, who had barely touched her food. I had forced myself to eat a good portion of it out of politeness and to lesson suspicion. Ryan had done a lot of talking, but I could see the question in his blue eyes, and recognized his growing concern.

We hadn't fooled him.

The moment dessert was over, Ryan took his plate to the kitchen, rinsed it, and stuck it in the dishwasher. He came back into the dining room and began to gather more plates.

Justine shot him a bewildered look. "What are you doing, Ryan?"

Ryan wasn't smiling this time. "I'm helping so you guys can tell me what's going on. I know something is, and it's driving me crazy." Suddenly, he stood still, a plate in each hand. "Someone died, didn't they? And you guys think I'm a baby and that I can't handle it."

"No, sweetheart," Justine said in a wobbly voice. "Nobody died. I promise." She got up and helped him clear the table while Brent and I sat staring at each other in mute agony. I wondered if he was wondering the same thing I was wondering—if we'd be able to keep the delicious food down.

All too soon, we were seated in the living room, waiting awkwardly for someone to make the first move. I looked at Brent, Justine looked at me, Brent stared at the fireplace, and Ryan skipped his glance around, growing more and more solemn as the adults continued to remain silent.

"Just tell me!" Ryan finally blurted out. "You guys are scaring me."

His choice of words made us all wince visibly. Justine began to cry, and Brent did his best to comfort her.

That left me holding the bag, as I suspected would happen all along. I cleared my throat, praying I didn't sound as hopeless as I felt. "You were right, Ryan. We do have something to tell you, and it isn't good news. Your mom wanted me to be here." I looked at Justine, willing her to look at me. Finally, she did. I tipped my head in Ryan's direction, letting her know that I thought she should be the one to tell him. She frantically shook her head, so I transferred my gaze to Brent. I'd never seen him cry before, and the sight of his tears nearly broke me down.

But I couldn't break, not when I was the only one left standing besides Ryan. With a fatalistic sigh, I looked into my son's anxious, expectant face and said, "The doctor's found out that you have a very serious disease, sweetheart."

Ryan blinked. "Mom said I might have mono. Is it that serious?"

I swallowed my sudden surge of anger at my sister. "It isn't mono, Ryan. You have leukemia."

For a long moment, Ryan just stared at me. I watched his Adam's apple bob, and then he said: "That's cancer, isn't it? People can die from it?"

"No—" Justine began frantically.

"Yes," I interrupted forcefully, shooting her a quelling glance. "Sometimes, they do, and sometimes the doctors can make it go away for long periods of time. Sometimes, they can even cure it completely."

"Can—can they cure mine?" Ryan asked in a pitifully hopeful voice.

This time, I had to look to Justine and Brent for an answer. I didn't know what type of leukemia we were talking about, and silently cursed myself for not asking earlier. To my relief, Brent answered his son's question.

"We're not certain yet, son. We should know something in a couple of days."

Ryan stared at the carpet. Everyone else remained silent, waiting for his reaction. Would he burst out crying? Start screaming, "Why me?" Or, would he hold his fear and grief inside?

I knew his favorite cereal. I knew his favorite sport. I even knew that he still slept with a doll named "Woody" from Toy Story.

But I didn't have a clue how he was going to react to finding out he had cancer. One glance at his tense, expectant parents told me they didn't, either.

Surprising us all, Ryan began to ask rational questions. "Is that why I sometimes get tired for no reason?"

He was staring at Justine as he spoke. Mutely, she nodded.

"And that's why my gums bleed when I brush my teeth?"

Again, she nodded.

"Oh." He fell silent again, his gaze on the carpet. I wanted to go to him, but I didn't know if he was ready for comfort. I was afraid I'd start his hysteria.

When he looked up again, his eyes were brimming with tears. He swallowed several times before he asked in a raspy whisper that seemed to have aged in the last few moments: "Am I—am I going to die?"

He was staring straight at me, as if he suspected I was the least likely person to fall apart at the question.

I don't know where I found the strength, but I do know that I resented Justine and Brent at that moment. They were his parents; they should have been talking to him, not me! I should've been free and clear to fall apart like I badly needed to.

"I hear—" I stopped to clear the frog from my throat. "I hear they're making a lot of headway in the treatment of leukemia these days." I wasn't lying, but I couldn't, for the life of me, remember where I'd gleaned this information. I don't think any parent cared to dwell too much on the subject of childhood leukemia, including myself.

"So the doctors can get rid of it, right?"

The hopeful note in his voice tore at my heart. As I opened my mouth to say some kind of drivel just to fill in space, Brent spoke. I was so relieved that I almost fainted.

"We're waiting on some more tests, son. In a few days, we'll go back to see the hematologist and talk to him about what to do next."

The twelve-year-old boy frowned. His freckled face crumpled, and big fat tears began to fall from his eyes. He got up and flew at his mother, knocking her back into the sofa as great sobs racked his adolescent frame.

I couldn't tell who was crying the hardest, Justine or Ryan. Brent looked on with tears streaming down his face, one hand on his son's back and the other clenched helplessly at his side. I couldn't stand it a moment longer. I rose and quietly left the room, locking myself in the guestroom before flinging myself onto the bed. I cried until my eyes were sore and my throat felt raw and clogged. My chest hurt, too, but I didn't care. I never imagined in a million years having to face such an ordeal.

When I found out I was pregnant at thirteen, I thought it was the end of the world. I truly didn't think there was anything worse than being pregnant at thirteen. I was only in junior high school! Slowly, I rolled over onto my back and stared at the ceiling, thinking back to that time in my life when I was convinced nothing short of death would help me.

The boy's name was Nate Carteris, and he was from Alaska. As if that wasn't impressive enough, he was also two years older than I was, yet in the same grade.

He was a smooth talker, too. Within a week, he talked me into meeting him at his house while his parents were at work. Another two weeks found us going to "third base." Nate was experienced, and he didn't mind bragging about it. As I got older and wiser, I realized that he'd planned every step of his seduction. He'd teased me, aroused my curiosity as well as my passion, and then told me to go home.

By the fourth week, I was begging him to go all the way with me. I promised him that I wouldn't regret it or tell anyone. I just had to know what was at the end of the sexual rainbow.

Nate was a smooth talker and he talked me into doing it again and again, until finally, I began to enjoy it.

It's a wonder it took me three months to get pregnant, as many times as we had sex. All the while, my unsuspecting parents believed I was at my friend, Morgan's, house. She didn't like covering for me, but she did it, anyway. The only thing she demanded in return was all the juicy details. . . .

I wasn't stupid; I knew that since I'd gotten my period I could get pregnant. What I believed, what I had convinced myself, was that I wasn't old enough to get pregnant, and that Nate wasn't old enough to get me pregnant.

Of course, that was naïve and stupid. I did get pregnant, and it was definitely Nate's. On the night I told him, he laughed at me and threw my clothes in my face.

"I'm only fifteen! I'm not gonna have no kid right now!"

"You might not," I said, choking back sobs, "but I am, and I'm only thirteen!" But Nate wasn't listening. He merely turned up the music and flopped back onto his bed, deliberately ignoring me.

My parents flipped, of course, as did Justine. Daddy wanted to kill Nate. Justine stormed out of the house and was gone for hours. Later, I found out that she'd gone to talk to Nate, and he had laughed at her the same way he'd laughed at me.

Bewildered, scared, and feeling about as miserable as a person can get, I waited for my parents to guide me on what to do. Days passed. The house became a picture of gloom, except for the occasional cough or muffled curse. There were a lot of secret talks in my parents' bedroom, more often than not with Justine and her husband, Brent. Justine and Brent had been married for two years. I knew they'd been trying to have a baby, and the realization increased my guilt.

I was thirteen and going to have the baby that my sister longed for.

The knowledge sparked an idea. At that point, I didn't realize that the grown-ups had already been discussing the possibility, but I knew the moment I opened the bedroom door and told them my idea.

They'd looked shocked, then relieved. Mom had hugged me tightly and told me that I was good girl, despite my present condition. Daddy cried, and Justine could hardly contain her excitement over the prospect of getting my baby.

Our plans were simple, and they worked. Since Brent was a photographer, he could work anywhere. After announcing to family and friends that they were expecting a baby, Justine and Brent made a temporary move to San Diego, taking me with them. They made up some believable excuse about me taking a computer class that my own school didn't offer.

Mom and Justine were with me when I gave birth to Ryan, and then handed him over to Justine and Brent. I waited until they left before I cried. I didn't want them to know how hard it was to give them my child. Even at fourteen, my maternal instincts had kicked in when I saw my baby.

But I knew giving him to Justine and Brent had been the best thing I could have done and I've never regretted it. Now I was a grown woman with three children of my own; I could never make that sacrifice again.

I put my hand on my flat stomach, wondering if Doug and I would finally have a boy, and if we did, how Justine and Brent would react. My sister had never been spiteful or jealous, but then, she'd never lost a son before, either.

No, think positively! I berated myself for thinking of Ryan as if he'd already died. They had made remarkable strides in the treatment and cure of childhood leukemia recently.

My son . . . my nephew, the little boy who had his heart set on becoming a basketball star, would get better. He would live.

The hematologist said: "The first step we're going to take is a bone marrow aspiration and biopsy," he said, his voice gentle and kind.

The four of us sat together in his little office. Ryan perched on Brent's knee while Justine and I huddled close and held hands.

"And after that?" I asked, wincing as Justine clamped down on my hand in anticipation. Ryan leaned forward on his daddy's lap, his young face intent and apprehensive.

"After that, we'll discuss doing a bone marrow transplant. We've had great success with it."

Ryan nearly fell off his father's lap. "I've heard about that!" he exclaimed. He turned his excited face to his dad. "I read about it on the Internet, and sometimes they can get rid of it completely, Dad!"

I bit my tongue to keep from telling him not to get his hopes up. Why shouldn't he?

"The problem we have with transplants," the doctor interrupted gently, "is finding a donor. Siblings?"

Justine and Brent solemnly shook their heads. I think they honestly had forgotten for the moment that my girls were Ryan's half-sisters. I bit my tongue to keep from blurting out something that should probably be discussed in private with Brent and my sister.

"What about the mother?" Justine asked.

The hematologist frowned. "It's possible, but not as probable as a donor sibling. He only gets half of your genes, while a sibling might share the same genes from both the father and the mother."

"But you said that it's possible the mother could be a match?" Justine persisted.

I thought about my baby girls donating bone marrow and shuddered. They were too young to be subjected to that, but what if I

40

had no choice? Doug would fight me, and the prospect of telling him my long-buried secret made me break out into a cold sweat.

Ryan's disease was like a tidal wave . . . slow creeping over all of us and sucking us in. Ironically, it affected my family and me the most.

"Why do you have to tell Doug at all? Why can't you just say that as his aunt, you might be a match and leave it at that?"

I sighed and thought about Justine's advice. It would definitely be the coward's way out, but it wasn't my way out. "I just think I need to go ahead and tell him. He's my husband; I should have told him before we got married."

"But you agreed—"

"I know I agreed not to tell anyone, but at the time, I wasn't thinking about a husband or children. It's not fair to keep this from them. Can't you see that?"

Justine gave her head a violent shake. "No, Gwen! If you tell them, then Ryan will find out. I can't bear him knowing that I'm not his real mother, or that Brent isn't his father! Do you have any idea what that might do to him? My God, he's just been told he has leukemia! I can't believe you're considering dropping another bombshell on him!"

We stared each other down. As usual, I gave in. "Okay. I'm going to tell Doug, but not the girls. Doug can be trusted."

"But—"

I stood up, my voice grim and determined. "I'm not going to argue about it anymore, Justine. If I'm tested to see if I'm a match and possibly be a donor, then Doug's going to know why." It would have been the perfect time—and ammunition—to tell her that I was pregnant, but I just didn't have the heart. I didn't know if donating bone marrow would endanger my child, but I suspected there would be some risk involved.

As long as nobody knew, then I could make the decision—take the risk—on my own. The next day, I flew back home with the full knowledge that I would be coming back, probably with the girls. Justine had given me a credit card and some cash.

Doug looked vastly relieved to see me. Yes, the house was a mess, but as far as I could tell, nothing catastrophic had happened while I was gone. After we got the girls to bed, I told Doug that I needed to talk to him. I didn't know how he was going to react, so my stomach was full of butterflies as we went around turning out lights.

We ended in the den. I turned off the blaring television and took a seat on the sofa. Doug sat beside me, his hand on my leg. I knew he'd missed me as much as I had missed him, but I had to wonder if he'd want to make love after hearing my story.

Gathering my courage, I told him everything in a rush of words. I watched his face, watched as his eyes got wider and his mouth got grimmer. When I finished, I stared at my hands, waiting for his reaction.

"You should have told me. I can't believe you didn't trust me enough to tell me, Gwen!"

He didn't raise his voice, but I flinched as if he had. It was the disappointment I heard in his voice that crushed me. That, and a big dose of hurt. "I promised my sister and Brent that I would let them be his parents. The less people who knew, the better. I'm sorry. I know that I should have told you."

If I'd have been standing, my legs probably would have given out on me when he pulled me against him and held me tight.

His voice was gruff as he said, "I'm sorry that you didn't trust me enough to tell me, but I'm not mad." He pulled back and gazed into my face, his eyes shining with love. "You're a special woman, do you know that? To give your sister your baby . . . to make this sacrifice now. You went through quite an ordeal."

"I—I don't know if I'll be a match. He said the chances were slim."

"I know, but it's the thought that counts, right?" Doug smiled his endearing, crooked smile. "No wonder you're so crazy about Ryan."

"He looks like Rachel," I said.

Doug looked thoughtful, then surprised as he nodded. "He sure does, doesn't he? I never really noticed before. Maybe someday we'll have a boy that looks just like him."

My smile was pained as I said, "Yeah. Maybe someday." I couldn't tell him I was pregnant. Maybe it was wrong of me, but I knew Doug. He loved his family, but it seemed hard for him to care for anyone that much outside his little circle. Even for Ryan, he might not want me taking a risk. I didn't have the energy to fight him.

So I tucked another little secret beneath my breast and surged forward.

"I'm amazed to say that you're a match," the hematologist exclaimed the moment Justine and I entered his office. His brow furrowed as he shot me a slightly accusing look. "But I wished that you had confided in me earlier about being Ryan's birth mother."

"You and Doug both," I mumbled beneath my breath as I took a seat. Justine did the same, then reached for my hand. She was smiling.

"You're a match, sis! You hold Ryan's life in your hands . . . or . . . bones!" She bounced in her seat, giggling like an intoxicated teenager. Her happiness was infectious. "So, when can we do this?"

"Well, we'll have to run some further tests on Gwen, but I don't think that will take too long. She looks healthy to me."

And pregnant, was my silent thought. I considered discussing the risks with the doctor, but decided against it. What if he adamantly refuses to let me donate the marrow? I couldn't take that risk. I was a

42

hearty, healthy woman. I'd had four children without any difficulties. My unborn baby would weather the storm just fine.

I wished I felt as confident as my silent lecture sounded. What if I lost the baby? Would Doug forgive that transgression? Could I forgive myself? One thing I did know; if I didn't help Ryan, I couldn't live with myself.

One month later, everything was ready. Doug took off work to come with me; nothing I said put a dent in his determination. The girls were thrilled to get to stay with my parents.

The transplant went off without a hitch, but we were told it might take some time before they knew if the treatment would be successful.

When I was able, I went to visit Ryan in his room. He opened his eyes, gazed at me a moment, then said, "You're my hero, Aunt Gwen."

I'm your mother, I silently whispered. Tears flooded my eyes. I gave him a bright smile and a thumbs-up before letting Doug lead me back to my own room. I'd felt a few mild cramps earlier, so I was anxious to lie back down. Hold on, little one, I urged fervently.

My baby turned out to be one hell of a fighter. He not only weathered the storm, but also came in weighing a whopping eight pounds, fourteen ounces.

Ryan's not out of the woods yet, but he's in remission and things look very promising. He's back at school, playing basketball, and lighting the world with that bright, wonderful smile of his.

But I'm saving the best news for last. Justine and Brent are finally going to give Ryan a brother or sister. Talk about a triple blessing!

THE END

TWICE THE JOY
OR TWICE THE GRIEF?

I'd always heard that twins skipped a generation. That appeared to be the start of the pattern in my own family. My grandmother was a twin. I was also a twin, and I assumed that I would be the grandparent of twins.

However, after three years of marriage, life threw me a pleasant curve ball.

"We're gonna have twins!" I said excitedly, struggling to keep my feet on the ground. I wanted to jump up and down, but instead, I waited for Billy's reaction to my news.

Billy's mouth dropped open, but he didn't say anything for a good thirty seconds. When he did speak, his first word came out on a croak. He cleared his throat and tried again. "As in two babies? Is that what you're saying?"

I nodded and this time I gave in to my impulse. I threw my arms around his shoulders and hugged him tight. This was the second happiest day of my life, and a simple squeeze just wouldn't do.

Being pregnant didn't really surprise me. We'd been trying for over a year. To me, these babies were simply a double blessing to show for all the effort we'd put into it. Without kids, our life had been good. But now, I knew it would only get better. We were two people with lots of love to share. Even holidays and celebrations would take on a whole new meaning now that we were on our way to becoming a true family.

Because he was an only child, Billy desperately wanted a baby. He especially desired a son to carry on his family's name. When I didn't get pregnant right away, Billy didn't voice his concern, but I could tell that he was getting a little worried. That was all in the past. Soon, we would have two babies to cuddle and fawn over. Maybe we'd even have a boy and a girl. What more could we want? Our lives would be complete.

"Wow," Billy said, the shock and disbelief still evident in his voice. He pulled back slightly and looked into my eyes. "When we finally did it, we did it big time." He brought his hand to my tummy and gave it a loving pat. "Are you sure there's only two in there? I am a high achiever, you know."

I laughed and joked along with him. Our happiness was a tangible force that day. Nothing could cloud our joy. Maybe we were being overly optimistic, but neither of us could fathom anything going wrong. Women gave birth to multiples every day. Triplets, quadruplets, and even more were safely delivered. How complicated could twins be?

The answer to that came during my third month of pregnancy.

"Nicole, from the look of things, you're having identical twins." Dr. Blume moved the ultrasound wand around a little and paused. "Everything appears normal, but this type of pregnancy is considered higher risk."

I propped myself up and gazed down at my jelly-covered, still-flat belly. "I don't understand. At my last visit you said everything was going perfectly."

Dr. Blume's eyes were still focused on the screen. With his index finger, he pointed to a small, bean-sized structure. "This is the placenta. Normally each baby will have its own, but in the case with some identical twins, they will share a placenta."

I nodded, still not comprehending his concern. "But you said everything looks fine. The babies are healthy, right?"

"Anatomically, everything looks normal." He pointed to the two fluttering shapes. "Their hearts are beating at a good rate and their sizes are appropriate for this stage of your pregnancy."

"Then what's the problem?" Billy asked, speaking up for the first time.

"Potential problem," Dr. Blume corrected. "If everything goes according to plans, Nicole will deliver perfectly healthy babies." He pulled a few tissues from a box and wiped the goo from my belly. "However, sometimes with identical twins with only one placenta, problems can arise. Occasionally, one baby will get the lion's share of oxygen and food. That baby will grow and thrive."

"And the other baby?" Billy asked cautiously.

Dr. Blume reached for my hand and helped me into a sitting position. "The other baby would be underdeveloped and underweight."

I gasped lightly, not realizing I allowed the sound to escape my lips. I quickly turned to Billy, but he looked just as confused as I did.

"Let's not worry at this early stage," Dr. Blume said, patting my leg in a reassuring manner. "We're going to monitor your entire pregnancy and we'll spot any problems early on. For now, go home and relax. This is supposed to be a happy time. Make the most of it."

I expelled a heavy breath and felt the tension leave my body. I couldn't dwell on fear or doubt. My babies would be okay. They had to be. Billy and I pinned so many of our hopes and dreams on a life filled with giggling, happy children. Nothing would dare mar the perfect future that I had envisioned.

The next few months flew by in a blur of activity. We had a nursery to prepare and baby paraphernalia to purchase. Billy even took a week's vacation from his job as an accountant just so he could help me out around the house.

We probably overdid it a bit, but our excitement was contagious. We spent hours reading up on the safest and best baby equipment. We educated ourselves on the proper parenting techniques, and we even involved our family members through long-distance phone calls.

"Help us choose the perfect names for our babies," I requested. "We want everyone's input."

"Okay, would you like girls' names first or boys' names?" Billy's mother asked.

I smiled as I considered her question. I hadn't yet told her our news, but now seemed the perfect time. "Well, I think we can eliminate any girls' names." I held the phone away from my ear as I anticipated her shout. She didn't disappoint me.

"Boys, you're having boys?" A high-pitched squeal of joy escaped her lips.

"Two perfect, little boys," I confirmed, looking at the tiny ultrasound picture that clearly depicted male body parts.

"Joel would be so proud," she said, referring to Billy's father who had died of a stroke the previous year. Her voice turned heavy and filled with grief. She sniffled lightly and attempted to disguise the pain I knew she was still feeling. "I'm very happy for you and my son."

"Oh, Kathy, I know this has been a hard year for you," I replied, wishing I could be with her. "Maybe you should come out and stay with Billy and me. Just for a while—"

"I wouldn't hear of doing that," she said, cutting me off. "This is a time of new beginnings for you and my son. I can't intrude on that."

I tried to assure her that she wouldn't be intruding, but I couldn't convince her. Finally, I shrugged and gave up. "Okay, but at least consider coming out when the babies are born. We would love to have you share our happiness."

When she told me she would visit after her grandsons' birth, I let up. She was getting her life in order and the last thing she needed was a daughter-in-law hovering over her and hounding her. Besides, I had my own hands full with a set of twins due to arrive in less than five months.

Most people told me to expect double the amount of aches and pains and pregnancy complaints. I can honestly say that I had never felt more wonderful. I was energetic, my skin glowed, and mentally, I was on top of the world. That all changed at a routine doctor's visit during my fifth month.

"You're measuring large," Dr. Blume commented, stretching the tape measure over my taut belly for the second time. "I'm going to double check my findings." He frowned and deposited the tape measure back into his coat pocket.

Billy moved forward and placed his hand on my tummy. "What's the big deal? I mean, there are two babies in there. She's bound to get huge. My mom said I weighed over nine pounds at birth."

I rolled my eyes. "Let's just hope I don't get too huge and our babies aren't that big."

Dr. Blume jotted something down on my chart. "Yes, we could just be dealing with a couple of good-sized babies," he said offhandedly, though his demeanor was anything but casual. "But, just to be on the safe side, I'm going to schedule another ultrasound for this afternoon. You were due for one next week anyway."

I couldn't resist a tiny smile. I enjoyed every opportunity that we had to take a peek at our babies. We already had quite a collection mounted on our refrigerator. As far as I was concerned, we would soon be adding another black and white photo to the collage.

"So how does everything look?" I asked the technician an hour later. She and I had become familiar with one another over the past few months. She'd performed my last three ultrasounds, so I was used to her excited chatter as she pointed out the various structures in my babies' bodies. This time, her manner and attitude were entirely different. She was so quiet and almost too professional. I immediately knew something was wrong.

"Tell me what you see, Linda." My heart began to pound and my palms became damp. "I really do need to know."

Linda turned off her equipment and handed me a tissue to clean off my belly. "Nicole, I'm sorry, but I'm not at liberty to say anything. Dr. Blume will get the results, and he'll tell you everything.

"But why? You've always told me when everything looked good. Why can't you talk to me about it now?" My distress was mounting, and instinctively, I knew the news was going to be bad.

She touched my hand, her eyes showing compassion. "I'm only following hospital policy. If I do otherwise, I could lose my job. Go to your doctor's office and wait until he can see you," she advised.

The next forty-five minutes were horrible. I prayed for the best while I prepared myself for the worst. For the life of me, I couldn't imagine what might be wrong. Structurally, we already knew our babies were healthy. From what I saw on the screen, they still looked normal. I saw their tiny hearts beating and their little legs kicking. They looked exactly as they had at my previous ultrasound—only bigger.

"Let's just wait and hear what Dr. Blume has to say," Billy suggested. "Maybe Linda read the ultrasound wrong, or else she's blowing it all out of proportion. And remember, she didn't actually say anything was wrong."

"But she was acting so strangely," I argued. "She saw something that didn't look right. She just couldn't tell us what it was."

He cupped my face between his hands. "It won't be long and then we'll know for sure if there's anything wrong with the twins."

Dr. Blume's face was grim and he didn't mince words. "There's a big discrepancy between the sizes of your babies." He flipped on a switch and pointed to the blown-up image of one of my ultrasound pictures. "Baby A is already over a half-pound larger than baby B. That's too big of a difference at this stage of your pregnancy." He used his index finger to show us what he was looking at.

"They both look the same to me," Billy said, his eyes straining to pick up on the tiny difference.

"Well, look at this region," Dr. Blume suggested. "This is the amniotic fluid surrounding baby A." He shifted his finger to the right. "And this is the amniotic fluid surrounding baby B."

Billy squinted. "I can hardly see any around the second baby."

Dr. Blume nodded. "That's the problem. Baby A is getting the bulk of the nutrition. We call him the recipient twin, while baby B is referred to as the donor twin."

I held up my hand. "Recipient, donor. I don't understand any of this."

"Just tell us what's going on with our babies," Billy interjected.

Dr. Blume nodded and pointed toward the ultrasound. "Since your babies share a placenta, they're also sharing some major blood vessels. The lower twin is getting the bulk of the nutrients. That explains his large size. The extra amniotic fluid is caused by increased urination. He's trying to rid his body of excess fluid."

I wiped away a stray tear that escaped from my eyes. "What do we do about it? There's a treatment, right?"

Dr. Blume's brow furrowed. "I'm going to be honest with the two of you. This isn't an easy thing. You need to understand that your babies are perfectly normal. The total problem lies in the placenta. There's nothing you could have done to prevent it and there's nothing you can do to change it now."

"Then what do we do?" Billy asked.

"At this stage, we watch and we wait."

I sucked in a deep breath as I felt my babies move within me. They were so active and they seemed so strong. How could something so serious be wrong with them? My mother's heart wanted to deny it, to say none of it was true. But the rational side of me knew that the road ahead of us was going to be long and hard.

For the first time since I'd gotten pregnant, Billy and I had a major blowout. At a time when we should have been drawing strength from one another, we were attacking each other.

"The worst thing you can do is get all hyped up about this," Billy said. "So we're going have one big baby and one little baby. What's the big deal?"

I tapped my palm against my forehead. "Did your brain take a powder when Dr. Blume was explaining all of this to us? This is a very serious condition."

Billy's eyes narrowed. "I heard him, all right. He also said the twins were normal."

"Normal and healthy are two separate things," I argued.

He slammed his fist down on the counter. "What difference does it make? He said we couldn't do anything to change it!"

Suddenly, realization dawned on me. Billy was scared. Maybe even more so than I was. He had been so excited about our babies and now something was getting in the way of that excitement. Since he couldn't change it, he was pretending that it didn't exist.

Billy and I were very different in our personalities and in how we approached difficulties. Like most men, he wanted to fix the problem. If he couldn't fix it, he would ignore it. Like a lot of women, I chose to educate myself. I scoured books and magazines for everything that I could get my hands on concerning high-risk twins. There was so much information available that I was surprised I hadn't noticed it before. I guess I assumed nothing bad would dare touch my family or me. I was very wrong.

My next doctor's visit turned up even worse news. The amount of amniotic fluid around baby A had reached the point where we had to intervene.

Using a large needle and guided by ultrasound, Dr. Blume withdrew the extra fluid in an amniocentesis-type procedure. "Be advised, this is only a temporary solution," he told me. He snapped off his gloves and tossed them into the trash. "We're not out of the woods."

From my reading, I knew he spoke the truth. I was no longer ignorant about the seriousness of our situation. I knew our babies were gravely ill. The tiny baby was struggling to get enough nutrients to grow on, and the larger baby's heart was being overworked as he struggled to cope with the extra blood flowing into his body.

Gone was the joy of pregnancy and new beginnings. In its place was an expectation based on fear and the unknown. No longer did I read the books and magazine articles dealing with child-care and normal infant development, but I concentrated on the ones that mentioned dealing with extremely fragile newborns.

Despite my doctor's warnings, I got my hopes up after the extra fluid was drained from baby A's amniotic sac. After the procedure, his heart rate picked up and both babies appeared to be more active. I even made a move of a different kind. I decided that it was time to name our babies.

"I'm not sure that's a good idea, Nicole," Billy said when I first suggested it to him. "I mean, what if something happens to them?"

I felt myself smile even though my body was filled with tension and stress. "Does that really having any bearing on this? Don't our babies deserve a name whether they live or die?"

Billy bit his lip. I knew that for my sake he was clamping down on any negative emotion that might try to escape. Though I didn't advocate holding grief or sadness in, we both knew that if he lost control, I would soon follow. I appreciated his strength and wisdom.

"I think naming our babies is a wonderful idea," he murmured at last. "It's about time we called them something other than baby A and baby B."

We decided to name the bigger baby, Joel, in honor of Billy's father, and we named the tiny baby, Devon. It seemed like a small thing, but providing our sons with names also gave them an identity and a special place in our hearts.

I was put on bed rest not long after that. I was beginning to have pre-term labor, and Dr. Blume said that neither of the babies was big enough to survive.

"Twenty-eight weeks," he said, flipping the calendar page over. He touched a date with his pen. "We're going to shoot for right here."

My jaw dropped open. "But that's next month! Are you telling me that you want me to deliver in four weeks?" I couldn't believe what I was hearing. I knew the chances were high that I would deliver early, but I never really considered the possibility that I would have extremely premature babies.

Dr. Blume sat down and rolled his stool closer to where I was perched on the exam table. "I know you're shocked and disappointed, but we have to be realistic. As soon as baby B is big enough to survive, we need to schedule a C-section."

"His name's Devon," I said flatly.

Dr. Blume nodded. "That's a beautiful name. And the other baby?"

"We're calling him Joel."

He scratched his head and looked down at the floor. "Though Joel is the bigger baby, he's the one who's actually weaker. His heart is having an extremely difficult time handling the extra blood volume that Devon's body is diverting to him."

My eyes captured his and refused to look away. "Please, just spell it out to me."

"We're walking a fine line here, Nicole." He once again pointed to the calendar. "The key is delaying delivery until the smaller baby is big enough to survive, but to not wait so long that the larger baby suffers heart failure. As I said before, circumstances can turn grim very quickly."

So there I had it. Either baby might live or both babies might die.

My pregnancy and the babies' health were monitored twice a week. The first thing they would do is strap a fetal monitor on my belly for a non-stress test. This is a procedure where the babies' heartbeats were measured after they kicked or made some sort of movement. If their heart rate rose in response to the movement, it was considered a good sign. After that, I would get a quick ultrasound to monitor the things that we couldn't see. For two weeks, everything continued to look good and we were hopeful.

But then we received the news that we were dreading.

"We've got to deliver." Dr. Blume pushed his glasses up on his nose and leveled a steady gaze at Billy and me.

"You said I needed to get to twenty-eight weeks," I argued, shocked and confused by the sudden turn of events.

"Yes, the outcome would improve if you and the babies made it to twenty-eight weeks. That's not going to be the case. The scores from your last non-stress test were lousy. This latest ultrasound confirms it. Joel is fading fast, and if we don't deliver, he's going to die before birth."

I felt hot tears sting my eyes, but I didn't cry or yell or show any other emotion. I gripped Billy's hand and put my babies' lives in God's care. It was out of my control. All we could do was hope and pray.

Due to my slightly medicated state, my C-section went by in a haze. The atmosphere in the operating room was serious and almost grim. It wasn't anything like I expected childbirth to be.

My boys were born less than a minute apart. The first baby, who I later learned was Joel, cried weakly and squirmed on the warming table. The second baby, tiny Devon, was silent.

Since I didn't have my contacts in and my glasses were back in my room, I could only make out the blurry outlines of the doctors and nurses as they worked over my babies. So far, they were both alive. I took that as a good sign.

A few hours later, I was feeling well enough to go see the babies. Billy had already spent some time in the NICU getting to know them. He informed me that they were both stabilized but were in very critical condition.

"But they're so beautiful," he said, handing me a couple of instant snapshots. "And they're fighters."

I took the photos from his fingers and stared at the babies who had been the center of my universe for six months. He was right. They were gorgeous. A light sprinkling of hair covered their tiny heads, and their little features were miniatures in perfection. I was so enthralled by the beauty of my babies that I barely noticed the tubes or machinery attached to their bodies.

"Joel weighs nearly three pounds. That's huge for a twenty-six-week preemie," Billy said, a measure of pride in his voice. Then he turned more sober. "Of course his little brother is a lightweight at one-pound, four-ounces. But he's strong. I can tell that about him."

I put the photos on the nightstand and allowed the nurse to help me get into the wheelchair. Billy pushed me while she pushed my IV pole.

It was only a short walk down the hall and through a set of double doors. We passed the newborn nursery, and at the end of the hall, was the ward where they kept the sickest babies. It was the place that would be home to my twins for the next several months. With a little luck and a lot of prayer, they would live that long.

The nurse helped me wash my hands and don a protective gown. Then we entered the large, brightly lit room that was filled with sophisticated machinery. Strange beeps and hisses filled the air. The nurse motioned to a couple of men in white coats who were approaching us.

"Mrs. Shandling, I'm Dr. Haas and this is Dr. Fox. We've been taking care of your babies."

I shook their hands and looked past them to the babies who were either in incubators or lying on an open table-like contraption.

"Joel and Devon are over there." Billy pointed to the far end of the room.

When I nodded, the nurse pushed my wheelchair and the doctors followed. I saw Joel first. He was on one of the tables. He looked so tiny, his little body dwarfed by the various tubes and wires entering and leaving his body.

"So far, he's doing better than we anticipated," Dr. Fox said. He pointed to the heart monitor. "His cardiac output is good, but the next forty-eight hours will be critical."

Devon was occupying his own table a few feet away. If I thought Joel was tiny, nothing prepared me for the sight of my smaller baby. His skin was loose and nearly translucent, and he looked smaller than a doll. The rhythmic pump and hiss of a machine reminded me of his frailty.

"The respirator is a necessity for babies this size," Dr. Fox said, answering the question before I even had time to vocalize it.

I closed my eyes and bit back the tears. At this point, information was much more important than giving in to my urge to cry. I wanted to know everything I could about my babies and what their odds were for survival.

For the next two days, my life consisted of daily walks down the hall to visit the twins. Family and friends showed up and gave their support, but I barely felt their presence. I was engrossed in the two tiny babies who were struggling to survive. I would stare at them and tentatively touch them. And for now, that would have to be enough.

Joel, larger than his brother by over a pound, was the weaker of the two. This surprised me. I had always equated size with strength even though the doctors told me not to be deceived and think along those lines. Joel was very large for being a twenty-six-week preemie, but his size was due to the increased blood flow through a faulty placenta. His condition was very critical, and his delicate heart was struggling with every beat it took.

I almost hated getting discharged from the hospital. It would mean separation from my babies. At least while I was in the hospital, I could be there in a moment's notice if they needed me. Not that they needed anything I could give them. Doctors and nurses surrounded them and machines monitored their vital signs. The only thing I could do was pump breast milk every four hours. There was no telling when they would be able to drink it. For now, I faithfully froze it in little plastic bags. It wasn't much, but at least it helped me feel like a mother.

The second night I was home from the hospital, the dreaded phone call came. Billy and I talked about it and wondered if it would happen, but we never discussed how we would feel if it did occur.

"Calm down, Nicole. It might not be serious," Billy said, as he hurriedly slipped his arms into his shirt. "Just get dressed and we'll go down there."

I reached for my pants, moving slowly because of my still-painful incision. "Didn't the nurse tell you anything?"

He shook his head and was already fishing in his pockets for the car keys. "Let's just go and see why we're being summoned in the middle of the night."

Just as we feared, it wasn't good news. The activity level in the NICU was even higher than normal. Most of it was centered on Joel. Before Billy and I had a chance to enter, Dr. Fox intercepted us.

"We've been working on him for the past hour. I'm afraid it doesn't look good."

Billy pulled his fingers through his uncombed hair. The weariness and fatigue showed in his eyes. "What, exactly, does that mean?"

"We've known all along that Joel's main problems were associated with his heart. Apparently, we thought he was doing better than he actually was. Everything looked fairly good until tonight. . . ."

His voice drifted off and he looked over his shoulder to the people still fussing with my son's monitors and equipment.

"What happened tonight?" Again, Billy spoke up, echoing the question that was going through my troubled mind.

"His heart stopped several times. We were able to revive him, but his latest tests show his condition is extremely serious. We don't think he's going to make it through the night."

His words were blunt, but we needed to hear them.

Billy took a step backward. "Can't you operate on him? Give him medication, treat him—"

Dr. Fox held up a hand. "We're not talking about a heart that is damaged. If that were the case, we would call in a surgeon and attempt to repair it. What we're dealing with is a weakened heart and a baby that is not strong enough to pull through."

His words cut clear through to my own heart. I'm sure an actual knife wound wouldn't have stung as badly or stabbed as deeply as the words spoken by the doctor.

When they led us to our baby, I couldn't believe how much he'd changed since the last time we'd seen him. Though a lot of it was probably in my imagination, he appeared even more fragile and vulnerable. He was now hooked up to a respirator, and the constant beeping of his heart monitor reminded us of the doctor's bleak prognosis.

"Nicole, he looks peaceful," Billy commented softly. He reached out and stroked one of Joel's tiny arms. "It's going to be okay, son," he whispered. "Everything's going to be okay."

We stayed with him through the night. We watched on the monitor as his heartbeat became more and more irregular. Over the course of the early morning hours, we came to a decision. We would follow the doctor's advice and say good-bye to our son. They were of the opinion that Joel was going to die, but even if he did live, he would very likely suffer from brain damage. That wasn't the kind of life we wanted for him. With heavy hearts, we released him. If he died, we would always remember his short time on earth, and if he lived, we would love him and accept him.

As the first rays of light were coming through the brightly colored curtains, Joel slipped away. He didn't struggle or seem to be in any pain or distress, but he simply went home. I like to think that he went to the place where all innocent babies go when they are taken before their time. It was a place of peace and tranquility where the children run freely and aren't burdened by the mundane things of the world.

Two days later, we buried our boy and we dealt with our grief. Whereas I tended to want to talk and to rationalize, Billy was more silent and brooding.

"What's the use going over it?" he asked. "We can't change what happened. We have to move on."

"But communicating about it might make it easier. I just want to know why—"

"Nicole, you deal with your grief your way, and I'll deal with my grief my way. Okay?"

I was going to argue that we needed to talk, but I let it go. He was right. He needed to grieve in his own way and in his own time.

Something changed inside of me after Joel's death. I held onto the hope that Devon would be okay. He had to be. I couldn't bear to lose another son.

"You need to guard yourself," Billy advised. "Devon's only ten days old, and he's hardly out of the woods. He's even lost a few ounces in the past week."

I nodded. "I know that, but it doesn't matter." I reached out and touched Billy's chest. "I have this knowing feeling inside that everything's going to be all right."

A muscle twitched in his jaw. I thought he was going to protest or argue but he didn't. He wrapped his arms around me and drew me close.

"I love you, Nicole."

Devon's health went up and down. He would have a few good days and they would be followed by a setback. I would get so excited when he would gain an ounce or two, but then frustration would set in if he got an infection or a test result came back with poor results. On top of this, I was still having a hard time coming to terms with Joel's death. I don't how many times I brought out the memory box that held the mementos the hospital gave me. A birth announcement, a receiving blanket, a hair clipping, and some photographs. That was all I had of a son that I had carried in my body for six months.

Peoples' attitudes were another difficulty. Friends and even a few family members didn't quite know what to say to me. Oh, everyone was nice enough. They just treated me differently than they did before.

"They're just afraid," Billy said "They don't want to say the wrong thing or upset you."

I rolled my eyes and pushed myself up from the couch. "They're afraid? I'm the one whose baby died. I can take people saying the wrong thing. I just can't take the silence anymore. People act like Joel didn't exist or like Devon is going to die, too!"

"Honey, you're not really mad at our family and friends. You're just frustrated because you feel so helpless."

"How come you know me so well?" I let out a long sigh.

Billy leaned back and braced his feet on the coffee table. "Didn't Devon look better to you today?" he asked, effectively changing the subject. He knew I loved talking about the strides our baby was making, and with a few simple words, he derailed my outburst. "He even seemed more alert and more active."

"I thought so, too. His weight's back up, and the nurse said he tolerated the breast milk well." For the past week, they had been giving him minuscule amounts of breast milk through a tube fed through his nose and down into his stomach. It was a frustrating process because the feedings would cause a setback and would have to be halted. When his condition improved, they would be started once again.

Billy smiled and nodded. "See, they said he would get the hang of handling food. Before we know it, the kid's gonna ask for a steak."

I laughed and sat back down next to him. I grabbed his hand and swung it over my shoulders. "I think that might be a ways off."

"But it's coming, baby. You were right. You said Devon's going to be okay, and now I believe you."

For some strange reason, his words brought a rush of tears to my eyes. Though Devon's progress was a wonderful thing and was nothing short of a miracle, it still brought up the fact that I once had two babies, and now I only had one.

"You're thinking of Joel again, aren't you?" Billy's arms tightened around my shoulders.

"How can I not think of him? He was a part of me and I feel the loss every single day." I snuggled further into the shelter of his arms. Though he handled it differently, I knew he understood what I was going through. Last year his father had died. And now his son, the one who bore his father's name, was gone, too.

"I had a client today that heard about our boys, and he gave me his take on the situation." Billy wiped a stray tear from my cheek with his thumb. "He's what you might call an 'unconventional' psychologist."

My curiosity was piqued. "So were you his accountant, or was he your therapist?"

"Actually, it was a little bit of both. I did his taxes, and he helped me realize something."

"What was that?" I asked, sounding a little more cynical than I intended. I didn't hold much stock in psychobabble and I was all set to discount it with a sharp retort.

Billy's eyes caught and held mine. "He said maybe it would be easier if I quit thinking of Joel as a baby who was born just to die, and instead, to think of him as a special soul. A soul who came into this world and who had a purpose. Not only that, but Joel was the one who chose when he was born and when he would die. There was nothing we could do to prevent it."

"That sounds pretty farfetched there to me. And besides, what purpose could a baby who was barely six days old have?" I asked bitterly.

Billy shrugged. "I don't know yet, but I'm sure that someday I'll find the answer."

Though they were hard to take, his words did offer some comfort. In my heart, I already knew that I had to separate my pain over losing Joel from my relationship with Devon. I couldn't continually remind myself that every time that Devon accomplished something, Joel should be accomplishing the same thing. That would only lead to feelings of guilt for Devon. He wasn't simply an identical twin or an extension of his dead brother. He was our son, and in our hearts and in our lives, he would have to stand alone.

I brought my focus back to Billy. "I think we'll find Joel's purpose together." I hugged him and brought my lips forward to meet his. We'd been through a lot in the last few months, but we were strong.

We had many more hurdles to overcome in the next two months. Devon had two serious brain bleeds. He contracted meningitis and almost died. Life with an extremely premature baby is very difficult, and ours seemed to be especially riddled with complications and trials.

Nevertheless, two months later we brought our son home. He was still very tiny at just over four pounds, but he was going to be okay.

"We still have to be concerned about developmental delays or even cerebral palsy," Dr. Fox warned. "A preemie is monitored very carefully for the first two years."

I smiled and listened, but I was confident Devon would do just fine. But if he wasn't, we would love him just the same. Through the difficulties, I'd learned what was important and what wasn't. I would love my son and do everything in my power to help him grow and thrive. The future would take care of itself.

Devon is now an active three-year-old. He goes to preschool two days a week, and he isn't much different than the other children. Physically, he does show some signs of his rocky start. He's very small for his age, but his pediatrician says that is quite common for preemies. He also wears glasses for vision problems, another consequence of his early birth. These are minor things considering where he is now and where he could have been.

Billy and I have decided not to have any more children. Though our next experience with pregnancy would probably be totally different, the time we spent in the NICU has scared us permanently. And besides, we have our miracle boy and our life feels complete.

THE END

Loving Tribute:

MY MOM—A WOMAN AHEAD OF HER TIME

Some women take life by the reins and lead
the way for those who follow.
My mother was one of those remarkable ladies. . . .

Back in the late Forties, one of the most creative women of her time and community moved from new project to new adventure in a town called Atlantic City on the eastern coast of New Jersey.

She never learned to drive a car, but you couldn't help but notice how many different venues she embraced with attentive and joyous involvement. Any review of her time choices could easily inspire the stir of talk and wonderment amongst her contemporaries.

On sunny days, she confidently wore strange straw hats that were not on any fashion lists. In the winter, her beautiful hair seemed to dare snowflakes to land. With pride, she introduced herself as Lenore Coleman. She walked with a full stride long before the word aerobic became part of spelling-bee land.

Her lifetime resume included being a young dancer in a ballet company, her left leg scarred forever from a fire that destroyed her big dreams long ago on the East Coast. Still, during some outdoor big band dance nights on the Jersey shore—and any other time and place for a waltz or swing—Lenore and her husband, Harry, could come together in a glide and a twirl in such a smooth fashion that all of the young people would stop and form a circle and watch her early-evening outdoor dance floor grace.

This lady—with some Basque blood and those effervescent Spanish genes—was the mother of three sons, so her list of full-time responsibilities could've been stifling and an unwelcome burden. It was not.

She was a full partner with her husband in organizing great Labor Day picnics, complete with a menu of fun and games and food and crowds—something quite common in New Jersey those many decades ago. Her sons could tell you about how a famous governor knew and said her name as easily as he wore bow ties. How could a woman without a fancy car do so much?

Her secret seemed to be her comfort in chasing dreams without feeling any shackle of constraint or concern about back-fence gossip.

58

Oh, yes, mothers have dreams. Lenore had the knack of slipping away from and into new dreams if some doors were locked or traditional gender clouds tried to keep her from new sunshine.

She was a writer. One of her stories was in an anthology that made it into the public library. She was a freelance writer with many newspaper bylines. At times, she worked full-time covering sports like bowling, archery, football, ice fishing, and many a winter carnival or an outdoor event. She was a woman of easy, open dreams long before the politics of gender. Hardly an election was held without her covering it in some way for a newspaper or the radio. Many of her poems made it into print.

Her eldest son tells how she left her own writing career to edit other people's work. She loved being involved in rewrites and final copy. She had many fascinating projects while saving time to teach creative writing classes.

It is strange that her son has many stories about his mother; however, he doesn't have any pictures. Lenore filled books with photos of family and friends and events, but it wasn't until years later that her family realized she didn't stop moving long enough to do much posing. While Lenore didn't collect photos of herself, her eldest son swears he saw a great black-and-white of her fly-fishing in the Fifties. He remembered it vividly, because it was the first picture he ever saw of any woman casting while standing knee-deep in a stream.

Later in her life, she devoted many hours trying to help the female inmates at the county jail. She loved to teach them to read and encourage them to seek high school diplomas. When she died, she left instructions to have most of her books donated to the same jail.

Among the stories her son tells about his mother, surely most centered on her creative and steady parenting. Some stories make you laugh—like the time she took her son's school shoes away. The new shoes were being misused in mud puddles and such and they weren't placed under the bed immediately after school.

In their place, Lenore had purchased moccasins. Her son only needed to hear the taunts from his classmates for several days about his unfashionable footwear in the fifties before he learned his lesson.

Among his memories, the favorite one her son tells concerns his mother's ability to avoid being locked into any facet of parenthood. His mother created great forms of loving care as often as she changed her dreams. In her lifestyle, new approaches were handled by instinct rather than by fad self-help books. How did she do so well without experts hammering at her senses?

He tells of the great bus ride with his mother. Lenore decided to pursue one of her dreams of working in Hollywood as a screenwriter. With her husband's blessing, she headed to the West Coast for the new adventure. Joining her was her eldest son—and his immense collection of comic books.

His grandfather once took him to a drugstore and bought one copy of every comic book there was as an incentive for reading so many books at such a young age. Over the next several years, Lenore's boy collected several hundred—enough to fill a sizable cardboard box—popular comic books. He was quite protective of the collection and insisted on bringing them along for the long, cross-country bus ride. After he'd read them once, all he did with the comic books was constantly count and arrange them.

While the trip was a story in itself, Lenore helped her son grow up somewhere on the highway outside of Little Rock, Arkansas.

Whenever they had to change buses, it was a chore to lug the great box of comic books into and through bus terminals. Lenore never complained as she patiently waited for her firstborn's small and measured steps. Things seemed to be going fine. Even at those smaller towns, where rest stops were but minutes long, the comic books were always safe—even if spread out on the long, rear seat.

In Little Rock, Lenore told her son it was a several-hour layover, yet they would be continuing on the same bus. It was bus number 1347 and they had a nice, long meal in the depot with a big piece of apple pie for dessert. When they returned to board the bus, the son's trauma exploded. While it was still bus number 1347, it was a different, newer bus. The bus was clean; all the windows were clear. As the son rushed down the aisle to the last seat on the bus, he knew the comic books were gone.

Reports were made. Bus drivers were understanding; a search message was relayed to the bus company, although they continued on the trip. The boy recalls hearing Lenore not being alarmed, because she was sure the comic books would not be destroyed. Of course, they wouldn't be destroyed—they'd been given to a passenger that had been sitting with Lenore since they left Indiana.

It was many years later that Lenore told her son that she felt he was fencing in his dreams by holding onto unnecessary stuff. She knew their great adventures in California would be easier to accept without the burdens of holding onto childish things. She'd also taken care to mention that the lady sitting next to her was returning home to her own family and her own young sons after a long hospital stay in Indiana, and she felt sad that her meager resources prevented her from bringing her children any gifts. Lenore immediately decided that those comic books would have a new home and that her son would someday agree that the California experience was better served without any cardboard box of old stuff.

Lenore was right again. Losing the comic books did become a

warm and precious memory. Her son said it was great to wake up in Burbank land without any responsibility and the chance to collect new stuff. Do mothers still manage their son's possessions in such a caring way today? Perhaps mothers load their children down with such an inventory that they have little extra time after toy and collection review to seek out brand-new dreams. Lenore's son would insist those parents might be less than creative managers of their children's time.

The season came when Lenore was leaving this world. As she struggled with her last days, she shared these last words with her firstborn son. From her hospital bed, she said, "Do two things, son," pausing as she fought for breath and her face tightened, yet keeping her eyes wide open and fixed on her son, she continued, "promise me you will never padlock your dreams." Then she smiled. It was the last time he saw her smile as she said, "And someday, maybe you can write something nice about your mother."

Yes, Lenore was my mom. While she might be surprised by the going rate for such a vintage comic book collection today, she could not be surprised by how visiting museums and art shows and travel are still new adventures for me to this day. She knows—oh, she must surely know I still haven't padlocked any dreams because of her being my mom. It seemed about time to honor her very last wish with these long-overdue words.

THE END

MOM WON'T LET ME
HAVE A BOYFRIEND
I hope she finds the courage...

That got their attention.

I had never seen my mother and my grandmother so angry with each other. I knew they didn't get along, but this was outrageous.

"Sit down!" I barked.

My mom sat down next to me, my grandmother on the opposite side of the table.

"Julia, are you really pregnant?" my mother asked.

"Had you going, didn't I? Would that make you happy? Then you'd finally stop harping on me, wouldn't you?"

Mom glared. "Don't lie to me again."

"You've been lying to me, so I thought I'd lie to you, to let you see what it feels like."

"That was a dirty trick," Mom said.

"Sorry." I pushed the cereal bowl away from me. "What is wrong with you two, anyway? You're acting like children."

"I'm sick of your grandmother's meddling," my mother said. "You're my child and you belong at home with me."

My grandmother said, "Don't listen to her, you can stay here as long as you like. She's not being a good mother, anyway, she's putting her own happiness ahead of yours."

Well, Grandma didn't to convince me of that.

Mom said, "What's so wrong with my happiness? Why can't I marry for love?"

Grandma said, "Marriage isn't about love! Marriage is about doing your duty!"

"Grandma! That sounds awful," I said.

"Julia you're young and you've still got stars in your eyes. Marriage is hard work. Nobody tells you that, but it's true."

"But what about love?" I asked her.

"What about it?"

"Didn't you love Grandpa when you got married?"

"Grandpa and I didn't worry about such things. Our parents wanted us to get married, so we did."

"Arranged marriages. Yuck."

"We did better than your mother and father."

Mom said, "That's not fair and you know it."

Grandma said, "You spent your teen years telling me how stupid I was. Your getting pregnant was the best thing that happened between you and me. It took you down a peg, showed you what it was like to be human."

"Grandma!"

"It's the truth. She should suffer for what she put me through."

"All those years in a loveless marriage isn't suffering enough?" my mother screamed.

"Mom!"

"I'm sorry you had to find out this way," my mother said. Tears threatened to spill out of her eyes.

"Why didn't you tell me you were pregnant when you got married?" I crossed my arms across my chest and leaned away from her. "I'm not a baby. Stop treating me like one."

"Sometimes the truth isn't pretty," she said.

"Now I know why you never celebrated your wedding anniversary," I said. "What else haven't you told me?"

She sighed deeply. "Let's go out in the car."

Grandma muttered to herself but didn't stop us from going outside.

We settled in the front seats. "I met your father at a college party. It was my first time away from home and his, too. We got drunk, one thing led to another, and we woke up in bed."

"We are talking about Victor, aren't we?"

My mother shot me an angry look. "Yes, we are talking about Victor."

"Well, there might be something else you haven't told me."

"No, Victor was your father. There was no doubt about that."

"What happened next?"

"We didn't see each other again for a couple of months. I was embarrassed. It was my first time."

"The first time you had sex?"

Mom nodded. "Then I found out I was pregnant."

"What did he say when you told him?"

"He was shocked, of course. So was I."

I felt a dagger plunge into my heart. "Obviously, you didn't want me."

"Now, don't be like that. Just because you were a surprise doesn't mean we didn't love you the minute you were born."

"But you didn't love each other. I always suspected something was wrong. I just never knew what it was."

My mother twisted in her seat. "How could I love him? I didn't know him! But we did the right thing. We got married. Your father insisted on it. "

I added, "I suppose Grandma insisted on it, too."

"Yes. She knew I wasn't in love with your father then, but she said that didn't matter. His parents didn't approve of me. They wouldn't even come to the wedding. We got monthly checks until your father graduated from college, then no contact with them after that."

"You told me they were dead."

"I'm sorry. That was another lie."

"Mother!"

"When your father was so ill, I tracked them down and found out your grandmother had died several years before. Maybe your grandfather is dead now, I don't know. But he still refused to come visit even after he knew your father was dying. And he's never asked to see you, never acknowledged your existence. How could I explain something like that to you?"

"Oh, Mom, that's horrible! How could you stand it?"

"How could I stand it? What choice did I have? How do you think I could watch your dad suffer and die like he did? Their coldness was just something else I couldn't change. I thought if I sent them pictures of you, they would soften in their stubbornness, but they never did."

"And you never loved my dad?"

"I wouldn't say that. I came to love your father in my own way."

"But if you hadn't gotten pregnant with me, you wouldn't have married him."

"I don't know. I'm sure you'd like to hear I would have married him anyway, but you said you wanted the truth. Are you sorry you asked?"

"Maybe a little bit. But now I understand why you are so worried about my reputation."

"It was so embarrassing, Julia, getting married in a hurry because I was pregnant. And it was hard to watch my friends drift away because we had nothing in common anymore, giving up my dreams of an education, becoming a mother before I was ready. I've never regretted having you, but it was hard. And in some ways, my situation was easy. Your father wanted to marry me. With so many girls, the man disappears. What would have happened then?"

"Yes, but Mom, that's not me."

"You say that, but I know how strong the pull of hormones are. We're all genetically programmed to reproduce, you know."

"Ron and I aren't you and Dad."

"I know you're not, honey, but I worry. Especially after we move in with Steve. You'll be living in the same house with Ron. How can I protect you?"

"Mom, I'm seventeen years old. I know what I'm doing."

"Well, I was eighteen years old and I didn't know what I was doing until it was too late. I'd like to keep the same thing from happening to you.

That's why I want you to date other people after Steve and I get married."

"I can't do that, Mom. My love for Ron is just as important to me as your love for Steve. Why can't you understand that?"

She sighed. "I do understand. But I'm frightened."

"Don't be," I leaned over and hugged her. "I promise we won't do anything wrong."

"How can I be sure of that?" Mom asked.

"You'll just have to trust me," I said.

"I don't know if I can," Mom said.

"You'll have to if you want me to live with you. Otherwise, it's me living with Grandma, and let me tell you, that's getting old fast."

Mom laughed. "She can be difficult to get along with."

"You said it. I can't believe she slapped you."

"It wasn't the first time, Julia, just the first time she's done it in front of you."

Mom said she'd ask Steve and Ron to meet us for dinner that night. Until we figured out a solution, I insisted on staying at Grandma's. I kissed her good-bye.

"See you later," she said.

After Mom drove away, I went back into Grandma's apartment. Grandma was in the kitchen, planning dinner.

"I'm going out tonight," I told her.

"With Ron again?"

"And Mom and Steve. We're going to discuss living arrangements." I groaned. "Again."

"Why don't you stay here? Problem solved."

"I love you, Grandma, but I don't like the way you treat Mom. I think you owe her an apology."

"What for?"

"For slapping her! That was terrible, Grandma."

"Oh, she'll get over it. She always does."

"Maybe, but do you have to treat her so mean? She's just doing the best she can."

"I thought you were upset with her. She's trying to make you break up with Ron."

"I am! But I do want her to be happy. And I don't want to give up Ron. Surely we can come up with a compromise that will still let me live with her."

"Spoken with the optimism of youth," Grandma grumbled. "Don't count on it."

"Just because you're miserable doesn't mean everyone else has to be," I countered.

"You'll see. Life has a way of making pessimists of us all," Grandma predicted.

That evening, Steve and Ron were already at the Chinese restaurant when Mom and I arrived. We walked over to the booth where they were sitting next to each other, Ron on the inside, Steve on the outside.

Every time I saw Ron, my heart beat faster. "I want to sit next to Ron," I said.

"No!" Mom snapped.

Steve laid his hand over Mom's. "Yvette, they can sit together. It isn't a big deal."

Mom shrugged, looking embarrassed. "All right, then."

Steve stood up and let me slide in next to Ron. Steve and Mom sat on the other side.

"Who wants mu shu pork?" Steve asked. Mom must have told him that was my favorite.

"I'm not very hungry," I said. I linked my fingers together and placed my hands on the table. If Mom was going to keep me from being with Ron again, she had another thing coming.

"Me, either," Ron said. Ron covered my hands with his.

Glancing over to him, I was reminded why I loved him so much. He was handsome like his father, but also considerate of my feelings.

Ron said, "I know why we're here. You can't break us up. Julia and I love each other."

Mom said, "But surely you understand how bad it would look to date your stepsister."

Ron shrugged. "I don't care how it looks."

Steve said, "Yvette and I realize that the only reason we met was because you were friends. But we worry about you living in the same house."

Ron said, "Just because you get married doesn't mean Julia and I will stop loving each other."

The waitress came to take our order. Steve waved her away. He turned back to Ron. "That's true. But what would you do if you were in our situation?"

I spoke up. "You would trust us to do the right thing."

Mom shifted closer to Steve. "Sometimes feelings can overpower people, and they do things they may regret later. And while men don't worry about what other people think, it's still true that a girl only has her reputation."

I made a face. I said to Ron, "I told you she'd come up with that reputation crap."

Ron said, "Mrs. Baker, I would never, ever hurt Julia. Not in a million years."

"Ron, now that your Dad and I are going to get married, I'd like you to call me Yvette."

Ron smiled, but he tightened his grip on my hands. "Okay, Yvette."

Mom said, "You're a great kid, Ron, and I like you a lot. But you have to promise that you won't date my daughter once your Dad and I are married. This is very important to me."

Ron let go of my hands and put an arm around me. He pulled me close. "I'm sorry, Mrs. Baker. I mean, Yvette. I can't do that to Julia. I love her too much to stop seeing her, even to please Dad and you."

Mom turned to Steve. "What are we going to do now?"

"Let's eat dinner," he said. "I'm sure we'll be able to think better on a full stomach."

We ordered several dishes to eat and green tea to drink. The food was good, but I didn't have much of an appetite. Steve tried to teach Mom how to eat with chopsticks, which was actually pretty funny. But by the end of the meal we still couldn't come to an agreement. We decided to continue the discussion at Steve and Ron's house.

Ron and I sat together on the love seat, Mom and Steve on the couch.

"We've been going around and around for hours. It seems to me the only solution that will work is to have us all live here," Steve said.

Ron said, "Fine, but I'm not going to break up with Julia."

I said, "And I'm not going to break up with Ron."

My mother raised her hands, palms up, in defeat. "I can't win. That's obvious."

Steve said, "It isn't winning or losing."

I said, "I know why you can't trust us. It's because you couldn't trust yourself when you were about my age."

"Julia, that's enough."

"No, it isn't enough. I think we should have everything out in the open."

"Steve already knows."

"Well, Ron doesn't."

Steve said, "Julia, that isn't necessary."

"I think it is. Are you going to forbid me to speak? You're not my father, you know."

My mother swore. "Julia, knock it off. You're not being reasonable."

"You and Steve are the ones being unreasonable. Why should Ron and I give up each other?"

"We've been through this before."

"I know. And each time, it's the same. You lay down orders and we tell you we're not going to go along. We're not children. We have a right to our feelings. You could at least try to trust us, you know."

"Okay, that's it," Steve said. "Time out. You and Ron have half an hour to come up with a workable solution. Then we'll negotiate." He took my mom's hand and led her out of the room.

I said to Ron, "Okay. They want us to propose some rules. First rule: We don't break up."

"Yeah, but we're going to have to give them something, or else it won't work."

"Fine. What bothers them the most?"

"The idea that we might have sex together in the house."

I laughed. "Sex somewhere else is good, huh?"

Ron laughed, too. "No, I don't think we can get away with that."

"I guess you're right. What if we promise not to sleep together until we're married?"

Ron gasped. "What a novel idea!"

"Stop teasing," I said, poking him in the ribs. "I suppose we ought to agree that any dates we have are outside the house."

"Yes, I think they'd be happier with that idea. No romance in the house."

Steve and my mother came back in the living room.

"That was fast," I said. "Or were you checking to see if we were having sex already?"

Ron said, "Julia, you've got to stop that, too."

I made a face at him. "So now you're on their side?"

Ron said, "If you're going to ask them to treat us like adults, then you're going to have to act like one."

"Well, shoot," I said, playing with him. "What kind of a deal is that?"

Steve said, "Here's our proposal. Julia and Yvette will move in here. Julia will have the downstairs bedroom, the one we've always used for guests. Ron will stay in his room upstairs. And we're not going to ask you to break up."

"Hooray!" Ron and I both said.

"But no funny business," my Mom added. "If you want a date, it's a regular date like you've been doing. Absolutely no holding hands, no kissing, or anything other physical contact in the house. If you do, Julia's off to Grandma's."

"We thought you'd come up with that," I said. "Okay, we'll agree."

My mother said, "I talked to Grandma on the phone. She's going to come stay here awhile."

I groaned. "Grandma here?"

"Actually, she was quite nice. She apologized to me about the argument we had earlier. She said you told her she ought to say she was sorry. Thank you for speaking to her, Julia."

"I'm glad she apologized. But she's not going to stay her all the time, right?"

"No, just while we're gone for the honeymoon."

One week later, we had the wedding at a small chapel. Ron and

68

Steve looked great in their tuxedos. Mom and I both wore blue, my dress dark blue and Mom's light blue. We had dinner at a fancy restaurant, then went to Ron's house. I mean, my new house.

Grandma insisted she had to sleep in the recliner chair in the living room, so she placed her suitcases on the couch. She was a notoriously light sleeper. Even if I wanted to break my promise, I wouldn't get past her eagle eyes. That made Mom happy.

Soon it was time to say good-bye to Mom and my new stepfather.

"I'm sorry if I hurt your feelings," I said to my mother. "I know we can work things out. You can trust Ron and me, honestly."

My mother raised her eyebrows. "You'd better. I'm counting on it, Julia."

Steve kissed me on the cheek. "Good-bye."

"Have a great honeymoon," I said to them both.

"Don't worry, we will," Steve said. They looked so happy when they got in the car to go to the airport.

Living at my new house was great. I had plenty of space in my new room. The house was close enough to a coffee shop to walk, so Ron and I got breakfast there on the weekend. Grandma ate tea and toast at the house while we had gourmet coffee and scones. And kisses.

"This is wonderful," I told Ron. "I'm glad your Dad and my Mom decided to take the plunge."

"Yeah, you say that today, but tomorrow you'll be complaining that you're seeing too much of me," he replied.

I grabbed his hand and squeezed it. "I don't think so," I said. "Promise me if something does happen and we don't end up married together, we'll still be friends."

"Always," Ron said. He whispered in my ear, "You'll always be my favorite stepsister."

I whispered in his ear, "That's because I'm your only stepsister."

We both laughed.

Mom and Steve came back from their honeymoon in Hawaii with chocolate macadamia nuts and straw hats for everyone. Grandma grumbled that nuts were too hard for her to eat while she collected her things to go home.

Mom asked, "Did Julia and Ron behave?"

"I guess so," Grandma said. "I didn't see much of them."

"Yes, Mother, we behaved," I said.

Mom took Grandma back to her apartment. Later, we were together in our new home, sitting around the dinner table, ready to say grace. Normally, Mom and I held hands while we said the prayer.

I hesitated.

Mom nodded. "It's okay. Just for grace."

I held hands with Ron on one side, my mother on the other, Steve across from me. We formed a circle, a family. "For what we are about to receive, may God make us truly grateful." I squeezed Mom's hand and Ron's hand, then released them.

Mom said, "Julia, I worried about you and Ron while we were gone, but I also realized something."

I raised my eyebrows. "What's that, Mom?"

She smiled at me. "I realized how proud I am of you. You stood up for what you believe and you wouldn't let me force you into doing something you felt was wrong. That takes a lot of courage."

I smiled at her. I knew it took a lot of courage for her to admit that she might have been wrong. "Well, Mom, I realize now how difficult things have been for you. It sounds like this is the first time you've gotten to do something you've really wanted to do, without having to think of what you ought to do. It takes courage to stand up for yourself that way, too."

Steve said, "It's good to see you both happy for a change."

"Can we eat now?" Ron asked.

We all laughed.

"Pass the pizza," I said.

THE END

MY SON WAS A HERO
My Eleven-Year-Old, the Nursing Student

"Milla, your son isn't in nursing school, you are," my mother chastised. "He should be out playing with other boys his age. You shouldn't be letting him look at those books, let alone have him quizzing you for tests."

"He likes doing it, Mom," I said patiently. "It's our thing to do together at night. He reads the questions from the book, and I answer aloud. I have to multitask, as they say, to get everything done."

"You're pushing yourself too hard," my mother argued. "Working all the time and going to school, then trying to study. You've got to think of Harlan, too. You need to spend time with him."

"That's what I'm trying to do, Mom." By now I was bristling at my mother's tone. "I'm doing all of this for him, too. I need my nursing degree to get a good job and to be able to schedule around him. Besides, helping me study is a way we spend time together."

Wrong thing to say. I had to listen to my mother gripe another ten minutes about my son losing his childhood, going to that awful school, and riding the school bus. Then I had to hear her complain about all that I'd done wrong in my life, which was pretty much everything, according to her.

"He doesn't need to study with you," Mom said. "He's not the nursing student, you are."

Good, I thought. She's starting to repeat herself. Maybe this means the conversation is at an end.

No such luck.

"He needs to be out playing baseball with his friends. You've got him stuck in that apartment."

At that moment my eleven-year-old son called out to me and I had the perfect excuse to get off the phone. My mom drove me nuts. She was loving and supportive in many ways, especially since Harlan's father left us high and dry. But she also used his leaving as a license to keep telling me what to do. It rang loud and clear that she thought since I'd failed at my marriage, I'd fail at raising my son.

It was my worst fear that she was right. I did worry about Harlan losing his childhood. Any child of divorce loses some of their innocence, and he was no different. He'd loved his father, and neither of us could understand why his dad left to go "find himself". Since Mickey left us with little money and no forwarding address, Harlan felt abandoned, too.

I worried about Harlan being stuck in an apartment every day, too. I couldn't afford our old house, so we'd moved. I tried to make sure he participated in sports at church, but like so many parents, I was afraid to let him go outside in the afternoons.

I was also afraid I depended on my son as a friend, a surrogate partner of sorts. I'd read that was a real problem with divorced parents. Loneliness caused many to reach out to their children for companionship and for the children to be caretakers. Children who needed a parent, not a friend. Children who still needed nurturing.

As I laid my books out on the kitchen table I glanced in at my son, who was also studying. He was such a good kid. He was more intelligent than a lot of the adults I knew, so I did talk to him a lot. Was the time he spent quizzing me expecting too much?

I thought back to nights of him trying to pronounce Latin medical terms with popcorn in his mouth that made us both laugh. We'd had a good time. I don't think it was asking too much of him.

It didn't hurt that my grades were improving in nursing school and Harlan was now studying a lot better on his own. Still, I worried.

Mom had mentioned the school and the school bus. He went to a decent school. It wasn't a posh private school like one my mom's friends sent their grandchildren to. Maybe that was what was bothering her. Mom had always been one for keeping up appearances. Harlan's school was good, though. The teachers seemed to care, and he'd made nice friends with kids who had caring parents. What more could any kid or parent ask for?

I worried about the school bus situation. My son promised to tell me if there was any bullying going on or anything like that. A couple of situations on the bus had made the news the last couple of years. He kept insisting he and his neighborhood buddies were fine. They sat together and got off together. There were actually a lot of kids from the apartment complex.

But I worried. Just like my mom worried about me and everything possible. I was sure, though, getting my degree in nursing would help us financially and improve our quality of life. I had to believe all this work was worth it. I had to keep telling myself I really was doing it for Harlan as well as myself. If we could only hang on this last semester.

The weeks flew by, but winter seemed to linger into spring. I sounded like my mom fussing at Harlan every morning to take his coat to school.

"Mom, it gets hot on the bus," he protested. "Everyone takes their coats off."

"Fine," I said, "take it off, but you at least have it with you if you need it."

I went to my early morning classes, then to my afternoon job. I called Harlan after he got home for a school. He'd already had a snack and said he was tired and thinking of taking a nap.

Again guilt plagued me. He'd stayed up a little late the night before, each of us quizzing the other for our respective tests.

When I got home, the smell of food from my slow cooker met my nose. It was chili for dinner and I'd promised Harlan I'd bring some hot dogs so he could have chili dogs. He was playing a video game in the living room. The message light on the phone was blinking.

"Haven't you been answering the phone?" I asked.

"I turned the ringer down when I was trying to nap. People kept calling and waking me up," he said. "I forgot to turn it back up. Sorry."

When I started listening to the messages, my mouth dropped open.

"How does it feel to have a hero for a son, Mrs. Bradshaw?" the Channel Five News guy asked. "We'd like an interview with your son tomorrow about what he did."

And so the calls went. Another local TV news station called, a radio station, and the school principal. The principal left a number and asked me to return her call.

"Mrs. Bradshaw," she said. "I did something impulsively and I hope you don't mind. It was just that I was so proud of Harlan. I get so tired of the news only carrying stories about bad kids, I wanted everyone to know."

"Know what?" I asked having no idea what any of the calls were about.

"Don't you know?" she asked. "Haven't you talked to Harlan?"

"I've talked to him, but he hasn't said anything," I said. "What's going on?"

She told me the story and as she did, I started crying. Harlan walked in and I saw the concerned look on his face. "Come here," I said hoarsely as I hung up the phone. "Give me a bear hug."

At eleven years old he still gave me "bear hugs" like he did when he was four. What his principal told me and what the local news was calling about both scared me and warmed my heart.

When Harlan was riding home on the bus, his driver evidently had a heart attack. Thankfully, she knew something was wrong early enough to pull off to the side of the road, so there was no danger of an accident. None of the kids knew what to do. Harlan told them all to put their coats on the driver because she was probably in shock and needed warmth. He then instructed one of the kids to try to use the radio to call for help and two of the oldest kids who lived closest to hurry home and call 911.

They said when the police arrived they were rather amazed to see a stack of coats on the woman, but it had done the trick of keeping her warm.

"Why didn't you tell me, Harlan?" I asked.

He shrugged. "It was no big deal. She had all the symptoms of shock, like we went over in one of your textbooks. I remember it said to keep the patient warm when that happened. None of us were using our coats, anyway."

I laughed through the tears. Harlan was more interested in the prospect of chili dogs than being interviewed on the news.

"It was just some of that boring stuff I'm always reading to you for your tests," he said.

For the first time since my divorce, I felt confident that I wasn't failing Harlan. He was a great kid who'd be a great young man before I knew it. I couldn't wait to tell my mother that I might be the one in nursing school, but her grandson had already passed all the tests with flying colors.

THE END

I WENT INTO LABOR
And didn't know I was pregnant!

"Mr. and Mrs. Watford, I'm sorry," the doctor said, his face long and filled with pity. "Mrs. Watford, your tubes are blocked. Even if we unblock them, they're so filled with scar tissue that it's highly unlikely you'll ever conceive."

My heart sank at the terrible news. All my husband and I had ever wanted was a big, happy family. We both had good jobs, but money could never replace the love we knew we could give children. I glanced over at Evan and saw the same reaction that I was feeling.

"Isn't there something we can do, Doctor?" he asked, his voice hoarse and filled with anguish, which only made me feel worse. I watched his jaw tighten as he waited to hear the doctor's response.

"Not really," the doctor replied. "We can do surgery, but there's still no guarantee."

We discussed my condition in detail before Evan stood to leave. "Let's go, April," he said. "This whole situation has worn me out."

We were silent all the way home, so I had plenty of time to think. I felt awful. It was like I'd let my husband down and couldn't give him the most important thing—a child of his own. If he'd married someone else, he'd be able to have a house full of kids, just like he wanted.

When I told him that later, he shook his head. "That's ridiculous, April. I don't want children unless I can have them with you."

That was a sweet comment, but I still felt awful. "Maybe I should get a second opinion," I told him.

"If you want to, that's fine," Evan said. "But don't get your hopes up. Your doctor is the best in town. I've never heard of him making mistakes."

"He's human," I said with determination. "Everyone makes mistakes."

I went to another doctor on the other side of town. After a thorough physical examination, she called me into her office.

"I'm afraid I have to concur with what your doctor said," she told me. "Surgery is a possibility, but not a guarantee. In fact, your chances of ever being able to conceive look very slim to me. Have you thought about adoption?"

Adoption had never crossed my mind because I'd always assumed I'd be able to produce plenty of healthy babies. My mother had, my grandmother had, and as far as I knew all the other women in my family had. I never dreamed I'd have a physical problem that would cause me to be barren.

"We can discuss that at home," Evan told her. "In the meantime, I think my wife needs me to take her out to lunch."

I wasn't hungry, but I didn't argue. Evan was just being a good husband and trying his best to make me feel better. We didn't talk much. I suspect he was dealing with the second round of bad news like I was—in silent anger.

Once we got home, he told me to sit down and put my feet up. "You've had a hard day, April," he said softly. "I'll fix you a drink."

He was in the kitchen for several minutes before he came out with two glasses of tea. Then he sat down in the chair facing me and said we needed to talk.

I swallowed hard. "I'm so sorry, honey. I feel like I've really let you down. If you want to find another woman who can give you a family, I'll understand."

"That's out of the question," he said quickly. "You're my wife, and we're in this together. I didn't marry you because I thought you were a baby machine. I love you with all my heart, and if we'd been blessed with a family, that would've been icing on the cake."

Through my tears, I said, "I love you so much. You're the best husband in the world."

"But there are some things I'd like to discuss," he said.

I nodded. "Adoption?"

"Adoption, among other things."

Evan and I talked about adoption first, but we weren't ready to do that yet. Plus, it was very expensive. We had a small savings account, but it was nowhere near enough to pay an adoption fee.

"Maybe one of these days we can do that," he told me. "We should start saving for that possibility. I'd want to be financially secure before we make a jump like that. If you'd gotten pregnant, our insurance would've covered most of it, but adoption would wipe us out."

I agreed. From that day on, I began to put a chunk of my paycheck into savings, and Evan did the same. Not only did we find out that adoption fees could run into five figures, I wanted to stay home and take care of our child for a few years.

We continued to save money, but over time we quit discussing adoption. I'd begun to think that might not be the way to go because I'd heard and read so many stories about people's adopted children growing up and looking for their birth parents. I didn't like the idea of a person I'd raised as my own to abandon me as a parent just to see someone who'd given them up.

Evan had begun to work long hours because his company hadn't replaced workers who'd quit, yet the workload had remained the same.

76

When he wasn't home, I always ate more because food became my comfort.

All my life my periods had been irregular, but now they got really strange. I assumed it was because of all the stress of having my husband gone all the time and I'd been gaining so much weight.

We barely had time for each other but our sex life was still pretty decent, considering how much he worked. That was one area of our marriage that was nearly perfect. Even after I gained weight, he told me I still looked beautiful to him.

Then I began to feel tired all the time. When I looked at myself in the mirror, I noticed my eyes weren't as bright as they usually were.

"You don't look so good," Evan said one Sunday morning when we first got up. "You look a little green around the gills."

I smiled. That was what he always said when I was pale. "I'm fine, but I do feel a little sick to my stomach," I said. "Maybe after I eat something I'll be better."

Evan nodded. "Let me fix some eggs. That spicy food we ate last night must not have agreed with you."

He called me when breakfast was ready. I had to gradually sit up in bed and make my way to the kitchen, holding onto furniture along the way. I was very dizzy and more than slightly nauseous. For some odd reason, the floor felt like it was shifting beneath me. That was an odd sensation, because I rarely ever got sick.

"Maybe you have a bug," he said as he helped me into a chair. "I don't think spicy food would do that to you."

I nibbled at my breakfast but it didn't taste right to me. "I'm going back to bed," I announced. "I think you're right, this is a bug. I need to sleep it off, and I don't want you to catch it."

"Don't worry about a thing," he said in an assured tone. "Go back to sleep and everything will be fine."

I woke up several times that day, but mostly I slept. It had to be a virus for me to feel so tired. I was normally full of energy.

On Monday morning I managed to get up and go to work, although I didn't feel much better. Evan tried to convince me to call in sick, but I hated missing work. I knew if I stayed home I'd have to work overtime to catch up.

It seemed like it took forever to feel better, but it was only several weeks. Everyone at work was worried about me, so when the color returned to my face, people said they were glad it wasn't anything serious.

"The virus must've been a bad one," I told my boss. "It took forever to get over it."

She nodded. "I'm just glad no one else caught it. With this workload, we can't afford for the whole office to get sick. Not everyone's as dedicated to their jobs as you, April."

I went from feeling awful and having no energy to feeling like I was on top of the world. My color came back and Evan said my skin positively glowed. "That's because you've seen me looking really bad for so long," I joked. "Anything would be an improvement after that." After I recovered from being sick, I couldn't seem to do enough.

"Man, April," my coworker, Jane, said. "You're unstoppable. You keep going and going."

Even after I got home, I felt like doing things I never used to do. I cooked, cleaned, and even got into a little decorating. Evan thought it was funny. "I didn't realize I'd married such a homemaker," he teased.

"I don't understand what's happening to me," I told him. "It's almost like I've been possessed. All I can think about at work is having clean floors, and I'm dying to put new window treatments in the living room. Do you think I'm losing my mind?"

"No, I don't think so," he replied. "Maybe you're just ready for some changes."

"Apparently so," I agreed. "Maybe this is my way of working through some of that sudden burst of energy I have."

"Whatever it is," he said, "I like it. We've never had such great meals before."

That was another thing. I wanted to cook all the time. I clipped recipes from magazines that featured pictures of gourmet meals. Anything that looked good, I cooked. It all tasted wonderful to me, and I especially enjoyed Italian food—the rich sauces and pasta in all shapes and sizes.

"Maybe you should open a catering service," Evan said.

"I'm already growing big as a house," I replied. "If I cooked for a living, I'd have to join a circus."

"You're not fat, April," Evan told me lovingly as he gave me a big hug. "You just have a little extra cushion."

I stood in front of a mirror and took a long, hard look at myself. I'd gained weight all over—in my arms, my thighs, and especially my mid-section. I'd put on more than just a few extra pounds. It was definitely time to go on a diet.

"At least wait until we come back from vacation," Evan begged. "I want you to enjoy yourself on the cruise."

He'd talked me into taking a short four-day cruise to unwind. Both of us had been working so hard. Evan felt that we needed some time away and to be pampered, which we'd heard was what happened on some of the big ocean liners. We'd looked at pamphlets of people having fun sunning, playing games, dancing, and of course standing in one of the many buffet lines where there was an endless supply of food. I drooled at the mere thought of all that fresh seafood and fruit.

The pamphlet didn't do the actual ship justice. It was even better than we'd imagined. I loved floating along without a care in the world, and being able to eat anything I wanted without having to cook. It was fantastic.

When I expressed a short moment of doubt before taking dessert, Evan waved me on. "Go ahead, April. You can start your diet when we get home."

I ate to my heart's content and had a blast doing it. When we got back, I had a great tan and a great outlook on life.

"I think we need to do that more often," I told my husband.

He chuckled. "We'd have to dip into savings if we do it again."

I swallowed hard. That savings he'd mentioned was for an adoption that we'd never pursued. I'd almost forgotten all about it. Putting money into that fund had become so routine. I never even thought about what it was for anymore, even though I'd continued to save. It had grown into quite a hefty account, and we had plenty of money to adopt one child. But I still had some reservations.

"Can we talk?" I said to Evan. "I mean a real, honest-to-goodness, heart-to-heart discussion."

"Sure, sweetheart," he said softly. "What's on your mind?"

"I've been thinking about a baby."

With a big smile, he said, "Are you ready to look into adoption?"

"I'm not so sure I want to adopt, Evan," I said slowly, hoping I wouldn't upset him. "After all, we're starting to get close to middle age, and I don't want to be too old with a child still at home."

His face fell momentarily, but then he smiled back at me. "You're probably right. If we were meant to be parents, we would've done something by now." His comment came so quickly I suspected he was reacting and might not have really meant it. Evan's sensitivity was sometimes too much for me to handle because I often suspected he was neglecting what he really wanted to make sure I was happy.

"Don't you want to even talk about it?" I asked.

"Not really. I think we should take our savings and have some fabulous vacations. We should travel and do whatever we want. Both of us work hard, so we deserve decent breaks."

"Then let's start planning our next cruise," I said with excitement. "Maybe next year we can go on a long one, like for a whole week."

"Sounds good to me," he said.

"I do need to take off some of this weight before then," I reminded him. "Plus an extra five pounds so I won't feel guilty for standing in the dessert lines."

"Shouldn't be too hard, since you have a whole year to do it. Tell you what, April. I'll diet with you. I could stand to lose a few pounds, too."

I put all my energy into cooking healthy foods after that. Evan and

79

I went through the pantry and tossed out almost everything.

Even after weeks of eating healthy foods I still wasn't losing weight, although Evan had taken off nearly ten pounds eating the same things as me. "Maybe I have a more serious problem," I said. "I wonder if my thyroid is sluggish."

With concern, Evan nodded. "Maybe you better go back to the doctor."

I promised to call and schedule an appointment. Since my weight issue wasn't an emergency, the doctor's receptionist scheduled me for a couple weeks away.

"Want me to go with you?" Evan asked.

Shaking my head, I said, "I don't think that'll be necessary. You've been working so hard lately, I'd hate to take you away from your office."

"If you need me, I'll be there."

I knew he would, and I appreciated it. However, a physical examination wasn't something I expected to be a problem. I'd just tell the doctor that if there was bad news to call Evan in so he could hold my hand. Otherwise, I'd just deal with it and tell Evan about it later.

One day as I was getting ready for work, my back began to ache. I flinched as I reached for my shoes in the closet.

"What's the matter, April?" Evan said.

"My back feels like it's about to go out on me."

"Have you lifted anything heavy lately?" he asked.

"No," I said as I stood there and thought. "Not that I can think of. Maybe I just turned wrong."

Evan got my shoes for me and said maybe I should call the doctor and see if he could see me earlier than the scheduled appointment.

"I'll be okay," I assured him.

All morning at the office I had to shift position in my chair because my back kept hurting if I stayed in one spot for too long. Then, when a bunch of people mentioned going to lunch, I felt an odd sensation in my abdomen. It tightened and pulled, causing me to gasp for air.

"Maybe I better stay here," I said to some coworkers who'd invited me out to lunch. "I think I've pulled some muscles, and I'm pretty sore. Can you bring me back a salad?"

After they were gone, I began to feel better. A few minutes later the pain miraculously went completely away, and I felt like I could do anything. That's weird, I thought.

I worked for several more minutes before I got a call on my extension that I needed to bring some folders to accounting. I turned, grabbed the folders, and started down the hall. Suddenly, I felt that familiar sensation in my abdomen—the feeling I'd had fifteen minutes earlier. I dropped the folders and literally fell against the wall.

"April," one of my coworkers said as she rushed to my side, "are you okay?"

"No." I moaned. "I think I need to go to the doctor." Reaching up, I said, "Can you help me up?"

She held up both of her hands and shook her head. "No way. You stay right there. I'm calling an ambulance."

"No," I argued. "I really don't need an ambulance."

She ignored me and shouted for someone to sit with me while she dialed 911. Within minutes I heard the scream of sirens, then the commotion as the paramedics arrived.

There were three of them, and they were practically on top of me before I had a chance to argue. One of them was firing questions at my coworkers, while the other two were taking my vital signs.

"Is she married?" the paramedic with the clipboard asked.

"Yes," Jane said. "Want me to call her husband?"

"That would be good. Have him meet us at the hospital."

Then the pain hit again. That time I let the medical people do what they needed to do.

We arrived at the hospital in ten minutes and Evan was there waiting for me. "How'd you get here so fast?" I asked.

"Someone from your office called me and said it looked serious," he said. "What happened?"

"I have no idea, Evan. Right now I'm fine, but a few minutes ago I thought I was dying."

His worried expression broke my heart, but I was scared for myself. What if I was dying? I wasn't ready to go yet.

Evan was asked to leave while the doctor examined me. Fortunately my doctor was on call, and he wasn't far from the hospital when I was admitted.

"I'll take care of you, April. It's probably nothing serious. Where does it hurt?"

I rubbed my back and said, "Here, and my lower abdomen."

He was checking my heart when the pain began to wash over me again. I tensed. He pulled the stethoscope away and gave me a quizzical look.

"Is this what you've been feeling?" he asked.

I nodded. "Yes, and it hurts worse each time. I think it lasts longer, too." My voice was raspy from the pain, and I felt the sweat break out over my face.

The pain lasted a couple minutes then it was gone, just like that. "Am I dying?" I asked as he stood there shaking his head.

"I don't think so, April. How long have you been having these pains?" What I saw on his face was bewilderment, not deep concern. I was confused.

I thought for a moment before telling him. "It's really strange how they come and go so quickly."

"Yes, I know," he said. "How far apart are the pains?"

"They seem to be coming faster and faster. The last one was about ten minutes after the one before that."

He turned to one of the nurses behind him, mumbled something I couldn't hear, then turned back to me. "I want to check something else, April."

They wheeled me into another examining room, and the nurse put my feet into some stirrups. "What are you doing?" I asked.

"Ruling out possibilities," was all he said.

The nurse held my hand as the doctor gave me a pelvic examination. I watched his expression go from perplexity to genuine happiness.

"April, I think you'll be glad to know—"

Suddenly, the pain was back and I was hurting so much that I let out a scream. That time it was in my back, my abdomen, and my thighs.

"The baby's crowning," the nurse said as she pointed.

The baby? Then suddenly, the pain grew so intense I couldn't hold back.

The nurse squeezed my hand, the doctor nodded, and they all turned to me and said, "Push!"

Instinctively, I tensed my entire body and pushed. As soon as I relaxed, the reality of the situation hit me like a ton of bricks. I was having a baby. All this time, I'd been pregnant and not known.

"Once more, April," the doctor said. "We need a good, solid push, and the baby should be out."

"Can you get Evan first?" I asked weakly.

Again, the doctor nodded and one of the nurses by the door ran out and came back with my husband, whose face was white as a sheet. "Is my wife okay?" he asked.

My body tensed with another agonizing pain that didn't seem so bad now that I knew what was going on. Tears streamed down my face as I tried to smile at my husband.

"Push," the doctor said.

This time, I gave it my all. I pushed as hard as I could as I kept my eyes on my husband. Evan's eyes were bugging out of his head as he watched his baby being born.

"Oh, my God," he said.

"Surprise!" the doctor said as he lifted the tiny baby covered in blood. "It's a boy."

The chaos in the room right then prevented me from saying anything, which was good because my thoughts were totally scrambled. Evan didn't say a word as he came to my side and held my hand.

Over the next couple of hours people came and went, congratulating us, telling us we'd kept the best secret in the world. I was so dumbfounded, I didn't know what to say to any of them.

My coworkers thought it was funny that I hadn't told anyone. I tried to convince them that I didn't know, but they didn't believe me.

Finally, later that night, after we found out the baby was just fine and healthy, Evan and I settled down to discuss what to do now. He pulled a chair up beside my hospital bed, and he looked into my eyes, grinning like a fool. We were both in shock, but at least we were finally able to comprehend what had just happened.

"Have you thought of a name yet?" he asked.

"Are you kidding? That's the last thing on my mind. All I can think about is where he'll sleep when we get home."

"I'll go out and get a crib after I leave here," Evan said. "We have that savings account for the adoption."

"Oh, yeah," I said with a smile. "It's funny how that adoption never happened."

Evan shrugged. "I sort of wish we had adopted. Then we'd have two children."

I studied my husband as my love for him flooded my body. He'd really wanted children pretty badly, but he'd quit discussing it because he knew how awful I felt about not being able to get pregnant.

"That's something we can talk about later," I said. "But first, I guess you better go get that crib. I'll start on a list of names. It'll give me something to do between feedings when they bring him to nurse."

That was three months ago. Everyone from my office stopped by the hospital to see the surprise baby. Evan had a chat with my boss, who said my job would always be there if I wanted to go back after I take a leave of absence.

Now that I've been home for three months, I'm not sure I'm going back to work. There are times I'd miss my job, but I can't imagine leaving little Tyler every day. He's the sweetest child, smiling all the time, making sweet baby sounds. Evan says he wants me home because we have this miracle baby after I was told I probably would never be able to have a child.

The doctor was as stunned as the rest of us over my pregnancy. I had obvious symptoms all along, throughout the pregnancy, but I'd ignored them due to what he'd told me about my tubes being blocked. What baffled me was the fact that I didn't show my pregnancy like most women did. I'd put on weight, but not only in my abdomen. It was all over my body.

"I hope you're not complaining," the doctor said.

"No, of course not. In fact, I'd be willing to put on double that amount of weight if I could do it again."

With a grin, he replied, "Miracles do happen, you know."

THE END

Women Can Do Anything—And They Do It, Too!
SOCCER MOM TO
THE RESCUE!
Healthy, happy kids are my goal

Sometimes we make choices in our lives. Other times, things are just thrust upon us. Becoming a single mom was thrust upon me when my husband, Greg, was killed in a car crash. Being a working single mom after years of staying at home was also thrust upon me by necessity. We'd had only minimal life insurance, and what we had didn't nearly cover our mortgage payment, much less our other monthly bills.

When it came to becoming the coach of my daughter's soccer team, though—now that was a conscious choice. Not that I didn't have some reservations about it. I prayed long and hard that God would find someone else who'd be interested in coaching her team, but no one spoke up. And the fact that it wasn't a sanctioned team certainly didn't help matters.

The kids who wanted to be on this team were a group that had banded together on its own. They were the kids who, for various reasons, needed their own team. Of course, no one would ever admit that they weren't welcome on another team; that would've been discrimination. It was just that when some had gotten on a team, they were made to feel so inept or unwelcome that they eventually quit.

The fact that it was Lindsay's idea made me even more determined than ever to let them have their chance. Maybe I knew only a little about soccer, and I knew next to nothing about coaching, but I knew kids—especially the ones who didn't fit the mold. I'd been one of them, after all.

My daughter, Lindsay, was overweight and asthmatic, yet her doctor said exercise was good for her. Playing a sport would be good for her as long as she knew when she needed to stop and take a break.

At first, there were only a few girls interested in the team. They had to learn a lesson about discrimination when I suggested they ask a few boys to join them.

"Boys!" Lindsay said as she wrinkled her nose in distaste. At ten, boys were not high on her list of likes, especially after some of the experiences she'd had being the brunt of jokes and teasing.

"Yes, boys," I replied. "You know—the opposite of girls?"

"I know. But Mom, boys are just going to ruin our fun."

Hands on my hips, I faced my daughter. "Doesn't that sound familiar? I remember when your brother learned there was going to be a girl on his team."

"That's because Hunter thinks no one can play as good as he can. Especially a girl."

"And who's the best goalie they have on his team now?"

"Jenny Matthews." Lindsay giggled. "But she is the coach's daughter."

"He wasn't always the coach," I stated, then immediately watched my daughter's expression sober at the reminder that her father had been the coach before Lou Matthews. Perhaps for many reasons, it was not a pleasant reminder.

"Dad didn't want her to play, either," Lindsay reminded me. "Because she's a girl."

"Yes, but he let her."

"Because her dad was his best friend. What could he say?"

Okay, she had a point. But I had to turn my example around. "He didn't say yes because Lou was his best friend. He did it because he knew it was the right thing to do."

Lindsay shrugged. "But that's Jenny. She's not one of us."

"Listen to yourself, Lindsay," I started softly. "How can you expect people to treat you as an equal if you set yourself apart?"

She bowed her head.

I lifted her chin so I could look into her tear-filled eyes. "The kids on your team just need a chance, and I'm going to see that they get it. But you are going to have to be as open to others as you want others to be to you."

"Sort of like the Golden Rule."

"Exactly." I smiled, knowing my daughter now understood.

To prove it, her expression changed, looking like an idea had suddenly occurred to her. "So, besides boys who are fat—" she started—I winced at the three-letter word that might as well have been a four-letter word for all the pain it could cause. She'd heard it so often that even she referred to herself that way. "—we can ask the kids that everyone makes fun of because they're too skinny. Unless they're tall, because then they can play basketball."

I groaned, knowing my daughter still had more lessons to learn about stereotyping. But I'd just have to wait for another teachable moment. For now, one lesson at a time.

"There are a few kids who don't play on any teams because they spend all their time on the computer or reading," she continued, running with her idea. "And there's Tommy Sheffield. Do you think we should ask him?"

I knew the boy she spoke of had a twisted right foot that caused him to walk with a very profound limp. "If Tommy wants to play on your team, I'd say he can play. But, just like the rest of you, he needs to make sure it's okay with his parents and doctor so we'll know if there's anything he may not be able to do."

With that settled, my daughter went on a recruiting campaign that got us more than enough kids to start our team.

Before going to sleep each night, I read as much as I could about soccer. Then I said a prayer that not only asked for blessing for my family, but also that some miracle might happen that would make me a good enough coach for this very special team.

After our first disastrous practice, I knew I was going to have to pray a whole lot harder. I'd been naive to think I could coach; I knew basically nothing about the job.

Lindsay wore a frown as we parked in the driveway after practice. Though I'd praised all the kids for their efforts, I knew by the defeated looks on their faces that none of them were fooled. I also knew that their problems on the playing field had as much to do with my lack of skill as their own.

As we got out of the car and started toward the house, Hunter rode his bike into the driveway, returning from his own practice.

"So, Wheezy, how bad did you guys do?" he asked.

I grimaced at the nickname he used for his sister, and had to bite back the angry retort that was on the tip of my tongue. I'd learned it only made matters worse when I stuck up for his sister. Still, it was hard to be silent as I watched Lindsay's back stiffen at the same time her chin lowered to her chest.

Not for the first time, I thought of Greg and his "contribution" to the problem between our children. He'd been the one to call Lindsay "Chub" when she was just a toddler. And later, as she grew older, he'd pressed me to put her on a diet so she'd be more "normal," as he called it.

Unfortunately, he often said these things in front of Lindsay and the result was painful to see. I'd watch Lindsay cry because she thought her daddy didn't love her the way she was. Then I'd watch her struggle to try to be the way she thought he wanted her to be. She'd exhaust herself running and playing games, trying to keep up with her older brother.

Around this time, she'd had her first asthma attack. The doctor said it was as much from her activity as it was from her weight. He'd added that stress often triggered it, too, and then asked if she was under much stress.

"Only to lose weight and be active," I replied.

The doctor sighed. "It's a catch-22 situation," he said. "You need to figure out when it's best to intercede and break the cycle. A little activity will help her lose weight. But too much anxiety will only make her asthma worse and she'll probably end up with significant health problems."

I remembered so well what I'd gone through as an overweight child. I'd been teased and ridiculed mercilessly, and it wasn't until high school that I finally shed the pounds. It hadn't been easy. Fortunately, I'd had a lot of support from my family.

In Lindsay's case, she only had support from me. Her father always seemed disappointed in her, and Hunter had taken his father's lead and started picking on her, too.

It wasn't until six months after her father died that I noticed a slight difference in my daughter's weight. It was difficult to notice, since she was also growing taller.

Then after several more months, she'd brought up the subject of playing sports. I'd been the one to suggest soccer. When I went to the coach of the team for her age group, he'd told me that his practices were a strenuous workout, but if Lindsay could cut it, she could be on the team.

Unfortunately, the only allowance he'd made for her asthma was having her spend most of her time on the bench, watching the other team members play. The few times she got a chance to play, she'd pushed herself so hard she'd had another attack.

Instead of understanding, she got teased more and more by some of her teammates. The coach did little about it. When I finally complained, he'd told me that if Lindsay wanted to play with the big dogs, she had to toughen up.

I watched the nine-year-old kids running around the field and just shook my head, wondering how any intelligent person could refer to them as "the big dogs." I finally decided to pull her off the team.

Some might say it was the worst thing I could've done. After all, it made her look like a quitter. But the alternative of watching her get tormented when she couldn't perform the way she was expected, or watching her push herself so hard that she had an asthma attack and still couldn't perform, was too painful for me to even contemplate.

Lindsay was so angry and hurt—I think as much with me as with anyone else on the team. Within a few weeks, she started putting the pounds back on.

Then, several weeks before the start of the spring soccer season, she'd come up with the idea of forming her own team. This time, I supported her wholeheartedly. I wasn't going to let her down again—even if it meant becoming their coach myself.

I was in the middle of praying about it again that night when my prayers were interrupted by the ringing of the telephone. I answered it, surprised when I realized it was Lou Matthews calling.

Lou and I didn't see one another often, and even then, only in church. I suppose it had a lot to do with the painful memories. He'd not only been my husband's best friend, but he'd also been the paramedic who'd responded to the crash where my husband was killed. Lou had been the one to come to the house to break the news to me.

"I hear you're coaching a new soccer team," he started.

"I see word spreads fast," I replied. "I guess Lindsay's brother was making one of his jokes about it."

There was a moment of silence. "Actually, it was just the opposite," Lou said. "I wasn't going to mention this, but I pulled him and another boy out of practice today for fighting. Neither would admit to what happened, but Jenny told me the other boy made some kind of wisecrack about you coaching a misfit team, and Hunter popped him."

I started to smile in surprise, and then I caught myself, knowing I shouldn't be proud of my son for fighting, even if it was for a good reason.

"I hope you don't punish him or anything," Lou continued. "I already handled it."

"I won't, but I appreciate you telling me." He had no idea how much.

"Anyway, I wanted to commend you for what you're doing."

I gave a grim smile I knew he couldn't see. "You better save that until we see how long it lasts. I think it's going to be a race to see whether the kids all quit or have me impeached—or whatever it is they do to inept coaches."

He chuckled. "It couldn't have been that bad."

"Well, let's just say that right now, I'm hoping they do the latter and I'm praying for a miracle so that we can find someone else to take over coaching. Someone who actually knows what they're doing."

"What about taking on an assistant coach or two?"

"If I can't find one person to do the job, what makes you think I'll find a couple of people to help with the job?"

"I wasn't saying find someone. I'm volunteering."

"You? But you're already coaching a team."

"I have a good team. Most of the kids have been playing together for years. Pastor Paul said he'd like to help coach—his son is on our team—because he's basically on call all the time, so he feels he can't do justice to being a regular coach. I thought I could get him to help out as my assistant and I could split my time between both teams."

"That would be wonderful!" I replied. "But you said an assistant coach or two."

"When I first heard about what you were doing, an idea started gnawing at the back of my mind. I think it would be good for some of my players to help, too. I'd let them miss one practice a month in exchange for helping out. Purely voluntary, though."

I doubted he'd get anyone to volunteer, but I didn't tell him that. His team was one of the best in the league. I'd say they'd be more eager to make my team the brunt of their jokes than to help them become a better team. Hadn't my son and the boy he'd gotten into a fight with proved that?

Boy, was I in for a lesson! I was ashamed to realize I was as guilty of stereotyping as anyone else.

My biggest surprise was that Hunter was one of the first kids to volunteer to help coach. Jenny was not as big a surprise; I figured she took her lead from her father. Perhaps Hunter's attitude was changing from what he was learning from Lou, as well.

Lou proved to be a great help. And he didn't come in and take over. When he'd said he'd assist, that was exactly what he meant. But he was quick to help by offering suggestions and guiding me in things I still didn't understand.

We still weren't going to get into the league that season, but by the time most of the teams had begun actual games, our team was definitely improving.

Lou didn't think that was enough. He felt the kids needed to have some actual experience playing against another team. He suggested it be his own team.

"You must be crazy or joking," I said, certain it was the latter. "They've improved, but not enough to play against a much older team. Especially the best one in the league."

"That remains to be seen," Lou said. "And I think it would be a good lesson for my team, too."

"Lesson?"

Lou nodded. "Invite me over after practice and I'll fill you in."

"Is this a plan the kids should hear?"

He smiled. "Make it about ten. The kids will be in bed, won't they?"

"Yes, but what about Jenny?" I knew that since his wife had died five years ago, Lou and Jenny lived alone.

"She's staying over with a girlfriend tonight. I'm at loose ends, anyway."

"Okay; ten o'clock it is."

It felt strange opening the door to Lou that evening. It was like déjà vu. I realized that it was the first time he'd been to our home since the night Greg died nearly two years before. One look at his face and I knew he was remembering that night, too.

"Greg would've appreciated all you're doing," I found myself saying.

"Maybe," he replied, and I didn't ask him what he meant. I think I realized then that Lou knew Greg had had a few faults when it came to being a father, especially where his daughter was concerned.

I needed to occupy my mind, to get away from those negative thoughts. I offered Lou a soda and finally asked him about his idea.

"I had a couple of ideas, but I threw out a few after I saw more cons than pros," he started. "Then I came up with this one. I need to know what you think."

He went on to explain that his plan was to divide both teams in half and put half of his team with half of my team and have them play against one another. He said that he was going to stress that the importance wasn't winning, rather that they try to help the younger kids do their best by trying to strengthen their skills.

"I'm sorry if I'm skeptical," I started. "You have fourteen-year-old kids and all they've ever known is to play to win." I knew, because up until the two seasons before, my husband had been their coach.

"I'm coach now," he said. "I've been trying to teach them different values."

I realized this was the closest he'd come to saying anything negative about Greg. He didn't want to be disloyal to a friend, but at the same time, I realized he knew Greg's flaws. The best thing was that he didn't share them. Perhaps, for that very reason, his plan could work.

"Do you think it won't really matter who wins?" I asked. "Playing devil's advocate, isn't it possible that the kids will just think the side that wins just had the best players from your team?"

"They might, if it were the only game we played. My thoughts are that we play a series of games, and switch players each time. There won't be a time where the same players are on the same team."

I smiled. "Yet each time, someone will win."

"Unless we tie."

I conceded with a nod. "I like the idea, as long as your players are sincere. I honestly don't want to have anyone playing who is out to make fools of the younger kids."

"I agree. And no unnecessary roughness. My team is older and bigger; I don't want anyone hurt."

I nodded again. "I'll put the idea to my team and see what they think."

"I'll do the same."

With that we shook hands on it, our hands remaining linked perhaps a little longer than would be expected for a handshake. Our eyes locked.

"You know, Candace, I'm happy we've been doing this," he started, breaking the uncomfortable silence. "I've thought about you often."

"I know. I've always known that I could call you if I ever needed anything," I said nervously. "But Greg always stood in the way."

Lou nodded, gently releasing my hand. "We were best friends, but that didn't mean I was blind to him. He wasn't always very nice, was he?"

I shrugged. "He just couldn't accept weakness or flaws, or anything that kept someone from living up to his expectations."

"That's what his father did to him."

"And he succeeded, as did Hunter, thankfully. Lindsay has been a different story."

"She has you, Candace. She's going to be all right."

He started to turn for the door, and then stopped as I blurted out my next embarrassing statement. "I'm glad Hunter has you for a role model."

"Hopefully, I can help him remember the good things about his dad," he said with a frown, and then headed the rest of the way out the door.

We started playing our games and as we suspected after the first one, there was banter among the kids that the winning side only won because they had the best players from the older team. The sad thing was, even the younger ones were saying it. It showed they still didn't have enough confidence in themselves.

I hoped Lou's plan of switching the kids around would help remedy this, and it did. Before long, each youth had a chance to be on a winning team. And they all had the opportunity to learn how to be good sports about losing.

Even after soccer season was over, my team wanted to continue having practice. And they wanted me to continue being their coach—with Lou, Jenny, and Hunter as our assistant coaches. Lindsay was nominated to ask each of us if we would agree to continue.

I, of course, said yes. I wasn't surprised when Lou and Jenny agreed, since they'd both gotten along so well with the younger kids. It was when Lindsay approached her brother that I was most concerned.

I watched as she knocked on his bedroom door. As the music playing in the background grew silent, I took a breath.

"Can I come in?" she asked.

"Sure, Lindsay," he replied.

Hearing those words, I slowly released the breath I'd been holding. I knew I didn't have to be worried anymore. God had answered all of my prayers.

THE END

I'M THE PROUDEST
MOM IN AMERICA!
Even though my daughter's lifestyle
is controversial—and
almost drove us apart for good

I'd looked forward to this day for weeks. My daughter, Nikki, was arriving home from college for a weeklong break. I'd planned all sorts of shopping trips and gabfests with her for whenever she wasn't busy with friends.

But as soon as she entered the house, dragging a large duffel bag behind her, I saw a fearful look in her eyes that told me that things were not quite right.

I'd seen that look before. Once was the time when she'd had an accident while driving my car. Another was the time when she'd failed an exam in calculus and didn't want to tell me.

Now, I silently braced myself for whatever she'd eventually tell me.

"Hi, sweetie," I said, and wrapped my arms around her. Her body was rigid beneath my touch. "You okay?"

She gave me a fragile smile. "I'm okay." She headed for her old room. "Let me put this stuff away."

Soon the phone started ringing for Nikki, and then she headed out the door. "See you later, Mom. I'm meeting Maggie and Linda."

That was it. A lump of disappointment welled up in my throat, but I swallowed it. I ate dinner alone and afterward sat in front of the TV with a photo of Nikki in my hand. I ran my hand over the photo. It was like looking into a mirror and seeing a younger version of me twenty years ago, when I was twenty. Nikki's hair was cut short and her eyes gazed trustingly at me. A pretty face, our friends and acquaintances said.

Finally, I went to bed telling myself that I would see her tomorrow. Before I drifted off to sleep, my last thought was that besides her friends, I'd have to share Nikki with her dad, my ex-husband. Bill lived in another part of the city and had remarried. I hadn't seen him for a long time. We'd been divorced since Nikki was three.

I could've called my friend, Greg Stanley, and invited him over or gone out to a movie with him, but then he'd ask me how come I wasn't spending time with Nikki, like I told him I was doing. I didn't want him to know that Nikki's friends were more important to her than spending time with me. Besides, I'd just met Greg at the plumbing company we both worked for. We'd only been going out for a few months. Our relationship was still in the beginning stages. I found Greg attractive. He's a big bear of a man. When he puts his arms around me, I feel safe and secure.

As I thought about him, I wondered if our friendship would ever develop into anything more. He was different from me in many ways. For one thing, his outlook on people and life was more optimistic than mine. He seemed to like everybody and thought nothing of inviting his friends over when he and I spent an evening at his place. I suspected a couple of his male friends were more than just friends to each other. I'd caught them hugging each other in the kitchen. When I mentioned this to Greg, he laughed it off and said something about "being tolerant" and "live and let live." I didn't answer him, because I frowned on homosexuality. I'd read about where people could change that aspect of themselves if they worked at it.

The week lurched forward, with me trying to find some time alone with Nikki. I didn't have the week off from work, so I kept trying to catch Nikki when I got off in the afternoon. It wasn't until Saturday, the day before Nikki was driving back to college that we actually sat down together for supper.

"Well, just in the nick of time, before you leave." I nursed a small grudge. After all, I was her mother and yet she couldn't seem to find any time for me. I wondered how she'd feel if the situation were reversed.

"Mom," Nikki said, her words running together, "I have to talk to you—tell you something."

Alarm bells went off in my head. Here it was, whatever had been bothering her all week and she'd been too afraid to tell me.

This is different, I thought. This is no trivial thing she has to tell me. This is serious.

I waited for her to continue and watched her run her hands through her short hair in a familiar gesture of frustration.

"I'm a lesbian," she blurted out in a soft voice, her eyes averted and staring at something unseen.

My head jerked up. My mind said: I'm not hearing this. "It's a joke," I whispered aloud. "It's not true. You—you're saying this to. . . ." My voice trailed off. It was one of those moments in time when everything becomes unreal. I thought I might faint as the room began to whirl.

"Mom," Nikki said sharply. "It's not like I have a fatal disease—it's just that I prefer women. I have a partner. . . ."

"This isn't true." My voice sounded harsh to my own ears. "All you need to do is get back to church—get some counseling for this nonsense." That's what she needs, I thought, some common sense drilled into her head. "I've heard you can change. All you need to do is go to a good counselor."

Nikki shook her head, her face ashen. "No, Mom. This didn't just happen the day I went to college." She shredded her napkin into tiny pieces. "I've known this for a long time, maybe even since I was a child. I always felt left out—different. I can't change it. I didn't necessarily choose it," she said, still shredding the napkin. "It chose me."

Anger churned in my stomach. How could this be? Was it my fault because Bill and I had divorced when Nikki was so young and she didn't have a full-time father? Maybe it was Bill's fault, because over the years he'd taught Nikki boy things like how to drive a motorcycle and drive a pickup truck.

I jumped up from the dinner table, spilling a glass of water, and stomped out of the room. My voice was shrill. "I suppose it's my fault. I don't believe it. How could you do this to me?" In my rage, I turned and rushed back to face my only child. "I don't ever want to see you again—until you come to your senses!" I hissed.

The next morning the house was eerily quiet. I went to Nikki's room and saw it was empty. Her bed, with the pink bedspread, was neatly made. The sight of her empty closet made my heart lurch. She was gone. I'd driven her away. Well, I was right to do that. Surely, it would bring her to her senses. After all, she was old enough to know she was committing a sin—a particularly horrible sin and I sure wasn't going to forgive her.

In my new resolve, I phoned my best friend and neighbor, Ruth Mosley. She'd understand and—I was sure—assure me that I'd done the right thing by banishing Nikki. But why did I feel so rotten?

After I told Ruth, she commiserated with me. "Beverly, I believe it's the only way to bring these kids to their senses." Ruth had kicked her only child out a year ago when she found out Wendy was taking drugs. "You'll see. Nikki will be phoning you within a few days."

"Did that happen with Wendy?"

"Well, sure. She called a few times, but Curtis told her she had to clean up on her own. She got on the drugs all by herself, so she could just get off them by herself. You know how dads can be."

"Hmm. Maybe some of them. I don't think Bill would do that," I told her, and then asked, "She's never come home, has she?" I already knew the answer.

"No, but we did the right thing—and so did you. Besides, Curtis wouldn't allow Wendy back into the house until she cleaned up her act."

"I remember." But talking to Ruth didn't make me feel much better.

She'd kicked her daughter out to make her own way when Wendy was sixteen.

"Do you even know where she is?"

"No. I don't want to know—until she smartens up. You'll see. Nikki will be calling you in no time to tell you she made a mistake. Then you can invite her back on your terms."

Later that day, Bill phoned. "It's your loss, Beverly. I heard from Nikki and she's heartbroken."

Angrily, I said, "So, I presume you're going to continue paying for her college education and condone her deviant lifestyle."

"Hey, of course I am. And I'm hanging up. You're not even rational. Besides, I don't think Nikki told herself, 'I'll become a lesbian to hurt my mom and dad.' "

"You'll see. She'll come to her senses and stop all this. . . ." I stopped talking when I realized I was talking to a dial tone.

I didn't talk to Greg about it at all because I was too ashamed. What would he think? Even though he had a couple of friends who were obviously living a depraved lifestyle, he wouldn't understand my feelings. Besides, Nikki would change. I was sure of it.

The Christmas season came and I jumped every time the phone rang—hoping, praying that it was Nikki and that she'd realized how wrong she was. I knew the only way I could forgive Nikki for her sick lifestyle was for her to come around and be a normal person. On Christmas Eve, Greg and I sat near the Christmas tree, drinking eggnog, when the call display indicated a call from Nikki. I snatched the receiver. "Nikki. I'm so glad you called."

I heard her voice, sweet and hesitant, and waited for her apology. "I couldn't let Christmas go by without wishing you a Merry Christmas."

"Thank you. Are you coming home for the holiday?" I held my breath because I knew if she said yes, she'd come to her senses.

Her voice suddenly seemed distant. "No, Mom. I'm going to be with Angela."

I gripped the receiver tightly and pressed it to my ear. "Who's Angela?"

"My partner."

"In that case, I don't wish to speak to you—or see you," I told her as I slammed the phone down. I sat on the couch and stared at the Christmas tree. Its lights winked at me and I could smell the pine odor.

I might as well take the tree down, I thought. This isn't going to be a Merry Christmas.

Greg's voice brought me back to the world. "Beverly, are you okay?" He put his arm around my shoulders and pulled me close. "Tell me what's wrong."

Haltingly, I told him about Nikki and the whole sordid mess. "You

95

can see that I'm waiting for her to come to her senses. I know she will—it's just a matter of time."

"Beverly, what world are you living in? Your ideas are at least fifty years behind the times. Get with it, girl." He put his hand on my chin and turned my face toward him. "Don't you realize that in Massachusetts, for example, two people of the same sex can marry each other?"

I pulled away from him and sat rigidly. "Not in my world, they don't. Can't you see that this phase will pass? It's only a—"

"No. It's not a phase. You remember meeting some of my friends? They're gay and they have lived together happily for many years." Greg stood then and reached for his coat. "I can see by the stubborn look on your face that you can't see anything but a narrow tunnel. Maybe I'd better go."

Stubbornly, I said, "Yes. You've said enough."

I ended up spending the holiday with Ruth. I helped her cook a ham and made a special cranberry dish for dinner. Ruth's husband watched television all day, so Ruth and I were on our own. She knew that Nikki had phoned and I'd told her not to come home. I even told her about Greg and the argument we had. "Looks like that budding romance will never flower."

"Not when he's so wrong in his thinking. He even has gay friends. I pretended not to notice when I met them, but he brought it up to me. He thinks it's quite normal!"

"You don't seem that disappointed about Greg."

I felt a constriction near my heart and said, "I do feel sorry. I thought maybe there was something there. But obviously there's not."

I changed the subject to our church group and said, "I don't want the group knowing about Nikki. If I don't say anything, maybe she'll be back to normal and I won't have to tell them."

Ruth picked at some leftover ham and said, "I never told them about Wendy, but they found out somehow—you know gossip."

"It sure doesn't make us look like very good parents, does it?" I said.

"Makes us look like terrible parents—what with one a drug addict and the other a lesbian." Ruth stuffed some more ham into her mouth. "Food is my only comfort, besides having you as a friend."

"We're lucky to have each other, Ruth."

As I was leaving Ruth's, I told her, "You know, when I think about Nikki in high school, she never dated. It didn't concern me; I just thought she was so busy with her friends and schoolwork. I never thought it would come to this."

"You'll see. Nikki will come around."

Winter turned into spring. In early April, Nikki called again to tell

96

me she was moving. "We've found a cheaper place to live until we both finish school. Angela finishes this year and already has a job with a big insurance company. I have another two years to go." She rattled on as if we were on good terms. For a moment my heart ached for us to get back to being friends again, but I ignored the feelings. Nikki was wrong and if I held out against her foolish behavior, I was convinced she'd get over it.

"I'm not interested until you change. It doesn't matter that you're going to be a lawyer in a few years—it only matters if you change your lifestyle."

After I hung up the phone, I decided to vacuum and wash the floors, which is something I often did to get rid of nervous energy. As I worked, I wondered why Ruth and I had driven our daughters away. Why couldn't we be like Bill and go along with whatever our daughters wanted? I was convinced Bill was taking the easy way out and knew that in the end, Ruth and I would be proven right.

I hadn't seen Greg since Christmas. We'd talked once, but it was strained. Neither of us knew what to say. I saw him at work and we treated each other strictly as coworkers. I regretted that we were so far apart in our beliefs, but I was convinced that he was wrong. Gays marrying, I thought. What next? I sure didn't need a guy like Greg in my life. It would be like another Bill, someone I couldn't get along with and who had divorced me after only five years of marriage. To tell the truth, I didn't believe in divorce, either. When my mother was alive, she used say, "She made her bed; she better lie in it." Those were her words when the subject of divorce came up. I knew she'd feel exactly the same as I did about Nikki, too.

In early April, Ruth and I were spending some time in her backyard, drinking coffee and chatting. It was an unseasonably warm, sunny morning. Ruth was eating a cinnamon bun and complaining about her weight while I sipped on black coffee and said, "Cinnamon buns aren't really health food, Ruth."

"I know. Don't care."

I heard her phone ring and she went inside, saying, "I'll answer it and bring the phone out."

It was only a few moments before Ruth walked back out to the patio. Her face was frozen in an expression of disbelief.

"What is it?" I asked. I felt tinges of alarm making my breathing uneven.

Ruth stared at me, but I knew she wasn't seeing me. Her mouth opened and closed, but no sounds came out.

I ran to her and put my arms around her. She sagged against me and I staggered backward, holding her until I reached the chair. I eased her into the chair and she let out a piercing cry that froze my heart.

"It's Wendy!" she cried. Tears coursed down her cheeks and dripped off her chin.

I wiped the tears with a tissue and put my hands on her heaving shoulders. "What happened?" Dread forced its way into the back of my throat. I thought I might be sick.

"She's dead—an overdose."

The words hit me like a slap and I reeled back. "Dead? Dead? Who called? The police?"

She crumpled in the chair, her head touching her knees, her shoulders heaving. "No. Curtis. Dear God, now she can never come home!"

It was at that moment that I saw a part of Ruth die. I could see that for all of her tough talk about Wendy and how she acted as if she didn't care that much, she cared a whole lot. After all, Wendy was her daughter—her only child—just like Nikki was mine.

I stayed with Ruth until Curtis came home. I finally convinced her to go and lie down, but the tears would not stop for her.

"The tears will never stop!" she told me. In between sobs, she said, "I feel like a murderer! I should've at least helped her get into a treatment program—not leave her out there to die!" She sighed heavily and added, "It's all so clear to me now—when it's too late."

I spent days with Ruth. Fortunately, I was able to use some vacation time. She had no family, and neither did I. She and I had always said we were each other's family. I drove her to her family doctor, who gave her something to help her sleep. I helped Curtis make funeral arrangements and stuck by Ruth's side through the funeral. The church group we both belonged to brought over food that would last for weeks, and the pastor visited with Ruth. But she was inconsolable. She told me, "It's like I gave her that last, deadly shot. I sure as hell didn't help her in any way—except to rush her to her death."

As we reached the end of April, Ruth was locked into a deep grief. I didn't know if she'd ever recover. She said she didn't want to get better, that she just wanted to hide in her bedroom for the rest of her life. One day when I sat with her, she stirred and seemed to throw off the darkness surrounding her. She pinned me with a piercing gaze. "Beverly, you know we're all wrong, don't you?" Her eyes looked feverish in their intensity. "You must contact Nikki and welcome her and her partner with open arms." Ruth's voice rose. "You must do this as fast as you can!" she said, her voice breaking. "Go. Right now. Phone her and beg for her forgiveness."

I stared at Ruth. Her pain was obvious. I didn't know what to say to her, except, "I know. I finally know that we were both wrong." I felt a flood of relief wash over me, making my body feel limp all over. Watching Ruth and how she'd suffered this past month was almost too much to bear.

I put my arms around her. "Would it have made it any easier if you and Curtis had helped Wendy in any way you could, particularly by sending her to treatment?"

By this time, we were both crying and holding onto each other. "Yes." She sobbed. "How could we think we could give up so easily on our daughters? You and I are both so wrong—and for what? So the neighbors or the church group don't find out? Just because our lifestyles were compromised?"

I left Ruth's that day with a sense of urgency. I must contact Nikki immediately. I must get my daughter back before it was too late. Then I remembered that Nikki had talked about moving. I must find her quickly, and I had no phone number or address for her. Bill would have a phone number for her. I could call the college, although college was probably finished for the semester. In a panic, I dialed Bill's number. After four rings the machine clicked on and I left a message asking him to call as soon as he got in.

There was nothing left to do now except to wait to hear from Bill. Maybe he and his wife were out of town. Because I had to do something, I made it a point to gather all my courage and corner Greg at work. I blurted out words as fast as I could, so I wouldn't back down. "I don't know how to say this—except that I've graduated into this new world you were talking about."

Greg's eyebrows went up in a question. "How's that?" he said.

I told him about Ruth losing Wendy and how there was no turning back for her. As soon as I could get in touch with Nikki, I was going to beg her forgiveness for my wrong-headedness. "I only pray it's not too late."

Greg placed his large, friendly hand on my shoulder and squeezed. "Now you're thinking."

Greg was such a great guy. I felt warm all over just being near him—this big cuddly teddy bear. "You think you and I could have a coffee one day soon?" I asked.

"We sure can. I think we can do better than that and go all-out for a dinner."

I telephoned Bill's apartment again and got his answering machine. I figured he must be away. All I could do was wait. Believe me, I waited and suffered with so many doubts. What if Nikki told me she was through with me? She might tell me what a rotten mother I was to turn my back on her. And I would deserve her anger and disappointment because what kind of a parent was I? Only around for the good times and running away when things got tough. By the second Sunday in May, I was a basket case—especially when I realized that it was Mother's Day.

Greg and Ruth both kept in touch with me that day, both saying encouraging words—although Ruth sobbed so hard I could barely understand her. Around suppertime, a strange number came up on the call display. Could it be Nikki? My hand trembled so much I thought I'd drop the receiver. Quickly, I said, "Hello, Nikki?" I held my breath and waited for what seemed like forever.

I heard her sweet, hesitant voice. "Hello, Mom."

That's all she said and I started babbling. I know that I sounded like a crazy person, blurting out, "Sweetheart—I'm so glad you called—I'm sorry—so sorry. . . ."

I heard Nikki's lilting laugh. "Mom. Mom, slow down. I phoned to say—"

"Thank goodness, Nikki! I desperately need to talk to you—to tell you how very wrong I've been! Please, please forgive me." I had to stop to take a deep breath. "I don't care that you have a different lifestyle. How could I have been so foolish, to even think I could ever turn my back on you."

I heard Nikki's tear-filled voice: "Thanks, Mom. Of course I forgive you. When can we come to visit?"

"As soon as you can get here—both of you. And one more thing—I love you," I said softly.

Nikki said, "I love you, too, Mom. See you in about a week, then. Can you get a few days off from work?"

"Absolutely. Let me know which days."

"I nearly forgot why I phoned: Happy Mother's Day."

Here I'd been thinking that Nikki was a sinner who lived in sin with her partner, but I was the one who was the sinner—a mother who treated her daughter with contempt and anger. I could've lost her forever, like Ruth had lost Wendy. Somehow, for nearly a year, I forgot how short life is and how we must cherish our loved ones while we have them with us. It truly was the best Mother's Day ever.

THE END

WORKAHOLIC MOM
I didn't appreciate my kids

"Mary, Mr. Yardley is on line one," my secretary, Lucy, called.

"Put it through, I'm on my way," I said, grabbing my coffee and walking briskly to my office. I pushed the door shut with my foot and then sat in my leather chair.

The phone rang again, and before I took Mr. Yardley's call, Lucy buzzed my intercom.

"You have Marsha Baxter on line two and the editor of The Daily Post on line three. He wants to ask you about the Davis case."

"Put them on hold, and keep them coming, Lucy," I said before taking Mr. Yardley's call.

My desk looked as if a hurricane blew through the office. Manila folders, envelopes, and thick brown files bulging with court reports and depositions sat on the desk and even spread to the floor. My laptop sat open, but barely visible amid the confusion of paperwork. I was the top associate at my law firm, and my office was a beehive of activity. I juggled a caseload nearly double what most associates could handle, worked longer and harder, and brought in more money for the firm than any associate, but, most of all, I simply loved my job.

I no sooner finished with Mr. Yardley than Lucy poked her head in the door.

"Scott's on the phone, line four," she said.

I glanced the flashing buttons on the phone, sighed, and pressed line four. "What is it?"

"Can I make popcorn?"

"Scott, I'm busy. Just make the darn popcorn, and be careful."

"Okay, Mom. When you going to come home?"

Again, I looked at the flashing phone buttons, and irritation crawled up the back of my neck.

"Same time as always, now let me get back to work," I growled. Scott bid me good-bye, and I quickly took my next call.

"Good afternoon, Ms. Baxter. I've arranged for a court date," I began, but needed to put my client on hold when Lucy opened the door.

"I'm sorry to interrupt, Mary, but Erica's on the phone and she says it's an emergency."

I rolled my eyes and reached for the phone. "Erica, what's the matter?"

"Scott won't share the popcorn with me!" my nine-year-old daughter wailed through the phone.

I sighed and leaned back in my chair. Unnecessary interruptions like this aggravated me like crazy.

"Tell him I said to give you some."

I waited, tapping my foot and scanning the contents of my over-laden desk.

"Mommy?"

"I'm here," I said. My patience was near an end.

"I told him, but he's still teasing me. He said I can't have any popcorn because he made it and it's all his."

"Put your brother on the phone, right now," I said through clenched teeth.

"Hi, Mom."

"Scott, I don't need this sort of nonsense when I'm at work. Now share that darn popcorn with your sister or there will be trouble when I get home. Do you understand me, Mister?"

"Why should I share with her? She didn't make it; she just lies on the couch all day," he said, his voice reaching a high-pitched whine.

"Shut up and listen to me, Scott."

"But, Mom . . ."

"No. You shut up! You're thirteen years old and I expect you to take a modicum of responsibility and keep a lid on things when I'm not home. I do not appreciate this baloney, Scott. Now share that darn snack with your sister. Do you understand me?"

"Yeah, I hear you," he responded.

"Good. Now behave yourselves and don't call me at work again unless someone's bleeding!" I yelled, and then slammed the phone down on the receiver.

I leaned my head in my hands. Pain shot along my temple and across my eyes.

"Are you all right?" Lucy asked.

I looked up, but Lucy was a mere blur standing in the doorway. I blinked several times until my vision cleared.

"Yes, yes. I'm fine. Just more of the same."

"The kids getting to you?"

"They're tap dancing on my last nerve," I said, yanking the desk drawer open.

"If there's anything I can do, you know where I am," Lucy said cheerfully.

"Could you be a dear and get me a glass of water?" I asked, twisting the cap of a bottle of extra-strength aspirin.

"Sure thing," she replied.

"Stupid childproof lids," I muttered to myself. Another sharp pain shot through my head, and a wave of nausea slammed my belly.

I bolted from my desk and barely made it to the ladies room before becoming violently ill.

"Mary! What's the matter?"

"I must have eaten something bad. I feel much better now," I said, taking the cup of cold water from her hand. "Wow, my head's killing me."

"You better take care of yourself," Lucy admonished. "I think you need a vacation."

"Vacations are for wimps," I said. "Besides, I'm taking a working-vacation to the beach when school's out."

"Working vacation? That's not relaxing," she said, waving her hand in dismissal. "You're going to burn out."

"How can I? I love my job."

Lucy laughed. "Okay, whatever you say, boss, but it's five o'clock and I'm out of here."

"Have a good evening," I said.

After Lucy left, and the office quieted, I turned to my computer and spent the rest of the evening cleaning up the loose ends of the day. The phone on Lucy's desk rang several times, but I ignored the annoyance. No one of importance would call after hours.

Finally, at nine that night, I pulled into my driveway and flipped the switch for the automatic garage door opener. No sooner had I turned off the engine, than both my kids came pouring out the door, with our neighbor, Mrs. Raskin following close behind.

"Mom! Mommy!" they yelled.

"Hey, you guys being good?"

"Look what happened to me," Erica said, waving her bandaged hand in my face.

"What happened?" I asked.

"Erica burned her hand on the stove," Mrs. Raskin said, a look of disapproval on her face.

"Yeah, Mom. Mrs. Raskin took me to the emergency room, and I had to soak it in cold water and then a doctor put medicine on it. We tried to call you at work, but there was no answer."

Mrs. Raskin handed me an envelope. "There are further instructions in here, along with the bill, and the nurse said you are to call your family doctor in a few days so he can take a look at the burn."

"Thank you, Mrs. Raskin. I really appreciate your help."

"Any time, but, I worry about the kids being all alone over here. In my day, we just didn't leave kids alone like that. Besides, after Erica's accident, I called your office several times, but there was no answer."

I wanted to tell Mrs. Raskin to mind her own business, but instead I nodded politely and curbed my tongue. "I understand, but with Scott being thirteen and Erica nearly ten, I think they're able to be alone."

Mrs. Raskin peered at me through her glasses. "If you say so," she said, and then stood there, as if waiting for me to further explain myself. When I didn't, she said, "Well, I suppose I should get home. It's getting late."

"Good night, and thanks again," I responded curtly, leading the kids in the house and closing the door.

I set my briefcase near the closet and turned to the kids. "What were you doing with the stove on?" I asked, placing my hands on my hips.

"I made macaroni and cheese for dinner," Scott said.

"And I tried to help," Erica piped in.

"You're lucky all you got was a burnt hand! How many times do I have to tell you two not to cook when I'm not here?" I yelled.

"But it was late, and we were hungry," Erica said, tears filling her eyes.

"That's beside the point! Now both of you go to your rooms. I need some peace and quiet."

Erica stomped to her room and slammed the door, but Scott reached for his math book. "Mom, I need help. I can't figure out these homework problems."

"Did you try, Scott?"

"Yes! I worked on it all afternoon. I really need your help."

"Not now, Scott. Go work on it a while longer."

"But I'm really stuck. Please, Mom?"

"Don't plead with me. Go to your room. Tomorrow if you still haven't figured it out, ask your teacher for help."

Scott stalked to his room and slammed his door, and I was happy to finally have the kids out of my hair.

I went to the kitchen, grabbed a cup of yogurt from the refrigerator, and leaned against the counter. As I shoveled the yogurt in my mouth, I scowled at the stack of dirty dishes, candy wrappers, and sticky glasses sitting on the table. The mess would have to wait. When I finished eating, I hurried upstairs to my room, stripped my jacket off and tossed it over a chair, then unzipped my navy blue skirt, stepped out of it, and left it lying in a heap on the floor as I walked to the bathroom. Another wave of nausea hit my stomach, and a slight, but sharp pain, this time in the center of my forehead. I reached for my bottle of aspirin. This time I swallowed three, followed by a stiff dose of anti-nausea medicine. I had no time to fool around with some silly bout of food poisoning. I needed a good night's rest because the next morning I had to be in court at eight sharp.

I took a quick shower, tossed my nightgown over my head, realizing too late I put the darn thing on inside out, but no matter, I slid into my unmade bed and without even curling into a comfortable position, I was fast asleep.

By eight the next morning, I sat waiting for the judge to begin a case I'd been working on for the past three months. If I handled this case between two prominent businessmen properly, it could lead to a coveted partnership position at my law firm. Nausea and butterflies flitted in my stomach, but thanks to a double-dose of extra strength pain relievers, the pain in my head had quieted to a dull roar. I rubbed my eyes and shook my head to clear my vision, shrugging off the blurriness and slight dizziness as a bad case of nerves. However, when the court bailiff announced the judge, and I pushed my chair from the desk to stand, I lost my balance. The room began to spin, and suddenly my head was on fire with pain. I remember falling on the floor as everything went black.

"Ms. Lucien? Mary? Can you hear me?"

I wrinkled my nose at the antiseptic hospital odor. "What happened?" I asked groggily.

"You fainted in the courtroom. You're at Community General Hospital."

I struggled to sit up. "Oh, no. I have to get back," I said, but I was light-headed and weak.

"What's wrong with me, and who are you?" I asked the man who stood beside my bed.

"I'm Dr. Tischmann. I'm a neurosurgeon here at Community."

"Neurosurgeon? What? Why? What makes you think I need a neurosurgeon?" I asked frantically.

"Do you know what day it is, Mary?"

"Friday, of course. This morning I was in court."

"No. It's Tuesday. Tuesday afternoon. You've been unconscious for four days."

"What? That can't be right. You must be mistaken."

Dr. Tischmann leaned forward and showed me the date and time on his watch. "Oh, my! What's wrong with me?" I asked, near tears. "Where are my kids?"

"The nurses called the emergency number in your wallet and I believe your children are with their father."

"Oh, good. Okay. They're with my ex. That's all right; it was his turn to have them this week anyhow," I said, immediately dismissing any thoughts of my children. "Now, tell me what's wrong, and when I can get out of here."

"While you were unconscious, we took a few scans of your head," Dr. Tischmann said, and then reached into a folder and pulled several x-ray films out. He put them on a small screen and flipped a switch, lighting the pictures.

"See here," he said, pointing with the tip of his pen. "See this shadow?"

I squinted at the x-ray and nodded. "Yeah, I see it. Is that my brain?"

"This is your brain," he said, outlining a whitish-gray section of the picture. "But this," he said, pointing to the dark spot, "this appears to be a hemangioblastoma."

"A hema what? Is it serious?"

"A hemangioblastoma is a brain tumor."

"Are you serious?" I asked, completely shocked and terrified. "I have a brain tumor? How did this happen, and what can I do about it?"

Dr. Tischmann sat on the edge of my bed. "We don't know what causes this type of brain tumor, but the good news is that they are usually benign. We'll run more tests, a CAT scan and an MRI, and when we know exactly what we're dealing with, you'll need surgery to excise the growth."

"Benign? So, that means it's not cancer?"

"The likelihood of this type of tumor being malignant is very small, however, we won't know exactly what we're dealing with until we're in surgery. Unfortunately, brain surgery is very delicate work, and tumors can be unpredictable."

"Surgery? You can't be serious. I feel better already. My head doesn't hurt at all. Maybe the diagnosis is wrong, isn't it possible that I just have really bad migraine headaches?"

"Well, you're not in pain because you've been hooked up to a morphine IV for the past four days."

"Morphine? That's addictive, for heaven's sake!"

"Calm down, Ms. Lucien. I understand this is an awful lot to take in right now, but rest assured, the morphine dosage is very low, and studies show that in-hospital use of this drug is very effective and does not promote addiction. Also, I'm very optimistic that your tumor can be safely removed."

I grimaced at the tubes and wires attached to my arms. "I hope you're right. I'm so busy at work right now; I simply cannot afford to be sick! How long will all this take?"

Dr. Tischmann cleared his throat and stood. "Well, you're scheduled for tests today, once we get the results from those, I'd say we're looking at surgery by the end of the week. After which you'll have a recovery period. I'd say you could be back to work in as little as six weeks."

"Six weeks! That's forever! And when will you disconnect this narcotic?" I spat.

"That depends on how you feel. Generally, we slowly reduce the medication, and within a week after surgery it's not necessary."

"All right then, let's get on with it," I said miserably.

"That's the spirit," Dr. Tischmann said with a smile.

The next few days passed in a blur as nurses pushed me on a stretcher throughout the hospital for appointments with various experts and MRI technicians. Marc, my ex husband, brought the children to visit one evening, but I was so drowsy and disoriented I could barely focus on them.

Early the next morning, a nurse in blue hospital scrubs woke me.

"Ms. Lucien," she said, flipping on the bright overhead lights and waking me from a mixture of sleep and drugged disorientation. "I need you to sit up so I can prepare you for surgery."

I struggled into a sitting position as she adjusted my hospital bed. My heart sunk when I saw she had scissors and a razor among her equipment.

"You don't need to remove all my hair, do you?"

She sat on the edge of my bed and rested a hand on my shoulder. "I'm awfully sorry, but your entire head needs to be shaved for this surgery."

"Oh, no. This is the worst part," I said, choking back a sob.

She reached for a lock of my hair. "You have such beautiful hair, too," she said. "But you know, it will grow back quickly. You've no other health problems besides the tumor, so there's no reason your hair won't grow back thick and beautiful as ever. In a year, this ordeal will just be a bad memory."

"I hope you're right, but I guess I'll be bald when I go back to work."

"No, not at all. You'll be fitted with a very natural looking wig before you even leave the hospital."

"Are you serious? How do you manage all that?"

"We have a hair stylist on staff, and your insurance covers a wig in these instances. You'd be surprised how many women need our hair stylist's services. Most are getting chemotherapy for breast or other cancers. Try not to worry. When you're well enough, the stylist will visit with you and order you a wig."

"Same style and color I have now?" I asked

"I'm going to save a lock of your hair so she can match it exactly, and there are quite a few styles to choose from. Most women find something they really like," she said, trying to reassure me.

I nodded and tried to hold back my tears as she cut my hair, then shaved my head completely bald. She didn't offer me a mirror, and I certainly didn't ask for one. The last thing I wanted to see was my bare head.

When she finished, she covered my head with a paper cap that resembled a shower cap, and then she adjusted my IV's and rang for the orderly to wheel me to the surgical suite.

"Are you going to be there?" I asked the nurse as I rode the gurney down to the basement of the hospital.

"I'm not one of the surgical assistants, but I'll be in the operating area, and when you come out, I'll be waiting for you," she said, giving my hand a squeeze.

It seemed as if I waited for hours in the pre-op room, but eventually the anesthesiologist arrived and before I knew it, they rolled me into the operating room. In spite of the soft, classical music playing in the background, the operating room was horribly intimidating. Nurses and technicians bustled about as the anesthesiologist covered my face with an oxygen mask that, along with medication in my IV, would render me unconscious for my surgery.

I should've woken in my hospital bed, but what happened that afternoon defies logic. I remember being told to count backwards from one hundred, and I don't remember reaching ninety-seven, but the next thing I felt was a strange sensation of being pulled out of my body, exiting from the top of my head. I couldn't speak, but I was completely aware of everything happening in the operating room. At first, I thought there was a problem with my anesthesia that perhaps it wasn't working and I'd be doomed to feel and be aware of my operation, but that was not the case. I looked at the large clock on the wall. More than five hours had passed since I entered the surgical suite, but it seemed like only a few minutes. Then I wondered: How can I see the clock when there's surgical tape holding my eyes shut? Moreover, how could I even know there's tape over my eyes? It was then I realized I was looking at my body. I seemed to be hovering above the operating table, observing myself. Now, I should have been terrified, but I wasn't. I had a strange sense of peace, and oddly enough, a strong sense of curiosity. I felt intensely interested in the doctor's activities. Suddenly, Dr. Tischmann ordered the classical music shut off. Then the room was silent, except for brisk orders from the doctor and the metallic clang of surgical instruments. The doors swung open, and another doctor and two nurses silently rushed in, pushing a cart with more technical apparatus. I knew this was no dream, yet I was very much aware that I floated in the corner of the operating room, high near the ceiling. I had no sensation of discomfort. In fact, I had no pain whatsoever.

I watched with curiosity as the medical team worked feverishly over my body, and only mild surprise registered when I saw that my skull lay open, and a nurse stood beside me suctioning off a steady stream of blood while another nurse hurried to replace bags of blood attached to my IV. Then the nurses stepped back from the table as the doctor put two large paddles on my chest, and my body jolted and quivered in what I assumed was an attempt to restart my heart.

It was then I noticed a speck of light. This light grew larger as I moved effortlessly toward it, and a feeling of peace and utter contentment flowed over me. The scene from the operating room grew distant and surreal as this lit passageway became my reality.

It was then I heard a familiar sound. The friendly, comforting bark of my childhood pet, Bouncer. She came toward me, her long, tan fur knotted and as unkempt as always, her muzzle gray with age, but instead of the familiar limp, she loped toward me, her tail wagging furiously as she threw paws against my chest and wet my face with the kisses of a long, lost friend. If only I could stay here and experience this peace and comfort forever, I thought, because at that moment, I couldn't remember ever being so happy. Then, as if he read my thoughts, my grandfather walked toward me from the light.

"Mary, honey," he said, pulling me into his embrace. "It didn't take Bouncer long to know you were here. She's been waiting."

My voice choked with emotion. "Pop Pop!" I cried. "I've missed you."

He gently touched my face, as if to brush away a tear. "Don't fret over me, Mary. You have the kids to worry about."

"Oh, Erica and Scott would love to meet you. I've always wanted them to, but all I have are pictures."

"I'm right here," he said, pointing to my heart. "I'm always with you, Mary."

"But now I'm here with you, and Bouncer," I said, smiling. "Is Grandma here, too?"

"Oh, yes. She's here, and well, but now isn't a good time for you to be here. You have some unfinished business."

Suddenly, the sounds from the operating room intruded. "Unfinished? Yes, I became ill in court. I have a case to finish, and so much work on my desk," I explained.

Pop Pop smiled and shook his head sadly. "No, I don't mean law books and courtrooms. I mean my two grandbabies. Erica and Scott need a mother, Mary. Those kids will only be young once. Now go back and stop wasting so much time on the things that don't last. Tend your own house, and your children will flourish; ignore it, and they will be lost."

Before I had a chance to answer, I felt as if I'd plunged into icy water, then a horrible, painful sensation shot through my head and chest.

The next thing I knew I awoke, alone. My body was a mass of tubes and wires, constantly monitored by beeps and blips of machines. I couldn't move, and for a moment, I feared I was dead, but the faint, steady beat of my heart sounded throughout the tiny room, and a feeling of elation coursed through me. I'd made it. I survived my surgery. I was alive!

My moment of joy was short-lived. Soon the discomforts of my body became all too real. My mouth was dry, my legs and fingers felt stiff, but worst of all was the heavy, dull pain in my chest and head. A sudden wave of nausea came over me, but I was helpless, unable to even turn my head.

"Take it easy," a soft voice behind me said.

"Pop Pop?" I asked.

"No, I'm not your Pop Pop. It's Nicole, your nurse. Remember, we met before surgery? Do you know where you are?"

"I'm in the hospital. I had surgery on my head," I answered dully.

"Yep, you're right. Now, can you wiggle your toes for me?" she asked.

I gingerly wiggled my toes, and then my feet.

"Good job. How are you feeling?"

My eyes met Nicole's. "Like I've been run over by a bus."

She smiled. "I'd say that's a good estimation. You had a pretty rough time."

"I . . . I didn't. I mean I wasn't there."

"No, for a while you weren't there. You lost a lot of blood. You went into cardiac arrest and they lost you for a few minutes."

"Lost me?" I asked.

Just then, Dr. Tischmann entered. He sat on the edge of my bed and silently perused my chart.

"What does it mean that you almost 'lost me?'" I asked.

He was silent for a moment. Then he set the chart aside and looked at me. "Mary, we ran into complications during your surgery," he began.

"What kind?"

"First let me tell you the tumor is gone. We were able to excise it completely."

"So I'm going to be all right? I'm going to live?"

He took my hand and smiled. "You're going to live to be an old, old lady."

"But tell me what you meant about losing me?" I asked, already knowing what he'd say.

"Your tumor was in a tough position," he said, drawing a diagram on a piece of paper from my folder. "You see, when I began removing it, several of what we call, 'bleeders' developed. Bleeders are small veins, and it's a common enough occurrence, but unfortunately, there were so many at once, you lost a great deal of blood. Your blood pressure dropped dangerously and your heart stopped."

"I know," I said. "You looked worried. You even ordered the music turned off."

Dr. Tischmann's eyes widened. "How do you know that?"

I tried to sit up, but it was futile, so I clutched the rail of my bed and glared at the doctor. "I saw the whole thing. I saw the nurses giving me blood, I saw the tape over my eyes and my head cut open, I saw the tube down my throat, and I saw the doctors with the code-blue cart. I saw them put the big paddles on my chest, and when they shocked me, I saw a tunnel, and I left the operating room."

I thought he'd tell me I was insane or lying, but instead he nodded and agreed. "Your description of the operating room is uncanny, and it's true, because your eyes were taped shut for surgery."

"It was real," I explained. "I saw my grandfather, and my dog," I added with a smile.

"Oh, I believe you, Mary. You know, there has been a lot of research in this area. May I put you in contact with one of the professors studying this phenomenon?"

I shrugged slightly. "I guess so, but all I want right now is my children. I've wasted so much time already."

Dr. Tischmann stood and walked to the door. "They were here last night, but you were still unconscious. I'll have one of the nurses call your family; they've been waiting for word that you're awake."

That night when Scott and Erica visited, I saw them through new eyes. I saw them in a way I hadn't since they were newborns. Somehow, I'd lost touch with my children. Between my career and raising the kids, I let myself become detached. I wasn't raising my children. I was managing them. Managing them like a law case. Delegating their care to family and neighbors, and worse, leaving them alone for far too many hours, expecting them to be "tiny adults" instead of young kids.

That night I vowed to myself that I would no longer live my life based on my career. I remembered my grandfather's words, and I knew he'd offered me the very best advice I'd ever gotten. I would put my children first. Because at the end of the day, there is nothing more important than my kids.

When Scott and Erica arrived, I wanted so badly to gather them into my arms, but all I could do was grasp their hands and tell them how much I loved them. "I'm so sorry, kids," I said, tears slipping from my eyes.

"Mom," Scott said, "what's wrong? Why are you sorry?"

"Oh, sweetie, I'm sorry for everything. I've been a terrible mom, and I'm going to make it up to you."

"No," Erica piped in, "you're a good mom. We love you."

I sniffed and my lower lip quivered as I realized what wonderful children I'd been blessed with. "No, I've spent far too much time at work, and I've missed so much. From now on, I'm going to spend more time with you guys. I just love you both so much, and I'm not going to miss another day with you."

Scott smiled. "You're not going to be around too much, are you? You're not going to hang around the house and make us clean our rooms, I hope."

I tried to laugh, but the effort caused a dull ache in my head and neck. "Stop, Scott, it hurts to laugh," I said, chuckling softly. "I'm not going to make you clean your room; well, only when it starts looking like a fire hazard. I mean I'm going to be at your school events, I'm going to come home for dinner every night, and when we go to the beach this summer, I'm not going to take any work. It's going to be us; just us, and we're going to make sure we have fun."

Erica leaned across the bed rail to kiss me soundly on the cheek. "I love you, Mommy," she said.

Scott grinned and yanked his sister's long braid. "Yeah, I love you too, Mom. Just do us a favor, hurry up, and get out of here. It's lonely without you at home."

"I'll hurry, I promise," I said, giving his arm a firm, loving squeeze.

It's a bit embarrassing that I was so hardheaded that it took a life altering near death experience for me to wake up and realize my children are far more valuable to me than making partner in a law firm. Now I spend all my spare time with the people that matter the most. With my new schedule, it's fairly certain that I won't ever be a partner at the law firm. Law is my job, but it's no longer my heart. I've discovered my heart, and it belongs to my children.

There will always be legal cases, lawsuits, and divorces, but my children won't always be young, and when I'm an old woman, I want to be able to look back on my life with pride, knowing I put the love of my children before all else.

THE END

IT'S A MIRACLE!
Everybody please pray for Mel...

I spoke into the phone saying, "All right, honey, I'll see you in a few hours."

"You take care of my daughter," my husband, Brett, said.

"If she kicks me all night again, tonight, I'm going to be a real grouch tomorrow," I threatened.

"And how would that be any different than any other day?" Brett teased.

"Hey, I'm six months pregnant, and it's all your fault! The least you could do is take it easy on me," I teased right back.

"I love you, Donna. I'll be home as soon as I can," Brett said, gently.

"Love you, too," I said, hanging up the phone.

I smiled and patted my protruding stomach. Brett was going to be such an amazing daddy. I could hardly wait to meet our little girl. I wasn't due for another three months, but we had already decorated our extra bedroom as a gorgeous pink and yellow nursery. The baby's name would be Melissa Blair, and we were going to call her Mel.

Brett and I had only been married for a year, and the pregnancy had been quite a shock. Even though we had planned to wait a few years to start our family, we took the surprise for what it was—an unbelievable blessing. Just three short months from now, we would get to meet our blessing for the first time.

I lay down on the couch and turned on the television. Brett encouraged me to rest as much as I possibly could, because we both knew I wouldn't be getting much sleep after the baby came. I had become addicted to watching programs about delivering babies on cable TV. Brett couldn't understand why I wanted to scare myself half to death watching other women give birth. I felt like I was preparing myself for the worst—just in case. I never dreamed that I actually would experience that.

As I lay on the couch, watching a woman scream as she gave birth to twin boys, I felt an odd pain in my abdomen. The cramping got worse, and I thought I might feel better if I went to the bathroom.

The moment I sat down on the toilet, I felt my water break. I cried out, both in fear and pain. I was only twenty-three years old, this was my first baby, and I was home all by myself. As I started to cry, I felt something dangling between my legs. I assumed that the umbilical cord had come out. But when I looked down, I was absolutely appalled at what I saw. It was Melissa's leg!

I went to the phone and dialed 911 for help. I told them that I was six months pregnant, and that I was having a miscarriage. They promised to send an ambulance to me right away. Then, I called Brett at work.

"It's me, Brett!" I screamed into the phone. "Brett, I'm losing her. I'm losing Mel. The ambulance is on the way."

"Oh, my God, are you all right? It's going to be okay. I'll meet you there. I love you, Donna. I'll be at the hospital when you get there." Brett spoke quickly, and I could tell he was running toward his truck as we talked.

I heard the sirens, and I walked as quickly as I could toward the door. The paramedics ushered me onto the gurney and hoisted me into the ambulance.

One of them looked at me kindly, and he asked me when I was due.

"Not until April," I said, through my tears. I was crying so hard that I could hardly catch my breath.

"Have you had any contractions?" he asked.

"I'm not sure. This is my first pregnancy. My stomach hurt so I went to use the restroom. That's when my water broke and. . . ." I took a deep breath and continued, "Mel's leg came out."

The paramedic checked me and said: "You're not dilated yet, but to deliver a baby this size, you won't need to dilate all that much."

I was so upset that I couldn't even listen to what he was telling me. I moaned, "I can't believe this is happening to me. I can't believe I'm losing the baby."

"Losing the baby? Oh, honey, you aren't losing your baby. You're just having her sooner than you planned," the paramedic assured me.

My hopes soared. "I'm having my baby? Not losing her?"

"You are twenty-five weeks pregnant. Babies born at twenty-five weeks are viable with today's technology. She'll be small, but she's got a good chance of making it."

"A good chance? How good?" I needed to know exactly with what I was dealing.

Before the paramedic could answer, a stabbing pain went through my abdomen, and I cried out in pain. The paramedic checked me again, and he sucked in his breath.

"Donna, we're going to have to deliver the baby here in the ambulance."

I could hear the two of them whispering.

"We don't have the technology that the baby will need," one of them whispered, tensely. "She's only twenty-five weeks, so she will need to be admitted to the neonatal intensive care unit as soon as she's born."

"What do you think she weighs?" the other asked.

"Two pounds, maximum. Maybe a pound and a half."

I laid on the gurney, sobbing. I had never been so scared in my life. These men were talking about my baby as though she wasn't even a real person. Talking about her odds of survival as though I wasn't right in front of them, writhing in pain. I wanted Brett to be with me, to hold me, and comfort me. Even more than that, I just wanted my baby to be all right.

The pains were coming faster and harder. I knew it wouldn't be much longer. The paramedics encouraged me not to push, and I tried not to, but I felt Mel slowly slide out of my body, anyway. I lifted up my head to see her, but the paramedic who was holding her had turned his back on me. I didn't hear her crying, and even I knew that wasn't a good sign.

I could see the paramedics' hands moving over Mel's tiny body, but I couldn't see what they were doing to her. I had no idea what was going on, and it was the worst moment of my life.

Finally, I couldn't take it anymore. "What's happening?" I asked them, desperate for an answer. "Is she okay?"

The paramedics looked at me with sympathy in their eyes. "We're doing our best. We should be at the hospital in just a few minutes. The doctors there will be able to do more for her than we can here in the ambulance."

"So what does that mean? Is she going to be all right?"

"It's too soon to know. I'm sorry."

Suddenly, I heard a tiny cry come from my newborn daughter's mouth. It sounded weak and frail, but it meant she was alive. I silently thanked God for that small miracle. I prayed that He would continue to watch over her.

We arrived at the hospital, and a doctor was waiting on us to arrive. She threw open the ambulance doors and smiled at me, reassuringly. The paramedics rushed Mel inside.

"Hello, Ma'am. My name is Dr. Curtin. I'm going to be your baby's doctor. I'll get her set up in the neonatal intensive care unit, and then I'll come talk to you about her condition."

I smiled at her, weakly. "Thank-you, Doctor Curtin."

"What are you going to name her? I would just hate to call her 'Baby Sellers.'"

"Her name is Melissa. We're calling her Mel."

Dr. Curtin squeezed my hand. "That's beautiful. I'll take good care of her, and we should be able to let you see her soon."

I felt a single tear trickle down my cheek. "I haven't even gotten to hold her yet."

Dr. Curtin looked at me with sympathy. "I know, and I am so sorry about that. But the simple fact is that Mel came too soon. She's very tiny, and she's going to need to be on a ventilator for a while. We're going to need to make sure her lungs and heart are fully developed before we can let her leave the NICU. But I will let you see her as soon as I possibly can—as soon as it's safe for Mel. Okay?"

I nodded. The paramedics were back, and they were ready to take me into a recovery room. I had just arrived in my room when Brett came running in.

"Donna, honey, are you all right?" He looked at my stomach, frantic with worry. "You don't look pregnant anymore. What happened? Where is Mel?" He looked pale, and he was talking a mile a minute.

"I gave birth in the ambulance. They told me it would be better for her if I waited until we arrived at the hospital, but I couldn't help it. She was so tiny, and she just came out." I started to cry. "I tried to stop it, Brett, I really did."

"Oh, God, baby, this is not your fault. Don't you think for even one second that you did anything to cause this. So where is she, now?" He swallowed hard. "Did she . . . make it?"

"Yes, she's in the neonatal intensive care unit. She didn't cry, at first, for a long time. But when she finally did, it was the most beautiful sound I'd ever heard."

"So do they think she's going to be all right?"

"I'm not sure. The paramedics seemed really worried about her, but the doctor that came, promised to let me see her as soon as she could."

"See her? You haven't seen her yet?" Brett's eyes filled with tears.

My own tears flowed harder, now. "No, she wasn't breathing, at first, and the paramedics were doing all sorts of things to her. Then, they took her to the NICU as soon as we got here." I shook my head, sadly. "I didn't get to hold her or tell her that I love her or anything. I don't even know what color hair she has."

"Oh, honey, I'm sure she's beautiful, and she knows that you love her very much. You'll get to see her, soon." Brett put his arms around me. "Hey, I was so worried about Mel that I didn't even ask how you are. Are you sore? Did labor hurt a lot? I feel terrible that I wasn't there when you had her. I was supposed to be your coach." He smiled a sad little smile at me.

"Brett, she was so small that she just came out on her own. I didn't even have that many contractions. I'm sure you would have been a great coach, but everything happened so fast, that I didn't really need one." I reached for his hand. "I would have felt better if you had been there, but there was no way to know that I would have her so early."

Brett shook his head. "I am so sorry that I wasn't there for you."

"You're here, now, and that's what really matters."

"I'm not going anywhere. I'm not leaving this hospital for one minute until I can take you and Mel home."

I smiled at him, the love shining in my eyes. Brett was such a good husband.

Dr. Curtin walked into the room. She smiled apologetically. "I couldn't help overhearing what you just said. Donna can go home the day after tomorrow. But you'll have to wait a little while to take Miss Melissa home."

"How long?" I asked, holding my breath.

"It's hard to say, right now. But it's going to be quite a while. Generally, with babies born as prematurely as Mel was, they need to remain in the hospital until their original due date."

I heard Brett suck in his breath. "But that's three months from now!" He protested.

The doctor nodded. "I have to be honest with you both: Mel is a very sick little girl, right now. There are several health problems that are common with babies born as early as Mel. Unfortunately, she's suffering from nearly all of those problems."

My hand flew to my mouth. "What kinds of problems? I know you were concerned that her heart and lungs weren't fully developed."

Dr. Curtin nodded, again. "Her lungs are very tiny, and she has something called Respiratory Distress Syndrome. She is not able to breathe on her own, so we've hooked her up to a respirator. Her heart seems to be all right at this point."

I exhaled sharply. "Then she's okay, right?"

"Donna, Mel weighs only one pound, two ounces. With babies that small, problems can come up at any point. The next seventy-two hours are critical."

"What's that mean? Critical?" Brett asked impatiently.

"It means that if she makes it through the next three days, you'll probably get to take her home in a few months," Dr. Curtin answered softly.

"If she makes it? What are her chances?" Brett asked. I could hear the desperation in his voice.

"She weighs about five hundred grams, so her chances are about fifty percent," the doctor said. She seemed to be avoiding eye contact with us. "But she has a greater chance of complications like cerebral palsy and blindness."

"So what are you telling me about my baby? She may or may not live, we may or may not be able to take her home someday, and she may or may not be able to walk or talk or see? Is this what you're saying?" Brett asked, tears streaming down his face.

Dr. Curtin shook her head. "I know how upset you are, and I'm truly sorry that I don't have more definite answers to give you. As I

117

said before, we'll know more in seventy-two hours."

"What do we do in the meantime?" I asked. I had never felt such anguish.

"Pray for Mel. A nurse will come to get you in a few hours and you can see Mel for a few minutes. She'll be hooked up to several monitors and you won't be able to pick her up, but you can see her and touch her hands." Dr. Curtin sighed. "I'm sorry. Hopefully, we'll have some good news, soon."

After the doctor left, Brett and I held each other, and we sobbed for over an hour.

"Dr. Curtin changed her whole story," I cried. "In the ambulance, she made it seem like Mel would be all right, and I would get to see her soon."

Brett stroked my hair. "Honey, she probably didn't want to tell you the truth until you had a family member with you to comfort you. Anyway, I think sometimes, doctors have to give parents the worst case scenario, just so they're prepared in case something does happen."

I looked up at Brett's tearstained face. "So what if something happens? What if we turn out to be the worst case?"

"God, Donna, I don't know. You just can't think like that, I guess."

"I can't help it. I'm just so scared."

"I know, baby, I know."

Somehow, I dozed in Brett's arms. I think I was just so drained from the ordeal of giving birth and the emotional upheaval of hearing that Mel might not make it. Brett nudged me awake and whispered: "Babe, the nurse just came in and said we could see Mel if we wanted to."

I felt instantly awake. My heart soared at the prospect of seeing Mel for the first time.

The nurse made me sit in a wheelchair for the trip to the neonatal intensive care unit. I was not at all prepared for what I saw when we arrived. The NICU is a glass box with babies in isolettes, and on warming tables. The room was filled with the constant beeping and buzzing of the monitors and machines that kept the babies alive. Brett and I had to scrub our arms and hands and wear plastic gowns and gloves before we could enter the NICU.

"I don't even know which one she is," Brett whispered to me. "Isn't that sad that I don't recognize my own daughter?"

I nodded in understanding. "I feel the same way. She's probably the smallest one here, so we could figure it out that way."

The nurse smiled. "She is the smallest baby, but not by too much. Here, she is." She'd stopped by a warming table and pointed at the tiny being laying on it.

I sucked in my breath, and tears instantly filled my eyes. My poor baby was so tiny she would have fit into the palm of my hand. She was gray in color. She was hooked up to dozens of machines. Her skin was wrinkled as though her body needed to grow into it.

Before I could stop it, a thought jumped into my head: she looks like she might not make it. Disgusted with myself that I would think such a thing, I began to cry once again.

I reached in, and I touched Mel's tiny fingers. I silently promised her that I would love her forever—no matter what the future held for her. If she lived or if she didn't, if she was healthy or if she had problems, she would always be my daughter.

"Hey, sweetheart," Brett said, softly. "It's great to finally meet you. I'm your daddy."

I glanced over at Brett. Tears were streaming down his cheeks. He wiped his face on the back of his hand, and he continued talking to Mel. "You get well, okay? Don't you give up, because we're not going to give up on you. Mommy and I are going to be here every day, watching you, and praying for you. Then one day, the doctors and nurses are going to say that you're all right, and we can take you home. I'm praying for that day, Mel. I'm praying that you'll come home with us."

Before either of us could say another word, one of Mel's monitors started beeping wildly. Two nurses came running over. They looked very concerned.

"You'll have to leave, now," the nurse who brought us in, said.

"Why? What's happening to her?" I asked, panicked.

"Her blood pressure just dropped. Now please, step out!" she ordered.

We watched from outside as the nurses adjusted Mel's machines and monitors. Eventually, their movements seemed to slow down, and we knew that meant that Mel's crisis had passed. Silently, I wondered how many more harrowing experiences we'd have in the next few days and weeks.

I couldn't have begun to imagine. Mel had nearly every problem a premature baby could have. She had severe jaundice, she had anemia and low blood pressure, she had several infections, as well as some more serious conditions such as retinopathy of prematurity, and an intracranial hemorrhage—or bleeding in the brain.

Two days later, a nurse came in, and asked me if I was ready to go home.

"What are you talking about?" I asked. "I can't leave without my baby."

The nurse's eyes softened in sympathy. "I'm sorry, dear, but your insurance won't pay for you to stay here any longer. You'll have to go home, and you can come back and see your baby for a few hours each day."

I couldn't imagine leaving Mel there, even though I knew she was being well cared for. It broke my heart to think that it would be months before Mel and Brett and I would live under the same roof. Brett and I sadly gathered my things, and I went to say good-bye to Mel.

"I can't believe they're asking us to leave when Mel is still in critical condition," Brett grumbled.

"It's not their fault. The insurance company is to blame. They're too cheap to realize that we have extenuating circumstances," I said, far more reasonably than I felt.

We reached the NICU, did the required preparation to avoid spreading germs to the babies, and we went in. One of Mel's nurses smiled at us.

"Mel seems to be doing a little better," she told us. "She's gained two ounces." The nurse nodded her head with approval.

My heart soared. Maybe Mel would come home sooner than they had predicted.

"If she's doing so much better, can I hold her now?" I asked anxiously.

"Oh, I'm sorry. I didn't mean to get your hopes up. No, she has to be off the ventilator before you can hold her."

My heart sank. I would be denied a proper good-bye with my newborn daughter.

I reached inside and held her hand. "Hey, baby Mel, it's Mommy. We have to leave now, but we'll be back first thing in the morning. I wish more than anything that you could come with us now, but you're just too little. You keep growing, and we'll take you home real soon." I hope, I thought.

I knew that might be the last time I saw Mel alive. She was still critical, and there was the possibility that her little body would give out before the next morning. She was only two days old, and already, I couldn't imagine my life without her.

With tears in my eyes, I kissed my fingertips, and placed them softly on Mel's forehead. "Good-bye, sweet girl. We'll see you, tomorrow."

Brett whispered his loving good-byes, and we left the hospital.

As we drove home, we talked about the events of the past few days. "Mel shouldn't even be here for another three months. Instead, she's in the NICU fighting for her life. How can that be, Brett? How could God allow that to happen to our baby?" I asked tearfully.

"Donna, don't question God's judgment. He knows what He's doing."

"I can't help it, Brett. This is the most terrible thing that's ever happened to me."

"Think about something for me," Brett said. "Think about bringing Mel home from the hospital. Think about feeding her and holding her. How incredible does that feel, babe? The only way you're going to make it through the next few months is to focus on all the wonderful moments you'll have once Mel comes home."

I took a deep breath. "But what if none of that happens? What if she doesn't ever come home?"

"You've got to trust that God will do what He thinks is best."

I said a silent prayer, begging Him to save my tiny baby.

When we returned to the hospital the following morning, Mel was still with us, although she remained on the ventilator and other machines. In just a few hours, she would be seventy-two hours old, and out of the critical stage. We could then breathe a sigh of relief, and begin bonding with Mel.

Dr. Curtin came in to check on Mel. She smiled at me before saying, "Mel seems to be hanging in there. We're not completely in the clear yet, but she's proven that she's a strong little girl. She's a fighter, and those are the ones who usually make it."

The doctor's words were comforting and alarming at the same time. I didn't want to hear about which babies usually make it. I needed some kind of a guarantee about Mel. But of course, no one could offer me that.

I nodded to Dr. Curtin. "Thank-you for all you've done to help our baby. I know she's going to make it."

The doctor gave me a small smile. "I really hope you're right. I hope your little Mel is the one to beat the odds."

The next few weeks were grueling. Brett and I were at the hospital every single day. I spent all day there, and Brett came in the evenings after work. It was extremely difficult sitting next to my baby all day, but being unable to pick her up and hold her in my arms. I stroked her hair and her face and held her hands, but that was as much physical contact as we had for those first few weeks.

Finally, when Mel was six weeks old, Dr. Curtin suggested trying to take her off the ventilator. Many babies had a difficult time, and it often took several tries to remove them from it, she'd warned. But I just knew Mel would be fine. As soon as she was breathing on her own, I could hold her for the very first time. It was also a huge step toward her going home.

Dr. Curtin removed Mel's long breathing tube and within just a few minutes, she had crashed. They had to put it back in.

I was crushed. I called Brett and cried. "What kind of a life does she have? I can't continue to watch her live on machines."

"What are you saying, Donna? For Mel right now, it's live on machines or not live at all."

"I know," I sobbed. "But I hate it. I hate it for her, and I hate it for us. I can't even hold my own baby. Do you have any idea what that feels like?"

"Of course, I do. We're in this together, honey." Brett sighed. "She's only six weeks old. She's got her whole life ahead of her. She's going to be all right. Dr. Curtin sees improvements in her every day."

"Not enough improvement that I can hold her," I said, stubbornly.

"It's coming, Donna. You'll get everything you've been waiting for. Just give Mel a few more weeks. Remember that her due date isn't for another seven weeks. We knew things would be difficult until then."

"I didn't know they'd be this difficult, though."

"I know how awful this has been for you, and I'm sorry. I'd give everything I own to change it, but we can't do that. All we can do is hope and pray that she grows up to be a healthy little girl."

I sighed, and I wiped my eyes. Brett was always so sensible, and I was always so emotional. It was one of the things that made our marriage work, I suppose.

"You're right, Brett. I refuse to give up on Mel. Not now, not ever."

Brett and I hung up and I went back into the NICU to see Mel. One of the nurses came over. "Dr. Curtin wanted me to tell you not to be discouraged that Mel couldn't come off the ventilator this morning. Very few babies are successful the first time."

I hung my head. "I know. I just really wanted Mel to be one of the ones who could do it, though."

"It's not a race, Donna," the nurse said, patiently. "We can't rush Mel to do things she isn't ready for." She patted my hand and said: "Dr. Curtin said she would try to remove the tube again next week."

My eyes must have lit up because the nurse chuckled. "Don't get your hopes up too high. It may not work, and I don't want you to feel disappointed." But then, she winked and said, "It will give you something to look forward to, though."

The next week crawled by. Mel was seven weeks old, and I had still never held her. I was very concerned that she didn't realize that I was her mother. The nurses assured me that babies like Mel understand more than we think they do. They promised me that Mel could hear my voice, and that she recognized it.

Finally, the day came when Dr. Curtin had promised to try again to get Mel off the ventilator. The day I'd finally be able to hold my daughter. Brett had taken the day off work to be there when—and if—it was successful.

Dr. Curtin pulled out Mel's long tube, and she inserted a shorter one just for oxygen. We watched the monitors carefully, waiting for signs of complications. Nothing happened. Her color remained a healthy pink, and she was breathing on her own.

"Congratulations," Dr. Curtin said. "Donna, I think it's safe to hold her, now."

"Oh, thank-you, God," I said, my throat tightening. Tears threatened to spill over. I could hardly believe this day was here!

Brett pulled over a rocking chair. I sat down, and the nurse placed Mel in my arms. It was as close to heaven as I had ever been. She was so warm, and she seemed to snuggle right into my arms.

Brett knelt down beside me, not even trying to fight the tears. "She is so amazing, and so are you. Look at you two. You're a perfect fit. She's knows who you are, Donna, and she loves you already. She loves you for sitting by her side every single day, waiting for this moment. She loves you for your strength and your patience. She loves you for being her mommy."

"Thank-you, Brett," I murmured through my own tears.

The nurse took some pictures of the three of us, and then of both of us holding her. It was the best day I'd had since Mel was born.

Brett and I went to dinner that night to celebrate. "I wish Mel were here," I said. "It doesn't seem right to celebrate her health when she's not with us."

"She'll be with us soon, though. Very soon," Brett assured me.

Mel's condition continued to improve. Her jaundice was gone, and the anemia was being it was being taken care of with medication. The bleeding in her brain had turned out to be minor, and it would not cause her any long-term harm. The primary concern, now, was her eyes. She had retinopathy of prematurity, which could cause blindness in the most serious cases. Mel's case was moderate. She would need to wear glasses from an early age, and there was a possibility that she could go blind later in life.

Although we were still concerned about Mel's size and her development, it was hard not to be thrilled with the progress she was making. She weighed a whole six pounds— still not even the size of most full-term newborns, but to me, she seemed enormous. She was fourteen weeks old, and her original due date was just one week away. Dr. Curtin seemed optimistic that she would be going home soon.

I would sit in the rocking chair in the NICU, holding Mel for hours. The nurses often had to make me lay her back down.

"You are going to spoil her," they'd tease. "When you get her home, you'll have other things to do, and you won't have time to constantly hold her."

I would shake my head. "Nope, I'm going to make time for this one. Mel and I have lost too much time here, already. I don't care if she's spoiled. I'm not going to miss another minute of her life."

"She'll love that when she's a teenager," they'd tease again.

What an amazing thought—Mel as a teenager. Mel, who came way too early to have a chance at life, but fought back as hard as someone a hundred times her size. Mel, my one pound, four ounce living miracle, would grow up and be a teenager, someday. The thought brought tears to my eyes, and it made me realize, once again, how precious life truly was.

We brought Mel home from the hospital when she was seventeen weeks old. We'd spent one hundred and seventeen days, Mel's whole life, in that hospital. It seemed strange when it was time to leave. I felt insecure, as though I wouldn't be able to care for her without the nurses there to help me. Mel was still on oxygen, and she was just learning how to drink from a bottle. All babies were a challenge to care for, but Mel had additional needs to be concerned about.

"You're wonderful with her, and you'll be even more wonderful with her at home," Brett encouraged.

We said a tearful good-bye to Dr. Curtin and the nurses. We promised to send pictures and keep them updated on Mel's progress.

That first night was both exhilarating and exhausting. It felt incredible to have Mel home with us, sleeping in the bassinet next to our bed. She also woke up every two hours, and I hardly got any sleep at all. I was used to the nurses taking care of her at night, but now, it was my turn. I was wiped out, but I loved every minute of it. I just wanted to be a normal mom with my baby, and if normal moms stayed up all night, then I was happy to do it.

The weeks went by quickly—now that Mel was at home. She went back to the hospital for frequent checkups. She seemed to be doing well, although her development was a bit delayed because of all the time she'd spent in the hospital.

Mel will be celebrating her first birthday next week, a day I wasn't sure we'd ever get to see. But she's here, and she is such a blessing to Brett and me. She weighs twelve pounds, now. She's got curly brown hair and the biggest blue eyes you've ever seen. She smiles almost constantly, but the biggest smiles are always for her daddy.

Mel is developmentally delayed, as many premature babies are. She receives speech and physical therapy to help her catch up to other babies her age. She's nearly a year old, and she's just learning to sit up on her own. Her therapist says that it may be another year or so before she learns to walk, but that's just fine with me. I enjoy Mel so much, just the way she is.

Mel is healthy now, too. She is completely off the additional oxygen, and she has only mild asthma. She has to eat a special diet to help her gain weight. She is nearsighted, and looks positively adorable in her glasses.

When strangers see Mel, they think she is just a few months old because of her size and level of development. When I tell them what she's been through, they express sympathy for her—and for us. I always shake my head and say: "Don't feel sorry for Mel. That's like counting her out. I almost did that once, and she proved me wrong. She has overcome all the odds just by being here. And by being who she is, she has become a miracle!"

THE END

I REJECTED MY
OWN CHILD

I couldn't believe the harsh words I had said to my daughter. The poisonous venom had spewed forth from me as I turned into an unrecognizable monster. I had planned to be the perfect mother in a perfect family, but instead, the words I used with my fifteen-year-old daughter were unforgiving and unforgivable.

Maribel shrugged her bony shoulders, sighed, and went to her room, not even slamming the door. Then I knew that I had really made a big mistake, and that I was in a situation way over my head. I wondered how I had come to this crossroads, and why those basic instincts and good common sense I prided myself on hadn't served me well. I sat dazed, too stunned at my behavior and feelings of inadequacy to cry. I didn't cry on the outside, but my heart felt as if it had needles sticking through it.

I just didn't understand how our lives had come to this point. I started thinking about our lives before we got Maribel, and our hopes and dreams for our future.

Chris and I married right out of high school, when I was eighteen, and he was nineteen. At the time, I was working in the meat market of a grocery store, and he was working at a gas station. Even though the work was hard and I didn't like having the smell of meat on my hands, I learned about different cuts of meat and different ways of packaging. I also learned that sometimes prices go up from the packaging, and the same product can be found in a simpler package. I was the youngest worker in the meat market, and the ladies who worked with me exposed me to experiences I had never even read about in books.

One lady, Carol, a tiny lady with coarse black hair and dark black eyes that sparkled when she talked, came to work with blackened eyes and bruises. She talked about getting "spanked" for taking her baby to a bar where the oil field workers hung out. The "spanking" surprised me enough, but taking a baby to a bar was also an experience I had never heard of.

My parents were hard working, highly moral people. My mom was a housewife, and my dad was a bread route salesman. Our household was very basic, with the biggest discussion being whether it was all right to play cards on Sunday. Since I had never heard either of my parents, or any other adult, curse, I enjoyed being around these worldly ladies who weren't afraid to use any words they thought of.

126

I was fascinated to hear about this exciting and exotic side of life. I learned that in spite of their behavior that was so different from other people I knew, they were all protective of me, and were warm and generous in their affection. They teased me constantly, but were pleased that I didn't have the problems in life that they had. All of the ladies worried that I was marrying too young. They wanted me to be on my own before I had so many responsibilities. They didn't understand that I was in love, and all I wanted was to spend my life with Chris and have a family.

My mom and dad had married at eighteen and twenty-four, so they weren't worried about our ages. My two younger sisters thought the idea of romance and dating was exciting and a cause for great teasing. The three of us giggled, fought, and admired each other. Chris's family was just the opposite in make-up. He was the middle child of three rambunctious boys, who were always teasing each other and seemed to me to be very noisy. We never played games like "catch the alligator" where someone tackled and wrestled the "alligator" while the alligator screamed and roared and fought, gnashing teeth and body wildly. Chris's mom worked part-time at the school cafeteria, and his dad owned a garage door company. Both were much like my parents—good, solid, typical parents, or so I thought. Until I started working at the market, I had no idea that both our families were sheltering us from the harsher realities of life.

Chris and I couldn't wait to get married. When I was away from him, I thought of how many minutes or hours I would have to endure before I saw him again. I enrolled in a few classes at the local junior college, but instead of taking notes in history, I was writing "Chris loves Faith; Faith loves Chris." I also counted all time by when I would see him again. Now that seems childish, but I was completely enchanted by this intense, tall, raw-boned young man. Needless to say, my grades reflected my real interest in life at that time, and the meat market became a full-time job for me.

Chris and I married at the small church which I had attended since I was a child. The wedding was simple but lovely, and all the ladies from the market came. Carol wept throughout the whole ceremony. I think we reflected a kind of hope that would probably never be in her life, and she was happy for us, but sad for her own life that seemed hopeless. Both families were pleased, and both helped with the wedding itself as well as the reception.

Now the teasing turned to when we would provide grandchildren for them. The sooner the better, they all said. We decided to wait at least six months before trying to have a baby, so we practiced birth control diligently. Chris and I were also eager to start our family.

Our "daydreaming" times were filled with how many children,

perhaps four? What would we name them? We wondered how many girls and how many boys we would have since we both had same-sex siblings. We agreed on almost everything about rearing children as we talked late into the night about our plans. A larger house would be necessary, but that could wait until we had the second child.

Sometimes I worried that life seemed too simple, and that I didn't deserve the happiness that Chris and I shared. I compared my life to Carol's and the other ladies', and I knew that they were better-hearted and more generous in spirit than I could ever be. Despite their rough edges, these ladies had an honesty that would endure anything. They still teased me and tried to embarrass me about sex, but I knew they really liked me. They loved to tell me jokes and watch me turn red. They would have been disappointed to realize that I wasn't quite as naive or gullible as I acted because I was an avid reader of romance magazines and novels, but I knew they gained pleasure from thinking that someone was that "green." We just played games, and I shared with them my desire for children as soon as the six-month waiting period was over.

Finally, Chris and I had been married for six months, and we could start our family. I really expected to become pregnant that first month, and had already determined that the baby would be born in September. Much to my disappointment, no pregnancy occurred. We decided to increase our efforts, and listened to advice from Carol and the ladies as well as everyone else we knew who had a few tips on how to get pregnant. We were very open about our quest.

After three months, each period I had became a cause for weeping and frustration. Our relationship wasn't romantic anymore. I called Chris from work to dash home if my thermometer said it was time.

"Hurry, come home now! It's time. I know this time will work!" He felt used, and I felt obsessed. We started to argue over the intensity that I felt about getting pregnant. The ladies advised me to relax and forget about it. That wasn't possible for me.

Finally, after a year, we went to a fertility specialist. We learned that because of physical problems, I couldn't get pregnant. The news was devastating, and I felt like a complete failure. I just couldn't get over my sense of loss, and I grieved for the family that we could have had. Chris and I couldn't talk anymore, and I wasn't interested in anything remotely physical.

Chris's constant refrain was, "Faith, we had each other before, and we have each other now. This is just a setback."

What a setback. No matter how hard I tried, I couldn't make him understand that without children, my whole core of existence was missing. I had played dolls and house since I was a little girl. I mothered every puppy in the neighborhood, not even counting the number of young children I mothered around.

Finally, my doctor had a good, stern talk with me.

"Faith," he said, looking me right in the eye. "You are going to ruin your marriage as well as your health if you don't stop grieving over not being able to have children. Many children need good parents, and you are in an ideal position to adopt a child."

At first I couldn't imagine adopting, not having a child of my own blood, but as Chris and I talked it over, I realized that I needed a baby and could love any baby or child put into my care. We decided to try to adopt a child that was harder to place. We felt that we had the skills and love that could surmount challenges a special child would give us.

We asked for a "less than perfect" child. We were a little older than most adopting couples, and we had patience and a good background to give. I'd kept in touch with the ladies from the market after I stopped working there, and they warned me to be careful. That a damaged child was sometimes damaged for life, through no fault of her or his own. I explained patiently that I didn't agree. I never thought of how much more real life experience those ladies had seen. I just wanted my baby.

As we waited for the seemingly never-ending adoption process, we kept several foster children in our home. Keeping these children, and seeing the needs that are out there for a stable family, reinforced our determination to adopt a child of our own. Each time a foster child left, the grief over losing the child was almost heart-wrenching. I didn't understand why it took so long to adopt if so many children needed help.

When Mrs. Hill from social services called to say she had a child for us to adopt, a little three-year-old girl who was very undernourished and in great need of a loving home, we were delighted. We squealed with happiness.

Mrs. Hill warned us, "This baby girl is not a candidate for any kind of baby pageant award. We don't know exactly what has happened to her, but she has definitely been neglected."

We replied, "That's okay. We won't neglect her." We had total confidence in our ability to love and nurture this yet unseen child.

Mrs. Hill continued. "Her parents want total freedom from any kind of responsibility. They hardly acknowledged her while she was with them. An example of their attitude is in their name of her. On the birth certificate, she is named Venus."

I immediately replied, "We'll rename her and let her help us choose a name. We've waited so long for a child to love, and she will fit right in with our family. I know that she will have a last name that she can be proud of when she joins our family."

Mrs. Hill went on to explain that Venus hadn't been happy in any of her foster homes. She was withdrawn, wouldn't speak, and was so frail that the foster parents didn't know how to handle her.

An aide brought the child in, and this thin, pale, sad little girl watched us cautiously. Her thumb never left her mouth, and she seemed to fold into herself.

No one knew exactly what she had faced in her life, but we knew she had not had a happy or stable life so far. Chris and I both took one look at her, and with supreme confidence that only the untried can have, we shouted, "We'll take her. We'll make her a home." We thought we could make that little face smile, and I think we thought that we could just erase the first three years of her life with good intentions.

Our love alone would make up for any neglect she had suffered, and by loving and cherishing this child, we could face any obstacles. Our journey of life with a child was about to begin.

After our burst of enthusiasm, we noticed that our "new daughter" had not moved or responded in any way. She was obviously afraid of us.

I knelt down and looked her in the eye, and said, "Would you like to be in our family? Would you like to come home with us? I want to be your mommy, and Chris wants to be your daddy. We have always wanted a little girl just like you." I never questioned our decision that day, or had any idea of the power to hurt and to give hurt in return that we would all face.

The little girl finally looked up at me uneasily, but she still didn't respond. She did take my hand as I stretched it out to her. Chris held back a little because Mrs. Hill told him that the child was terrified of men. We got into the car, fastened her into the car seat, and started our drive home. She was so underweight that she still needed a car seat built for much younger children.

We talked very softly on the way home, and Chris started offering small bits of information. "Honey," he ventured. "Would you like to play with our dog? We have a very nice dog that has been wanting a little girl to play with. Now that you're in our family, the dog will be your dog, too."

Chris gently and quietly described the little dog that we had rescued from the shelter. He told her that the dog's other owners had been mean to him, and had not really wanted a dog after all. He explained that Cha-Cha hadn't really had a home until we found him, and we love him and love taking care of him. He lives with us and now is part of our family. We tried to mention the word "family" as often as we could without scaring her. Chris tried to keep her from fearing him, and I tried to show her that I could nurture her and accept her as she was by telling her that Cha-Cha was really shaking when we first brought him home, and he was hungry and afraid of everything. Now he is a happy dog and runs all over the place playing.

When we arrived home, she sat very still in the car and looked at the house, staring in amazement at the small, white three-bedroom house with cheerful pink periwinkles and a neat, well-kept lawn. Not so tidy was Cha-Cha, who, in his enthusiasm for chasing butterflies, had landed in mud somewhere. We carried a trembling, terrified child into the house.

The overwhelmed little three-year-old looked at her bedroom with its pink-checkered bedspread and matching curtains, a baby doll that I had hurriedly bought for her, and a few basic clothing items. She had nothing but the thin T-shirt and shorts she was wearing. Even her sandals were scruffy. She stood in the doorway of her room.

Finally, I asked, "Would you like a bubble bath and a nightgown?" She nodded.

As I bathed her, I had to turn my face so she wouldn't see the tears. She was all bones. She had never seen a bubble bath, and was afraid of the bubbles at first. This was a three-year-old! She should've been chattering, blowing bubbles from the foam, drawing bubble pictures on the side of the tub, making up fantasy stories for us, and asking questions. Instead, she still didn't speak, and she shivered with fright. I quickly dried her and put her nightgown on. She did seem to like the glamorous princess in purple that was on the front. She almost smiled.

Since we couldn't continue to call her, "Honey," "Darling little girl," or "Sweetie," we had to find a name. The child was still not speaking, so I decided to name her after one of the dear ladies at the market. I decided "Carol" was too old-fashioned, but I did like Maribel's name, so we decided upon the name "Maribel." I asked her if she like the name and she just looked at me, but at least she didn't shake her head. Maribel it was.

Gradually, Maribel started responding to Cha-Cha. She hugged him, chased butterflies with him, and whispered. Her vocabulary increased, and she started speaking in short sentences. Most of her talking was to Cha-Cha, even if she was saying something for us to hear. Cha-Cha was a good buffer.

Chris took his time with Maribel, and she allowed him to read stories to her. First she sat away from him, and then she started snuggling in closer. We were very careful not to rush her. She wanted to hear one story three or four times a night, and rejected hearing any other stories. We were glad that she was expressing her preferences. This little stubborn streak meant she had a mind of her own, and we saw that as healthy. She helped me to set the table, and I tried all the self-esteem building chores and ways to make her feel we really were a family that I could think of.

I thought back to the things my mom taught me, and I read parenting magazines. Sometimes I talked to my friends from the market even though I had not worked there for a year. They were still cautious. I stopped asking for their advice when I realized they didn't really approve of our decision to adopt Maribel.

Later, I realized it wasn't a lack of approval as much as a realistic fear of the future.

Maribel started kindergarten at the age of five, and even though she had learning disabilities, with the help of a tutor and developmental reading teacher, she was a happy, thriving little girl. Most of all, she loved her dog. She started having temper tantrums and not telling the truth to get out of trouble, but we thought that was normal child behavior, and was much better than the shy, frightened child she had been. I just kept reading my parent magazines, and Chris and I talked late into the night many nights about our strategies for dealing with this strange little girl that we loved so much.

The years flew by. Testing showed that Maribel had mild retardation, but she was now a very social child. She was still much smaller than the other children in her class, but that didn't stop her from having many friends. Other children were attracted to her nerve, and her willingness to try new things, especially if they were against the rules. Her grades were barely passing, and we had numerous parent-teacher conferences about her lack of following rules at school.

One time, when Maribel came home from school, I met her at the door. "Maribel, we had another call from your school today. Now that you're in junior high, I thought the calls about your behavior would stop."

Maribel looked puzzled. "What did I do?" I was amazed that she really seemed to be unaware of the problem.

"Maribel, when your teacher was giving instructions for the assignment, you were talking and passing notes. Then when she gave out the assignment, you had to interrupt other students to see what to do. She says this is a pattern of behavior. Why don't you listen?"

Maribel smirked. "That's no big deal. I get tired of listening to her. She has a boring voice, and I don't want to hear it. Thanks a lot, Mom, for making me hear about it at home, too."

"How did I become the villain in this? At school, pay attention. Period."

Maribel showed no guilt and just thought that I was overreacting. We went through junior high school with many conversations like this. By the time she was through the ninth grade, I knew all of her teachers. All of them had the same story—Maribel didn't talk back or speak rudely to the teachers, but she totally ignored anything they said. She didn't respect authority. We were finding the same truth at home.

I called Carol and she informed me that we had better rein that child in now, and fast, or we were in for a very rough road ahead. I decided not to call her again. She didn't understand modern parenting techniques. Out came the magazines and the late talks with Chris. He was getting very tired of her attitude, and couldn't understand why she didn't just behave at school. He kept telling her, "Maribel, that's your job. I have to follow rules and do what my boss says at my job. Your mom has to follow certain rules. All of us do. This is the way life is. Just shut your mouth at school, listen, and obey the rules. You're there for an education, not to socialize."

His words had no effect on her, either.

We kept telling ourselves that Maribel had come such a long way. Even though she was physically frail, this strong-willed child wasn't the least bit frail in mind-set.

By the tenth grade, Maribel had a group of kindred-spirit friends. They liked to break all the rules and defied authority. She snuck out of the house at night and seemed completely out of control. We couldn't talk to her about anything, because we were just too naive. Her room and clothes smelled like smoke that had the tell-tale sweet odor. School called two or three times a week to ask where she was. Chris and I tried everything. We grounded her, counseled her, assured her of our love, and explained that in our family we didn't do such things. We didn't realize that words such as these added to the problem. We spent most of every night trying to unravel this dilemma we were facing. We didn't feel equipped to deal with a child so unlike any child we had ever been around.

We asked her repeatedly, "Don't you care what we think?" and "Don't you want to behave in a way that shows respect for yourself as well as others?"

She never replied except by sighing. Those parents who named her Venus had damaged her far more than we had realized. Our leniency with her as we tried to assure her of totally unconditional love was the other extreme, and hurt her, also. We kept trying to nurture and love her. I will admit that I was in over my head, and I even questioned whether I should have ever taken this battle on. I kept reminding myself that parents of children who are born to them have problems like this, too, and that parents just resolve the problems one way or another. I asked questions, read more articles, and dealt with conflicting advice from "tough love" to "love immersion" and everything in between. By now Chris and I were arguing over the resolution, because he was tired of her taking every moment of time and energy that we had.

We took her to a counselor who was recommended by her counselor at school. The whole family went, but we were not successful because Maribel skipped the sessions.

Teachers and counselors at school told us that Maribel had a great deal of unresolved anger. We pleaded, "How do we resolve it?" And, "Why is she so angry?" We couldn't see that we had done anything but love and cherish this child.

Everyone encouraged us to talk to her. We talked and talked and talked and tried to listen, or to interpret her body language, those crossed arms, hunched shoulders, eyes looking toward the ceiling or floor, and the never-ending sighs.

Chris told her, "Maribel, you are going to shorten your life by sighing all the time. Think of all the air you're wasting." She didn't find that humorous.

We reassured Maribel daily. I read more books on building self-esteem, and I praised her for the slightest thing she did that was positive. She laughed when I said, "Maribel, thank you for closing the door more gently." That was a little ridiculous. We praised her for her sweet smile and her enthusiasm. Never mind that the enthusiasm was for getting into trouble. We were reaching.

If she did respond, it was with a shrug, and comments like, "Mom and Dad, you make a big deal out of everything. Just leave me alone. I'm not angry. Stop staring at me and talking about me all the time. It's my life."

She resented our talking to others about her, and she resented the books that I read about teenagers who were defiant and out of control. She loved to point out the teenagers on a television show who shouted and cursed at their parents, usually moms, and were really out of control. They made her look angelic. I kept thinking that I was close to finding the answer to her behavior. I saw it as the missing parts of a puzzle. I was sure I'd be able to put it together.

By this time, Maribel's grades were falling, and she wasn't bringing her weird friends with spiked hair and baggy jeans and multiple body piercings to the house at all. In addition to this, she was skipping school. Her teachers said she tried to sleep in class. This was because she was sneaking out at night and staying out late. She was now a sophomore in high school, fifteen years old. I was forty and felt eighty.

Her only positive behavior was toward Cha-Cha. We heard her whispering to him, revealing those heart-secrets that only he knew. We were at our wit's end.

Chris was sick of the tension in the house, and sometimes I thought that Maribel enjoyed the power she had of making Chris and me fight. Then I reminded myself that she didn't have that power unless we gave it to her, and apparently we had done just that. She was controlling the atmosphere of the house to that extent. Chris started going out with friends and staying away from the house as much as he could.

I didn't really care because I didn't have the energy to deal with him and with Maribel. I thought he should grow up and help me deal with our daughter.

Finally the day came when I erased in one short fight all the good will and love that we had built during those twelve years we had nourished this fifteen-year-old.

Maribel came into my room around midnight. Chris was visiting his parents and wasn't expected home until later that night. She said quietly, "Mom, do you feel like talking?"

"Sure, honey, I'll talk anytime you ever want to. Let's go to the kitchen and make a pot of tea."

Such a peaceful, easy beginning. Making a pot of tea was our comfort-talk ritual. I put the kettle on, waited for it to whistle, fixed the tea bags, and had the most terrible feeling that something awful was about to happen. I handled the tea very slowly and dreaded this pending conversation. Maribel looked at the table.

I poured the water into the teacups. "Maribel, sweetie, what has been troubling you? Are you ready to talk about why you're so angry all the time? What can I do to help?

I don't think I really wanted an answer.

She looked down. "Well, Mom," she said quietly, "I don't think you can do anything. I'm pregnant."

Silence descended upon us.

Then I slowly and deliberately said, "Maribel, you are fifteen years old. You can't take care of yourself. How in the world do you think you could take care of a baby?"

Maribel didn't answer, and she still didn't look at me. She put a spoon into her teacup; no sugar, just a spoon, and started stirring, clanging the sides of the spoon onto the cup in an irritating gesture. I wanted to shout, "Drink the tea! Don't play with it!" But I didn't say anything because I knew that the spoon in the tea wasn't the problem.

Finally, I said, "Sweetie, how did this happen?"

Even I knew what a ridiculous question that was. Maribel laughed shortly at my response, and said, still looking at her teacup, "The usual way, Mom."

I wanted a reaction from her. I wanted her to cry, to express regret, or to tell me that she knew that wasn't the way we had raised her. I instinctively lashed out to get some sort of response.

"How could you do this to us after all we've done for you?" The instant that question was out, I regretted it. She looked at me without any expression. Those aren't words you say to a child, especially to an adopted child.

"Mom, I know the story. I know you took an abused, ugly child that nobody wanted, and out of the goodness of your hearts gave her a 'perfect' home with all the good stuff, including a dog."

"Maribel, we never thought of you that way. We've loved you from the minute we saw you. We longed for a child. We have told you that over and over."

"Yeah, you've longed for a child in your image that would make you proud. Well, that's not what you got. I didn't plan this baby, and the whole deal isn't about you or the home you gave me. It isn't about the preachy morals or the books you read or the friends you talk to about your delinquent daughter. This is about me."

Now I know that we repeated words that many parents have said during one of these terrible conversations, with the mom feeling guilty, and the child afraid and hiding it by acting defiant. I couldn't think. I didn't know what to say next, and hated the thoughts of "What will people say?" that I couldn't keep from my mind. I thought of Carol, and wondered if she would have an I-told-you-so attitude.

Maribel continued to play with her tea bag, seemingly bored with our conversation, and with this bombshell she'd dropped on me. I kept thinking, How in the world am I going to tell Chris?

"What do you plan to do? Abortion is out of the question."

Maribel finally looked up. "Aw, Mom, I don't even want to do that. I'm not going to put this baby up for adoption, either. I don't want it to have to feel grateful to people who adopt it."

This statement left me seething. "Listen to me, young lady, and I'll tell you about being made to feel grateful. We have never done anything to you but love you, and I will not accept blame for whatever twisted ideas you have in your head."

I mentioned the idea that I was a little old to be raising a new baby, and that Maribel hadn't finished school. She had no mental or material skills to take care of a child.

Where was Chris when I needed him?

"Maribel, who is the father?"

She continued to clang that spoon against the side of the tea cup. It sounded as grating as high-pitched wind chimes. She yawned, and said, "I really don't know. I like to have a good time."

Then I lost it. I screamed at her, "Have a good time! I wish you had been brought up by those so-called parents of yours who named you Venus. They were on the right track. I wish I'd never taken you from that hole you were living in before the social workers found you." Then I collapsed, sobbing, regretting my words but regretting how much I meant them, too.

Maribel shrugged, sighed, and said, "That would be okay with me. At least they wouldn't have to preach to me and ask other people what to do about me. At least they would know me."

Her total lack of concern for my feelings, and her lack of

appreciation for what I had given of myself to fulfill this dream to have a child to nurture and love, made me livid and out of control.

Determined to get a reaction from her, I said in a steely voice, "You are a scrawny, pathetic, thankless excuse for a human being who is not and has not ever been a real member of this family."

She looked up, put her spoon on the side of the saucer, gave me a half-smile, half-smirk, and left. Then I sat at the table and realized what I had said. When she didn't even slam the door, I knew that my words had, indeed, gone very deep. I had been so desperate to get a reaction from her, a reaction over what she had done and what she had become, that I had gone way too far. I had crossed a line that must never be crossed. Neither of us slept that night.

When Chris finally came in, I told him what had happened. At first he didn't believe the news about the baby. Then when I told him what I had said to Maribel, he quietly held me and assured me that we would find a way to heal these wounds. He didn't say much about the baby except to agree that we wouldn't have an abortion, and that we wouldn't raise the child. His concern was in keeping our family together, and in finding ways to heal the wounds that I inflicted upon my child that evening. I had not been completely sure of his support, and this shocked him, too. This was a night for judging people's reactions incorrectly. This was also a night for facing harsh realities about our feelings.

Maribel came to the door when it was time for school the next morning. Her eyes were red and puffy, as were mine.

"Morning, Maribel," Chris said to her, and left it at that.

I asked, "Maribel, do you want some breakfast? I sliced some fresh strawberries the way you like them."

The air felt thick with tension.

Maribel's voice quavered. "No, I'm not hungry. I don't have time anyway."

"Maribel, honey, come home right after school. We are a family, and we will work this out. We need to talk, and to make some decisions."

"Mom, I think we talked enough last night to last me the rest of my life."

"Please come right home. We both love you."

Maribel snorted and looked me straight in the eye. "Mom, we won't be making any decisions. It's my life, my baby, and my decision. I don't want to hear any of your lectures."

I was so afraid that I'd lost her. "Maribel, I didn't mean what I said last night. I was trying to get a reaction from you."

She laughed very quietly. "Of course you did. You meant exactly what you said. You aren't sorry you thought it; you're sorry you said it. You should know that it didn't come as a shock to me. I've always known that you expected me to be like you, and I can't, and won't. I am really a Venus, aren't I?"

When she left again, closing the door gently, my heart sank. Now I knew the cause of her anger. She thought we were sorry that she had not lived up to our expectations. She thought we expected a perfect baby for a perfect family. I hadn't realized how much I loved, deep down, this quirky little free spirit.

I called the only friend I knew who had faced much of life's harder path. Carol was still in a rocky marriage, and she barely lived from paycheck to paycheck. In spite of her rough edge, she had more common sense and could "cut to the chase" better than anyone I knew.

When I called, I started with, "Carol, this is Faith. You'll probably tell me 'I told you so' but I've made a terrible mistake with Maribel and I don't know what to do." Then I told her in detail what had gone on the night before.

Carol immediately went to the heart of the matter. "What this kid needs now is a plan that will make her feel safe. You say you didn't mean the stuff you told her. Well, she didn't mean the stuff she said, either. Why do you think you're the only one to say stupid things to get attention? That's what teenagers do. They get you to say stuff and then they say they knew you meant that all along. It always makes you look dumb and like you don't love them. Then they have a case for acting out."

She also added that I needed to take a good long look at my reasons for adopting Maribel in the first place.

I talked this over with Chris, thinking all the time about Maribel's accusation that I asked other people for advice and didn't think for myself, but I needed some backup on this most difficult problem of my life.

I realized that the problem was Maribel's feelings as well as an unplanned baby. We needed to deal with one thing at a time.

All day long, I tried to think of what I should do. I was embarrassed to call anyone except Carol, and for once my parenting magazines and books didn't help. I had to reach deep within myself and let my mind be still. The day seemed to last forever until it was time for Maribel to come home. I still didn't have a plan, but I did have a calm mind-set.

Maribel didn't come home that Friday night. All night, Cha-Cha went to the door and whimpered, waiting for her. She'd at least felt unconditional love from this little fellow, now arthritic and a bit frail. Gray hairs covered his formerly black spots. Butterflies were safe.

We were so afraid our daughter died or would never be a part of our lives again. I thought irrational thoughts like: She can clang her spoon against the side of the tea cup all she wants to. I would have welcomed it.

When she finally came in Saturday morning, she looked tired and defeated. Chris and I both opened our arms to her. She looked as cautious as that little three-year-old girl she had been.

"Maribel, honey," I blurted out. "We love you. We love your feistiness; we love that different drummer you hear. Having you in our lives has brought us out of being stiff and getting set in our ways. You've brought joy into our hearts."

She wasn't too sure about this. She was thinking of all the problems she'd caused and all the late night discussions she had heard between Chris and me.

I just grinned at her and kept holding out my arms to her. Unlike the lack of expression from Friday night, she rushed into my arms, her frail body just reaching below my breast.

She sobbed. "I'm so sorry I said those mean things. I'm not pregnant at all. I just wanted to see what it would take to make you say you don't love me. I talked it over with my friends, and we decided that this would be a real test. They all thought you would just kick me out, and I wasn't too sure about what would happen. I had to know."

This was a bit of a shock. I had already formulated a plan to suggest an open adoption, with Maribel having an active part in the baby's life. Now I didn't know what to believe.

She continued. "I did go out with a lot of boys. I tried to pick those I knew you would hate, and I did have sex. I always wondered what would happen if I came home and told you I was pregnant. I guess I found out, but it wasn't as much fun as I thought it would be."

She looked up. "I do think if I had a baby, it would be mine, and my decision. I thought of trying to have someone to love me, but someone at school did that, and she doesn't feel loved at all. She feels tied down. Maybe I'd like for you and Dad to love me the way a little tiny baby would be loved. The way I wasn't."

She went on to explain that the boys she was with were losers, and she wouldn't want to have a baby with a father like the boys she had dated. She was afraid she wasn't good enough for a nicer boy who would treat her better.

"Maribel," Chris said softly. "We may get really angry and we may say mean things and try dumb ideas to try to understand you, but that's what families do. They make mistakes. We're learning here, too, and we make mistakes."

"Let's just all try to keep on trying," I added. "And let's try to communicate better. If you were testing us by telling a lie about such an emotional event, I was also testing you when I said such horrible things to you. I thought if you'd react, then we could talk. I lost my temper—no excuses. Maybe we shouldn't try that idea anymore. It sure hurts, doesn't it, honey?"

"Besides," Chris said. "Cha-Cha wouldn't love a loser the way he loves you. How about letting us see the heart that he has seen?"

She nodded and giggled.

We talked all morning. When I boiled the water for the tea, I thought about not putting a spoon by the saucer since none of us adds sugar, but I was so glad to have Maribel here with us that I would've given her a spoon for each hand so she could clang away at the side of the teacup. Actually, she didn't pick up the spoon at all.

We learned from this experience that testing is a negative way to find out whether someone loves you, and that we all fail these kinds of tests. We try to work through our problems, now that we've seen Maribel's point of view as well as we're able. I no longer consult outside sources for matters of the heart. Carol is an exception because she's also a free spirit. She and Maribel have become very good friends, and Maribel relates better to her than to us. She gives Maribel common sense advice, and Maribel can see what happens when I no longer consult outside sources for matters of the heart.

Carol is also an exception because she's had a very hard life. Carol also supports us, and encourages Maribel to talk with us. Sometimes she gives Maribel ideas about how to say things so we will not react defensively. She also steers Maribel away from dramatic bombshells created to get attention. She is helping Maribel to get attention by asking for it. We appreciate Carol's help, and we appreciate her friendship with Maribel. She can be much more plain-spoken than we can. Also, Carol can tell us where Maribel is coming from without betraying her confidence. Carol doesn't mind telling me if I am acting unrealistic in my expectations of Maribel, or if I am sending out messages of less than complete acceptance.

Our family is not "perfect," and we don't claim to be. We still have flare-ups about dates, school, and clothes, but we do rely less on shock tactics and more on our hearts. We expect to continue our journey as a family blessed by a quirky little sprite named Maribel.

THE END

I GAVE UP MY DAUGHTER
Now I want her back...

I watched the fifth graders as they walked into my classroom for the first day of school. This was my fourth year teaching. I loved teaching this age group, but this morning my heart thrummed and a cold sweat drenched me. This morning would be different. My own child might be in this class, the child I'd given up when she was an infant.

I'd taught at Jefferson Elementary for three years, then switched to Taft School. I told myself that Taft was a better school and I liked the principal better. But in my heart I knew I'd wanted to change because I suspected my daughter attended Taft. I could no longer deny the intense longing to see her—a longing that had been with me since the day the nurse took her from my arms forever.

The kids in my class were typical fifth graders. Many had been friends since first grade. They were boisterous and laughing as they dropped their new backpacks onto their desks, happy to see old friends after the long summer. They wore new clothes and carried new expectations.

I wrote the words Miss Bobbi Miller on the blackboard and asked them to find their assigned seats.

"You'll have plenty of time to get reacquainted today, but let me take attendance first," I said.

A groan murmured through the room, but I smiled. I was good at my job, and I knew I'd soon have them appreciating the discipline I used in my classroom. My students at Jefferson had the highest scores on the year-end tests, and I planned on repeating that performance at Taft.

I looked up from the list and glanced around the room. As always, the kids came in various sizes, builds, and ethnic backgrounds. They looked like a beautiful rainbow to me.

Then I saw her. I knew she was my daughter. She sat alone, a distant look on her face. She had my build, cheekbones, and mouth. Her father's eyes and hair. There was no doubt the girl was my daughter.

I swallowed and took a deep breath and checked my log. According to the seat assignments, she was Hailey Carter. I glanced up again and caught her eye. She gave me a tentative smile then looked away.

I breathed deeply once more and began the roll call. As each child answered, I checked off the name. When I called Hailey's name, I almost choked as she quietly answered, "Here."

Forcing myself to get my mind back where it belonged, I moved on to a discussion of who I was, what I expected, and what we'd be working on that year. I purposely kept my eyes away from Hailey. There would be time for that later.

That night, I nearly wept as I drove home. Maybe this wasn't such a good idea after all. I walked into my apartment, tossed my coat onto a chair, and collapsed on the sofa. The day I'd waited ten years for had come, and I was miserable.

If only my so-called "good family" hadn't forced me to give up my baby when she was born. I was only fifteen at the time.

I met Dan at my best friend's house when he came over to see Elise's brother. Dan let me know he was interested in me, and I was flattered. What fourteen-year-old wouldn't be? He was tall and well-built, with a cocky attitude.

He asked me out that first day. I was so excited I immediately said yes. I knew I'd have to figure out how to keep it a secret from my parents, but I'd handle that somehow. I'd never dated, not even once. My parents wouldn't even let me go to the dances at school.

"There's time for that later," my dad always said.

At fourteen, I was the ultimate innocent—and miserable—because my girlfriends were going to parties. Everyone but me had at least been kissed.

"Watch out for that guy," Elise told me. "He's too old. Besides, you haven't dated or anything yet. Don't start with him!"

I figured my friend was just jealous, and I ignored her advice. Later, I learned to regret being so impulsive. But I was riding high at the time, and told Dan I'd meet him at Elise's house, knowing full well my parents wouldn't approve.

Dan treated me so well on that first date. He was so much more mature than the boys in my class. He was also my first boyfriend, but I just knew the boys my age would never act so sophisticated. My parents thought I was spending the evening with Elise. That's how we managed to keep our dating a secret for a couple of weeks.

I thought I loved Dan. Mostly we just went to a movie or a fast-food place. It gave me bragging rights, though. I told all my friends about the wonderful guy I was in love with. At last I could talk about having a boyfriend and going on dates.

I wanted to tell my parents. More than once guilt invaded my thoughts, but I didn't tell them. Why should they object? I'd ask myself.

I learned the answer a week later. We'd gone to Dan's place for the first time, supposedly to pick up his wallet, which he said he'd

142

forgotten. Once inside his apartment, he kicked the door shut with his foot, swung me around, and planted a kiss on my mouth that overwhelmed me. We'd kissed before, but nothing like that.

Within a few minutes my clothes were off and we were on his bed. "Dan, no. I don't think we should."

"Shh," he whispered. "You know this is what I've wanted, that those innocent dates of ours couldn't continue forever."

Stunned with the sudden realization that I'd been a fool, I tried to push him off me. He snickered and continued to do whatever he wanted, as if I was a toy doll. And what he wanted was a lot. I thought I at least knew how people made love, but that night I learned how innocent I really was.

I was ashamed of what I'd done. When he finished, I grabbed my clothes, quickly dressed, and ran the six blocks to Elise's house. We went into the bathroom together and she helped me clean up while I sobbed.

"Don't tell anyone," I told her.

"But, Bobbi, the guy abused you. This should be reported."

"No! I don't want anyone to ever find out."

I never saw Dan again. At first I thought I'd escaped my shame without anyone but Elise knowing. I told my friends I'd broken off with my boyfriend, but now that I was considered one of the in-crowd, I didn't even care. I decided I'd never date again unless I'd known the guy for a long time.

A few months later I knew I was pregnant. I didn't tell my mom for another month—a miserable month. I felt sick. I couldn't eat, yet I gained weight. And my grades dropped due to my constant depression. Finally, my sister figured it out and a family crisis erupted, as if a volcano had blown up right in our living room.

My mother confronted me, hands on her hips, her lips pursed. "Bobbi, I know your sister is wrong. You can't be pregnant. You've always been such a good girl."

I simply sat down and cried.

"Our family has never had anything like this happen before," my father said. My parents decided I'd go to an aunt's house in Columbus, almost two hundred miles from my hometown in Cleveland, until the baby was born.

I had no choice. I sure couldn't afford to be on my own, let alone raise a child. I was only fourteen—and scared.

My aunt was good to me. She was a retired teacher and home-schooled me that year. If nothing else, I sure leaped ahead of the rest of my class. I never returned home once that entire year. My folks told everyone I wanted to go to another school in Ohio for a year.

The day my little girl was born I was alone. My parents didn't even want to see their first grandchild. It was the saddest time of my life. I held my daughter for a few minutes and then she was whisked away out of my life.

I returned to Cleveland and life went on as if nothing had happened, but my heart was broken. I had no desire to date or go to parties. Eventually I went out with a couple of nice guys during my senior year, and even attended the prom, but my thoughts were heavy with the memory of a sweet, little girl who would never know her real mother.

My parents and sister never discussed my daughter. Elise wanted to put it behind her. At least she kept my secret and never told anyone. I was alone with thoughts of my daughter.

I was never close with my parents again. I resented what they'd done; conveniently forgetting that I'd caused the problem in the first place. By the time I graduated from high school, my folks and I barely spoke, and they eventually focused on my sister, giving her their love and attention.

I easily earned a college scholarship with my good grades. I'd studied hard. In fact, that's about all I did through high school.

When I graduated from college four years later, magna cum laude, I was determined to start life over. I'd dated very little in college. My dormmates called me a bookworm. I didn't care. I just wanted to get my degree.

I toyed with moving to another city, but my little daughter was always in the back of my mind. I suspected she'd been adopted in the city where she'd been born, so I accepted a job in Columbus.

I'd never been told anything about the adoption except that a loving family had adopted my little girl. My aunt handed me a packet from the adoption agency, but I'd never opened it. I brought it with me when I moved to Columbus and stored it in the bottom drawer of a desk.

I just couldn't bear to open that packet, and yet I couldn't get rid of it. I'd look at the envelope in that drawer once in a while, pick it up, and pay attention to it once again. But I never opened it. Perhaps I was afraid of what I'd find.

I met Andy Sherwood at a party given by one of the teachers. Andy was alone, like me, and we easily struck up a conversation. He was an attorney and had just turned thirty. He was friendly, polite, and drop-dead handsome.

Andy asked me out that night. For the first time in many years I looked forward to a date. We ate at a small seafood restaurant, went to a park, and talked. His good-night kiss was tender and sweet, and when he stepped back, his eyes locked with mine. I think we both knew right then that there was something special between us.

We were a steady couple for several months before Andy asked me to spend the night with him.

"I'm not pushing you, Bobbi. I love you. I want you to be my wife. If you want to wait, then that's what we'll do."

I loved the man so much, and I didn't want to wait. My only sexual experience had been my one night with Dan. From what friends told me, it would never be like that with the right man. They were right. That night I learned the joy of sex with a caring man—a man who loved you and treated you like a woman.

Our wedding was planned for January. Torn about whether or not to invite my family, I only told Andy that we'd had a serious disagreement about something. He didn't pry, and said it was entirely up to me what wedding plans to make.

My life had finally reached a point of happiness, but I never forgot my little girl. I could tell Andy about her, but wondered if he was better off not knowing. I kept my secret and told no one. From what I understood, Elise had never said anything, either. No one in Cleveland, except for her and my parents and sister, knew that I'd given birth when I was only fifteen.

Now I wondered what would happen, knowing that Hailey Carter was probably my child. The dark evening clouds settled over the city, and rain softly tapped on the windowsills. I remembered the packet. For the first time, I decided to open it.

My hands shook as I snipped open the thick envelope and looked inside. There were copies of the documents my parents and I'd signed, along with an assortment of legal papers. I carefully stacked them on my lap and started to read. Most of them I'd seen before, although in my emotional state at the time I'd hurriedly tried to put them out of my mind.

At the bottom of the stack was a document I was sure I'd never read before. It was the adoption papers, listing the new parents—Phil and Megan Carter. It was confirmed. Hailey Carter was my daughter. I held that paper against my heart and took several deep breaths as jumbled thoughts and mixed emotions overwhelmed me. I felt as if I were in a whirlpool and being drawn deeper and deeper into the vortex, not knowing which way to turn for help.

I felt so empty inside. I almost decided to tell Andy, but then changed my mind. I would bear this cross alone—for a while at least. I'd be sure Hailey received love from me. How, I didn't know, but it would be done.

Andy was out of town on a case that week, and for once I was glad. Usually I missed him so much that I hated to see him go. This time I even had problems talking with him on the phone every evening, although I did my best to hide that fact.

The next morning in class, I watched Hailey as she walked in. She was alone once more, quiet, with eyes downcast. Was there something wrong, or was I just super-sensitive because I knew she was my little girl?

Within a week, I definitely knew something wasn't right in Hailey's life. She had the same new backpack and supplies as the other kids. She always had money for lunch and wore nice clothes. All the physical things were there. But she was such a sad little child who kept to herself. Even at lunch I noticed she solemnly ate her sandwich without talking much with the kids around her.

Hailey's homework and class assignments were flawless and always on time. She arrived early and ready for the day. She'd hand me her homework quietly, then return to her desk. She never caused a problem, but she rarely smiled. She was not a happy child.

In early November, Andy was assigned to a big case, an important one for his firm.

"This will take up a lot of my time," he told me one night as he cradled me in his arms. "The case involves a prominent family, and the partners want to win this case. It will be good for the firm. Good for my career, too." He gently kissed the top of my head.

"What's so important about this case?" I asked.

"Remember Bill Spector, the big real estate guy? His youngest daughter got into trouble—drugs, bad boyfriends, then had a child. The Spectors should've disowned her, but didn't. Now she's suing for help raising the child, plus other money, from the grandmother's estate."

An involuntary shiver inched down my arms. I remained silent.

"Anyway," he continued, "the Spectors have had nothing but trouble from that girl. I sympathize with them. It must be awful to have a bad seed in a good family."

Bad seed? Is that what Andy would think of me if I told him about my past? My teen years hadn't been wild, but I'd caused my family heartache and grief.

I knew I'd never love another man the way I loved Andy. I'd just have to make sure he never learned about my past life. Or my present life, too, if I admitted it. My relationship with Hailey would remain very private.

One evening, Andy did ask me, "Is everything okay, darling? You've seemed sort of distant lately."

I touched his cheek and smiled. "I think we're just both stressed from our jobs. Hopefully, things will soon settle down for both of us."

He took me into his arms and kissed me. I loved being in his arms, feeling him holding me. I hated myself for not telling him the whole truth, but I didn't want to lose him, either. He was my life. Andy and Hailey were all that mattered to me. If I could've had them both in my life, I'd have given anything, but I knew that could never be.

My father died the following week. Dad had been a good man, I realized. He'd tried to talk to me when I returned after giving birth, but I'd shrugged him off. Now it was too late for us to reconcile, and my heart ached for what I'd lost—the chance to really know my father.

I returned to the family home to find my sister in the middle of wedding plans. She also planned a January wedding. She was broken-hearted over our father's death, but in a different way than me. They'd had a close and warm relationship with him. I'd missed out on that, and had only myself to blame.

Many people attended the funeral, including Elise. She squeezed my hand as she entered the room and whispered, "I'll talk to you later."

As I listened to my father's coworkers and friends give eulogies, I realized that day how well-loved my father had been. Because of my bitterness I'd never recognized the depth of the man, nor had I thought of how he must've suffered to give up the rights to his first grandchild.

As we sat and ate at a friend's house after the burial, I felt Elise touch my arm. She motioned with her head, and I followed her out to the patio.

"How are you, Bobbi?" she asked. "I've wondered so many times how you were doing. I even called your parents, but they said they had little contact with you."

I shook my head and stared at the floor. "My fault, really. Guess I was always bitter about having to give up my baby." I looked up and met her eyes. "Elise, I have to confide in someone, so I'll tell you. My daughter is in my fifth grade class."

"Oh, no!" She held her hand to her mouth and furrowed her brow. "So that's why you returned to Columbus. What are your plans now?"

"Only to be able to see her and make sure she's okay." Then I told Elise that I didn't think that Hailey was okay. Still, I felt some relief in being able to finally talk about it with someone.

"You haven't told Andy?" Elise asked. "Why not? Surely he has a right to know."

"What if he can't accept it?" I said.

"Then I'd say he's not the right man for you. Either he loves you no matter what, or he doesn't. If he doesn't, then it's best to break up."

"That's easy for you to say. You have no big problems in your background. Andy is a prominent lawyer."

It was Elise's turn to shake her head. "Honestly, Bobbi, what's that got to do with it? Tell him now, or he'll find out on his own. Then he'll never trust you."

I bit my lip and looked away. "I can't—at least not now. He's such a good man. I don't want him to find out about my past. He's never questioned me about my disagreement with my family, and it's best left alone."

147

"I think you're wrong. I've never met the man, but from what you say, I have to believe he'd be there for you all the way."

Would he? I didn't want to take that chance. He came from a wealthy background. His mother was involved in charity organizations and entertaining, his father was a prominent physician. They'd accepted me from the first time we met, but that could easily change if they found out about my past.

The next week was busy with school conferences. I was nervous as I waited for Hailey's parents to arrive, but only Phil Carter arrived for the conference.

"Is your wife coming, too?" I asked.

He shook his head. "No, only me. I'll be the one coming to Hailey's conferences."

I wanted to ask more, but didn't. He was a nice man, very quiet, polite, and reserved. As with Hailey, I sensed a deep sadness.

"Hailey is doing very well," I said. "Her grades are always among the highest in the class. She turns in all her work on time." I hesitated a minute when Mr. Carter didn't respond. "She's very quiet," I added.

He nodded. "Yes, I'm sure she is. Life hasn't always been easy for her, Ms. Miller, but I love her dearly."

Now I really wanted to know about my daughter's background, but I didn't want to appear too eager. "Is there anything I can help you with?" I asked. My mind worked overtime from turmoil, but I did my best to appear composed.

He smiled. "Just give her all the attention you've got time for. She needs it. She's a wonderful little girl."

We looked over some of Hailey's school work and a project she'd completed. "This was turned in ahead of time, like most of her work." I turned the page. "I see she has a younger brother and sister. I'm sure she's proud of being the oldest."

"Sometimes that can be hard," Mr. Carter said.

There was really nothing else to say, although I wanted to ask so much more. Mr. Carter shook my hand and then he left. Before I had time to collect my thoughts, the next set of parents walked in. Their child was the proverbial troublemaker, and I knew this conference wouldn't be as pleasant as the previous one. It would be easier, though. Johnny wasn't my child.

Andy's big trial kept him busy into the evenings, so I was alone with my thoughts at night. My thoughts never left my little girl.

Then, as chance would have it, I meet Mrs. Carter a week later at a conference for a library fund-raising event. A friend introduced us.

"Bobbi, this is Aimee Carter. I believe her daughter is in your class."

So this was Hailey's mother. But I thought her name was Megan.

My mind worked in overdrive, but I tried to act natural.

"Oh yes, Hailey Carter. A very sweet girl."

She rolled her eyes. "Sometimes." And then she moved to her seat.

The speaker addressed the audience, and I sat down a few chairs from Mrs. Carter. She appeared to be much younger than Phil. She was a beauty and knew it. She wore expensive clothes, her hair was perfectly done, and she had on jewelry I'd never be able to afford. It wasn't my way, but she obviously spent a lot of time on herself. She sat ramrod-straight, aloof, as if the rest of us didn't quite measure up to her standards.

Why is her name Aimee? And why does she so obviously dislike my daughter?

I heard nothing the speaker said, although I was supposed to give a report a few days later on the meeting. I'd have to rely on someone else's notes. There was no way my mind would be able to focus on anything but the Carter family.

Fortunately, the speaker finished in less than fifteen minutes. Aimee Carter headed for the door, and I headed toward her, like a cat stalking its prey. I had to find out more.

"Mrs. Carter, I just wondered if you had any questions about Hailey, since you weren't able to attend the parent-teacher conference."

She shook her head. "No. My husband takes care of that."

That's all I learned. It was enough to make me even more apprehensive about my little girl. Aimee hurried out ahead of me. I watched as she drove out of the parking lot, wondering what motivated the woman, what caused her to be so cool toward Hailey. I vowed to find out, one way or another.

The next day, Hailey showed up at school with a bruise across her cheek. When I asked her about it, she mumbled something about falling down. I didn't believe it for an instant. I knew, just knew, that Aimee had hit Hailey.

That afternoon I looked up Phil Carter's work number and called him. "Could we meet again?" I asked him. "There's something I think we should discuss."

He was silent for a few seconds, then asked why.

I knew my job might be on the line, but at that point I didn't care. I intended to confront him with the fact I was his daughter's biological mother. Somehow, I knew Hailey's future was at stake. Finally, after telling him I was worried about Hailey, he agreed to see me later in the day. I told him I'd wait in the classroom.

Phil showed up thirty minutes late; it was the longest thirty minutes of my life. He looked haggard, almost distraught.

"There's something you should know," he said. He grimaced and looked away, then back at me. "Aimee is sending Hailey to boarding school. She leaves next week."

"Why?" I blurted out.

"I guess I should start at the beginning. My first wife, Megan, and I adopted Hailey as an infant. We'd tried for many years to have a child. When we learned a baby was to be born to an unwed mother and we could adopt that child, we were delighted. Megan loved Hailey as if the child was her own. They bonded immediately." He smiled at the memory, but then the sadness returned.

"What happened to Megan?" I asked quietly.

"She died when Hailey was just three. Megan had diabetes, maybe the reason she couldn't have a child. It ravished her and finally took her life." He bowed his head. "It was devastating for me and for Hailey. I didn't know what to do."

We sat in silence for a minute before he continued. "Then I met Aimee. I'm sure you've noticed she's younger than I am. We were married a few months later. I felt lucky to have found another woman—and such an attractive one—who was interested in me."

"Yes, she is very attractive," I said, seething inside. I knew the rest of the story wouldn't be any better.

"Aimee never liked Hailey and had no patience for an active three-year-old. I didn't want to interfere, so I let Aimee handle Hailey. Aimee was strict, too strict, and I knew it even then. Hailey reacted as all children will; she began to wet the bed again and have nightmares."

I almost lost it then and asked him why, as the father, he hadn't intervened. Instead I bit my lip and kept quiet.

We talked for another twenty minutes, and the rest of the story wasn't any better. Hailey had been raised by a woman who didn't like her, who only loved her own two babies, and looked at Hailey as an unnecessary intrusion in her life. Phil had refused to interfere, hoping to keep his pretty, young wife happy.

"But surely you won't let Aimee send her to a boarding school far from home, will you?" I pleaded.

"I feel I have no choice. You have to understand, I love Hailey very much. But I have my wife and two other children to think of. To be honest, my wife told me the other night that either Hailey goes or she'll go. I'm sorry to say, she lost her temper with Hailey and struck her on the cheek. That can't ever happen again. That's one reason I finally agreed to let Hailey go to the boarding school."

So that was it. He'd had to make a choice, and he hadn't chosen Hailey.

"There's no other family?" I asked.

"Not really. No one who could take her in. It's a nice boarding school, highly rated. I even picked it out myself."

I winced. I knew I had a big decision to make, and I had to make it quickly. "What do you know about Hailey's biological mother, Mr. Carter?"

"Very little. We were told she came from a good family and couldn't keep the baby. Surely she wouldn't want her now."

"What if she did?" I quietly asked.

He shrugged his shoulders. "Well, we don't know where she is, and I wouldn't want to interrupt her life anyway."

"It wouldn't be an interruption," I said.

"How do you know?"

"Because I'm her mother."

There. I'd said it. I was scared, but I felt better for it, too.

All sorts of thoughts flooded my mind. What do I do now? Andy will find out, and then what will he think? Will I lose my job? But none of that matters. All that matters is Hailey.

"I can't believe this," he said. "How did . . ."

"I knew she'd be in fifth grade this year, and I also suspected she'd been adopted by people who lived in this school district." Tears slipped down my cheeks. "The minute I saw her, I knew she was my daughter." I wiped my eyes with a tissue.

"I've never forgotten my baby," I said. "My parents made me give her up. I didn't want to. But I was only fourteen and couldn't raise a baby on my own."

I put my hand on his arm. "Please don't send her away. I'll take her if you'll let me."

The only sound in the room was the clock as it ticked the minutes away, as if telling me that time was slipping by and I'd better rescue my little girl. In that room, at that moment, time stood still.

"Let me think about all this," he whispered. He looked me in the eye. "I'm sure it would be best for Hailey." He touched my shoulder, then quietly stood up and left.

I'd promised Andy I'd attend a party with him that night at his parent's house. As always, his mother greeted me warmly and his dad put his arm around me and introduced me to people as his future daughter-in-law. I forced myself to talk to people, but I knew I wasn't fooling Andy. He knew something was wrong.

"What's the matter, Bobbi?" Andy asked me. "Can I help you with anything?"

I attempted a smile as I looked up into his eyes and put my hand on his. "Just a problem with a student is all."

"You take your job too seriously," he said as he kissed my cheek. "You've got to be the best teacher there is."

It was a long evening, but I did my best to mingle with the guests. I helped Andy's dad barbecue hamburgers and mix up the potato salad. I'd always enjoyed helping, but that night I also needed to keep busy.

The next day, Andy and I went for a walk in the park. We strolled along the path by the lake and watched the ducks and geese. It seemed so comforting to be with him there, to have his hand holding mine, as if all the problems in the world just floated away. But when we walked back to the car the world returned, and nothing had changed.

I didn't hear from Phil Carter for a few days. My anxiety level skyrocketed. On Friday, just as I was getting ready to leave for the weekend, I looked up and saw him standing in the doorway. He slowly walked over to me.

"Aimee is glad that you want Hailey," he said. "I have to admit, it makes it easier for both of us. I talked to Hailey about you last night. She doesn't talk much. Aimee never encouraged her to, but I know she likes you very much."

I was distressed and relieved at the same time. But now what did we do?

"I talked to an attorney," he said. "It can be worked out. It's a little involved, but I'm willing to pay for it." He held his head in his hand. I watched him struggle to gain control. "I love that child. But I love my other children, too."

I told him I'd contact an attorney, and we agreed to get together in a few days. "Please let Hailey know that something good is going to happen in her life," I said. He nodded, then embraced me. We held on to each other for a few minutes, then left together.

I knew I had to talk to Andy right away. He'd better find out about this from me. But we spent the weekend with his brother and wife, and I didn't want to bring it up then. We needed to be alone. I constantly worried about what he'd think of me.

Monday afternoon Phil Carter and I met at his attorney's office. It was a long, difficult meeting. Phil broke down and sobbed several times. I didn't feel much better. At least the process was started. I had to tell Andy, and I had to tell my principal.

As Phil Carter and I walked out of the building, we discussed Hailey.

"I'm so glad you've found your daughter, and that she'll be with you," he said. "If she has to go, I want her to be with you."

He said he'd bring Hailey over that evening to visit for a few hours. I stopped at the store and bought a pizza and ice cream, hoping that was what she liked. When they arrived, Hailey attempted a little smile, then she just rushed into my arms.

Holding Hailey in my arms was an experience I'd never imagined. I wrapped my arms around her and held on tight. Phil just nodded from the doorway and said he'd be back later.

Hailey and I ate pizza together, although my stomach was knotted up so much I had to force the bites down. For the first time, she really

152

opened up. She asked if she could call me Mom.

"You bet, darling. Because that's what I am, and what I'll always be from now on."

She looked up at the doorway, startled. I turned. Andy stood there, quietly, his keys in his hand, his brows raised.

"Guess I'm interrupting something," he said.

"It's okay. We've got lots of pizza," Hailey said. "My mom and I can't eat it all."

"Your mom and you," Andy repeated. "Well, I've had my dinner, just stopped by to see Bobbi for a bit. But I think I'll be going now."

"Andy, wait," I said. "I need to talk to you."

"Yes, I'm sure you do." He turned and left.

After Phil picked Hailey up, I called Andy. There was no answer. I knew he was home, and left a message begging him to call. When several more hours went by and he still didn't answer, I drove to his apartment.

At least he answered the door, but the scene that followed was a nightmare. He talked. I listened.

"I love you, Bobbi, and yet you couldn't seem to trust me enough to tell me you had a daughter. Let's see, she looks about ten, so you had her when you were only fourteen or fifteen, right? But you kept it a secret. From what I see, you don't trust me at all. Tell me, how did you plan on keeping this a secret?"

"I was going to tell you—"

"No more lies," he interrupted. "I won't marry a woman who can't own up to the truth." He shut the door in my face.

I'd won Hailey and lost the man I loved. It didn't seem fair. I wanted them both, but I knew I hadn't handled the situation correctly. I should have let Andy know from the very beginning.

I left several messages on his machine, telling him how much I loved him and how sorry I was. He never answered.

The next few weeks were busy with lawyers, a court hearing, and interviews with the judge and social workers. Hailey spent more time with me until she was finally living at my place.

One good thing came out of all this. My principal was understanding, even happy about what happened. My fellow teachers were thrilled, but my heart was empty because Andy was gone.

The judge agreed that Hailey belonged with me until the adoption could be finalized. Phil Carter seemed relieved.

"At long last, my little girl will be happy again," he told the judge. There wasn't a dry eye in that courtroom. Even the court reporter reached for a tissue to wipe her eyes.

Aimee was not around. She'd never adopted Hailey and had no say in the matter. That was fine with me. I hoped I never saw her again.

A month after my disastrous confrontation with Andy, I still hadn't heard from him. My daughter was with me now, and she blossomed. From the quiet, shy, sad little girl, she turned almost overnight into a boisterous, outgoing ten-year-old.

"Hey," I kidded her one night after school. "I miss that quiet little girl I used to know."

She looked at me, her eyes wide. "Only kidding," I said as I snuggled against her.

"I wish I still had you for my teacher, Mom. Mr. Benson doesn't explain things as well as you do."

"It was a choice, and not a hard one to make," I said. "You can't be in my classroom any longer."

We shopped for a bike and helmet the next day. She asked to take horseback riding lessons, so we went together and both rode. In the evenings we cooked dinner together, then she studied while I graded papers. Every Saturday we cleaned the apartment, just enjoying being together. It was as if we were soul mates, as tuned in to each other as if we'd never been separated at her birth.

My attorney assured me that all was going according to schedule in the adoption proceedings. Everything in life was just as I'd always dreamed. Everything but Andy.

I learned through a friend that he'd dated another woman. "I don't think he liked her, though," my friend said. "He only took her out once." Still, that cut through my heart like a sharp knife. I'd never get over him. Never.

"Where's that man who stopped by that night?" Hailey asked me one day.

I twirled my spoon in my coffee. "I'm afraid I don't know. I doubt he'll be around again."

"Is that because of me?"

"No, Hailey. It's because of me." If only I'd been honest with him. It was a lesson I learned the hard way.

The nights were the worst. I wanted Andy to hold me in his arms and love me, whisper in my ear, and be there in the morning when I woke up. I wanted him to hold hands with me and walk in the park. I missed all those little things that made me love him so much.

After three months, the adoption was finalized. Hailey and I celebrated with a movie and ice cream. Phil didn't come to the court hearing. I suspected it would've been too difficult for him. I felt sorry for him, but he'd caused most of his own problems.

School was over in no time. Hailey and I had the summer together. For the first time as mother and daughter, we had time on our hands. We bonded more closely, visited my sister and her family, went to an amusement park, and grew in our love for each other. She was only a shadow of the sad child she'd been. My friends marveled at the quick change Hailey had made.

Several men asked me out, but I politely declined. Only one man could ever enter my life again, and he'd made it clear he wanted nothing to do with me. Over six months had passed without a word from Andy.

Hailey received an invitation to a birthday party in the mail. "Look, Mom. It's at the park. That'll be neat."

The park. I couldn't think of that park without remembering Andy. I hadn't been back since we'd parted, afraid the memories would be too strong. But the invitation asked the parents to come, too.

"Sounds like fun," I told Hailey.

On the day of the party, dark clouds marched across the sky and suddenly broke, like a bucket of water being dumped into a trough. Hailey and I jumped from our car and raced for the picnic shelter.

We laughed and brushed water from our clothes and hair. Other people besides the partygoers also escaped from the rain and stood huddled under the shelter. Raindrops danced on the roof and lightning flashed in the distant sky.

"Hello, Bobbi." I turned and looked into Andy's gorgeous eyes.

"Hello," I whispered. "Looks like you got caught in the rain, too."

We stood there awkwardly. He'd lost some weight, even looked a little haggard. Had the past months been as hard on him as they were on me?

"Are you here with friends?" I asked.

He motioned for me to sit down on a bench beside him. "No, I'm alone. I come here once in a while. It reminds me of happier times, times I miss."

Did I hear him right? My eyes locked with his. "I miss them, too, Andy. Not a day goes by that I don't miss being with you."

"There you are, Mom," Hailey said. Then she noticed Andy. She smiled shyly. "I remember you. I keep wishing you'd come back. My mom misses you so much."

Andy looked at me with a little smile. "She does, does she?"

"Hailey, how do you know that, anyway?" I asked, wondering to myself if I wanted her to keep talking or shut up.

"I know you, Mom." She looked at Andy. "She never goes out with anyone else, and sometimes she just sits and looks at your picture. How come you guys don't get together, anyway?"

I felt my face heat up, but I also felt Andy's hand on mine. "I've been wondering that myself," he said. "I think it's my fault."

"No," I said. I squeezed his hand. "It was my fault. I should have been honest with you from the beginning."

He touched my check lightly with the back of his knuckle. "I

155

should have been sympathetic to what you were going through."

"Neat!" Hailey said. "Now you guys can get back together and my mom will be happy again."

As she skipped back to the party, I felt Andy's arm around my shoulders. He bent down and whispered, "Do you think she'd like a new father?"

"Well, do you have one in mind?"

"I was sort of thinking about me," he said, as he kissed my ear lightly. "What do you think?"

I turned and looked into his eyes. "No way, mister, unless you legally wed her mother."

"You sure are a stickler for rules, young lady." He sighed and smiled that sweet smile of his. "But I guess I can put up with it."

We were married the next week. Hailey was our only attendant. Andy's family and mine, our coworkers, and friends all came. It was a great night. But the greatest thing of all is that I'll be with my husband and my daughter from now on.

THE END

Medical Drama in Real Life!
"HELP MY MOMMY—
SHE'S DYING!"
A four-year-old calls 911. Will she make the difference in her mother's harrowing, life-or-death moment of terror?

"Time to get up, Mommy!" my daughter, Sindi, cried as she bounced onto the bed where I'd been sleeping peacefully moments before, carrying her new, favorite stuffed animal and constant companion, Mrs. Murphy the cat. "It's today! And it's real special, too, Mommy!"

"Is it? What's so special about it, honey?" I teased, tousling her dark brown curls.

Her lower lip popped out in a pout. "It's my birthday! You didn't forget, did you, Mommy?"

"Of course I didn't! Mommy was just teasing. I couldn't possibly forget my little girl's birthday, now, could I? It's the most important day of the year!"

She shook her head; the pout reversed itself into a beaming smile. "I'm not a little girl anymore, Mommy. I'm a big girl now!" she announced, holding her head high with pride.

"Are you really?"

She nodded, a serious expression filling out her Kewpie doll features. "I'm four! And that's real old," she earnestly declared.

"Is that right? And just how many is that?" I inquired politely.

Sindi obligingly held up four chubby fingers. "I'm all grown up now!" she exclaimed.

I laughed. "Well, if you're all grown up, then I suppose you won't be needing Mrs. Murphy anymore. I'll keep her here with me, though; after all, you wouldn't want her to be lonely, now, would you?" I plucked the stuffed, gray-and-white tabby from Sindi's arm, tucking her under the covers with me.

A look of shock mingled with fear streaked across her small face and the lower lip shot back out. Instantly, her big, brown eyes were glued to Mrs. Murphy. "I'm not really all grown up, Mommy," she decided.

I grinned, pulling back the covers so Sindi could crawl under with me. "Well! Both Mrs. Murphy and I are very glad to hear it! We'd be very sad indeed if you were too old to snuggle under the covers with us."

Sindi slid in next to me, cuddling close and hugging Mrs. Murphy tightly. "I'll never get that growed up," she said with a contented sigh.

"Happy birthday, baby girl." I kissed the top of her head and tried my best not to think of how fast the time was whizzing by. Or about how soon Sindi would outgrow Mrs. Murphy.

And cuddling with her mommy, as well, I thought with a poignant sigh.

Sindi wiggled closer to me. "I love you, Mommy."

I smiled, my heart full of joy. "I love you, too, honey."

I sighed again. She was growing up so fast. But then, I suppose all mothers must feel that way about their babies. Indeed, it seemed as though it was only yesterday that I held Sindi in my arms as a newborn. And yet that day, she was officially four years old.

Where did the time go?

Lying there under the comforter in our cozy bed with Sindi in my arms I thought back to when I was a teenager working as a waitress at the local diner.

One night this couple came in with a little boy who was about two years old. I watched them cut up his food and refill his blue, plastic sippy cup with its safety lid with chocolate milk. Then there was a trip to the bathroom for a diaper change, and once again later to clean up after the meal. With all the attention their little boy required, I was surprised either parent got to eat a bite of their own dinner.

At the time it all seemed like so much work to me—parenthood. I wondered why any rational person would actually want to have kids, what with all of the feeding, changing, washing little hands and faces, and endless cleaning up after them. It seemed like a vast pit of nothing-but-work to my teenage brain.

I remember saying something, in that graceless way of the typical teenager, to the lady about it and she just laughed. She claimed not to mind all the work involved a bit. That puzzled me as I stood there thinking about just how many years it must take before a child stops needing their parents to do every little thing for them. It seemed like an eternity to my sixteen-year-old state of mind.

So I made another comment about it and she just laughed again and told me that no matter how long they needed you to do everything for them, it simply wasn't long enough. I turned her explanation over and over in my head, but it never made sense.

And then I had a little girl of my own—four years ago today. Now I understood what that woman told me perfectly. Indeed, it wouldn't be very long at all before this darling, little, chestnut-haired angel lying in my arms would be a grown woman with babies of her own. Oh, yes—they grow up and stop needing their mommies much too soon.

A sharp pain jolted through my left arm and took me away from my mental stroll down memory lane. I sat up with a start, rubbing my arm vigorously.

"Are you okay, Mommy?"

"I'm fine. It's just another one of those cramps, baby. I should've been more careful yesterday at the gym."

Sindi nodded, her solemn features and brown eyes serious. "You should be very careful not to hurt yourself, Mommy. That's what you always tell me, right?"

I suppressed a grin at Sindi's expression and tone of voice. "Right. And from now on I promise to be more careful with myself. Why don't you get dressed and I'll make the two of us some breakfast? Then you can help me get the house ready for your party tonight, okay?"

Sindi giggled with excitement and bounced off the bed, keeping a firm grip on Mrs. Murphy as she bounded out of the bedroom.

The pain in my arm was fading by then. This is what you get for pushing yourself at Curves yesterday, Julia, I thought. To be perfectly honest it wasn't only my left arm that hurt, but my whole body, as well. I was nothing but one big ache all the way from the roots of my hair clear down to the tips of my toes. I couldn't recall ever being this sore; I figured I must be even more out of shape than I thought.

Granted, I gained a substantial amount of weight during my pregnancy and then I'd only packed on more pounds over the last four years of being a stay-at-home mom. A month earlier, when I discovered I could no longer get my jeans zipped—never mind getting the button fastened—I'd gone shopping for a new pair. The reality check that made me truly realize that I needed to do something about my weight occurred in the dressing room at Express as I stood sweating, trying to suck in my stomach in a futile, depressing attempt to force up the zipper on a pair of size-twenty jeans.

Enough is enough, I decided in the dressing room, and I started my diet that very day.

Now I stood up, stretching my sore muscles. Why is it that putting on weight is so darned easy to do while getting rid of it is next to impossible? I was hardly aware of the pounds as I put them on, but I was more than painfully aware of every single ounce I'd so far managed to lose.

"Only fifteen pounds to go," I reminded myself, pulling both jeans and a sweatshirt from the dresser drawer.

Indeed, I was only just then finding out how hard it really is to go on a diet and stick to it. Before I got pregnant I was always "on the go," as they say. I worked full time and then afterward, in the evenings and on weekends, there was always something that my husband

Jerry, also an active sort, had planned for us to do. We played a lot of racquetball together and I took Jazzercise classes twice a week. I ate whatever I wanted—to heck with the fat grams—and I was so busy that I burned off the calories before they had a chance to settle in on my hips.

And my goodness—how they settled, I thought depressingly, looking at myself in the bathroom mirror as I pulled on my jeans. I reminded myself once again that it takes time and patience to lose weight—and keep it off. I was proud that at least I was now doing very positive things, like working out regularly and walking a lot and eating a strict, low-calorie, nonfat diet. I'd even started playing racquetball again and taken up my old Jazzercise classes. I was determined that I was going to lose all the weight I'd packed on; it would just take a little time, that's all.

As it was, I knew I should be proud of myself for losing even just the first ten pounds of the whopping fifty-five-pound weight loss goal I'd set for myself. But I still felt a tad blue tugging up the zipper of my size-eighteen jeans. I was thinking of my pre-pregnancy days, back when I wore what seemed now to be an impossibly tiny size six.

I stuck my tongue out at my reflection in the mirror, but then I forced myself to smile at my own silliness and I refused to let myself remain upset over a few extra pounds.

What difference does a bit of extra weight make in the grand scheme of things, after all? I figured it was a small price to pay for the overwhelming joy Sindi had brought to my life.

I was tying the laces of my right sneaker when another cramp seized my arm, causing me to stop what I was doing. I rubbed at the sore spot and fought the slight wave of dizziness that washed over me as I moved to the bathroom in search of some lineament. I decided I was definitely going to have to take it easier at the gym from then on. I realized I must've been nuts to overwork my out-of-shape body like I had.

After I'd applied a liberal dose of fast-acting heat gel to my upper arm I left the bathroom to see if Sindi was dressed. Sadly, she'd informed me a few weeks earlier that she didn't need my help choosing her outfits anymore, much less help getting dressed. I sighed; her not needing me to help her tackle those particular chores was just another example of how fast she was growing up. Soon, she wouldn't need me for much of anything at all.

Oh, it's not that I didn't want her to grow up to be a normal, healthy adult. Because I did. It was simply a case of my not wanting her to do it all so darned fast.

"I'm very impressed. You look beautiful, baby," I announced as I strolled into her bedroom, tactfully ignoring the fact that she'd chosen a cherry-red sweater featuring an embroidered Scooby Doo face on the front, paired with a neon-purple skirt dotted with tiny, white flowers. I figured I had plenty of time before the party guests arrived to suggest a change of clothing. I glanced once more at her cartoonish get-up and smiled; maybe she did still need my help a little bit, after all.

"Thank you, Mommy. We're ready now." She picked up Mrs. Murphy, who was reclining in her usual spot on the pink, ruffled pillow at the head of Sindi's bed.

"Let's get to it, then. We've got tons of balloons to blow up and we need to get the crepe paper hung in the dining room." I ruffled her curls. "How about pancakes for the birthday girl's breakfast?" Pancakes are her favorite.

"Yum! Can I call Daddy?"

Just the night before Jerry had taught Sindi how to use the telephone and she'd called her grandmother in Florida for the first time by herself. Now, of course, she was positively addicted to making phone calls.

"Sure. Why don't you remind Daddy to pick up the ice cream on his way home?"

She nodded, clearly pleased to be entrusted with such a grown-up job. She took a few sedate steps toward the living room before exclaiming, "I love being four! I get to make phone calls all by myself!" She then broke into a flat-out run for the phone, Mrs. Murphy bobbing in her arms.

As I watched her go, for the millionth time, I wished desperately that I could have more children. Both Jerry and I had wanted a large family, a home filled with happy children. But we'd been forced to accept that it just wasn't meant to be for us.

Jerry and I married a mere two months after we graduated from college. So many of our friends decided to put their careers first and wait until they were established before starting their families, but that wasn't for Jerry and me. We bought a small home in a quiet, family-oriented neighborhood and settled in to nest, hoping to hear the patter of little feet very soon.

But after two years of trying and waiting only to be disappointed when "that time of the month" rolled around again, I got frightened and went to see our family doctor, Dr. Monroe.

Dr. Monroe couldn't find anything at all wrong with me, so he referred me to a specialist. Despite administering more tests than I'd ever dreamed existed to determine—and hopefully reverse—the cause of my infertility, the specialist was also baffled. She, just as Dr. Monroe had, found me to be in excellent health; in fact, she proclaimed me "perfectly normal." But in the end, largely due to my insistence, she referred us to a fertility clinic.

The doctor at the clinic, Dr. Stevens, after a thorough physical and still more tests that all indicated I was the very picture of glowing health, recommended I try fertility drugs. I was completely against the idea at first; the possibility of multiple births made me uneasy. Sure, I wanted a large family—maybe even four or five kids—but not all at the same time! And it seemed as though the newspapers and magazines were full of feature stories about women who'd taken those supposedly safe drugs and ended up having septuplets.

Dr. Stevens was very understanding and she assured me that while it's somewhat more common for a woman to give birth to twins while using fertility drugs, large multiple births are, in fact, rare. I dove into research on the Internet and I even spoke with several other doctors who are considered experts in the field and I found Dr. Stevens to be correct. It was highly unlikely that the low dosage of fertility medication she proposed would lead to me delivering eight babies.

So I cast my worries aside and started taking the prescribed medication. Dr. Stevens cautioned me to be patient—sometimes it takes a few months for the medicine to get into one's system and do its job. I was prepared to wait, resigned to the fact that it wouldn't happen right away.

But the medication's effectiveness surprised us all. I found out I was pregnant with Sindi after only one month of fertility drugs, just three months shy of my thirtieth birthday. After eight long years of waiting, counting, praying, and hoping, we were finally going to have our baby! It was the happiest moment of my life when I looked into that result window on the home pregnancy test and saw a second thin, pink line there—positive proof that I was, indeed, pregnant. Jerry and I danced around the bathroom, reveling in the sheer joy of the moment.

Needless to say, I threw myself into the joys of being pregnant. I was completely determined to do everything possible to ensure that our baby had the best start in life that any two parents could provide. I didn't have to worry about quitting smoking or abstaining from alcohol because I didn't indulge in those things, anyway, but I did make every effort to eat the most nourishing foods and I drank plenty of water, as well—no junk food for this mommy-to-be. I made sure to walk every day and do all the other pregnancy exercises recommended by my obstetrician.

I faithfully kept each appointment with Dr. Stevens, who would deliver our baby, and she assured me regularly that everything was progressing just as it should. My glucose level was fine, my pulse rate was wonderful, and my blood pressure was excellent. I was doing everything strictly by the book and I felt better than I ever had.

And then, completely without warning, at the end of my sixth month—everything fell apart.

I woke from a sounder-than-usual sleep with a pounding headache. My feet and hands were swollen—uncomfortably so—and a quick peek in the bathroom mirror showed me that my face was swollen, as well. At first I brushed my worries aside, thinking maybe I'd eaten too much salt the previous day. But when the swelling didn't go away by late afternoon and my headache worsened, I finally called Jerry at the office and he came home and took me to see Dr. Stevens right away.

The moment Dr. Stevens took my blood pressure she knew what was wrong. It was toxemia. There could be no doubt about it— suddenly, my blood pressure was through the roof. Suddenly, I was at risk of having a stroke or possibly a heart attack—I was in terrible danger, Dr. Stevens said. And not only was my health in danger, but so was the health of our unborn child.

Dr. Stevens immediately had me admitted to the hospital, where I spent the next two days under observation, with nurses checking my blood pressure every hour on the hour. When those two days of complete bed rest didn't bring my pressure down Dr. Stevens was left with no other choice but to prescribe medication.

Thankfully, the little pills worked quickly, bringing my blood pressure under control within hours, and I was sent home the next day. Although there were a few conditions to my release. The first was that I needed to take my medication every day without fail and the second was that I was officially on bed rest for the remainder of my pregnancy.

Well, I'm an active person, and the idea of lying in bed for the next three months wasn't a pleasant prospect for me by any means. But if it was necessary for the wellbeing of our baby, there could be no question about my compliance.

I wasted no time calling my boss and making arrangements for an extended leave of absence. Jerry also took Dr. Steven's orders seriously by hiring a housecleaning service to take care of our home and he started cooking all of our meals. I couldn't ask for a more compassionate, understanding husband than my Jerry. Many of my friends from work called to ask about my condition; invariably they'd tell me how much they envied me just lounging around in bed all day. I knew they were only trying to cheer me up so I refrained from telling them that I felt like a time bomb ticking away toward an inevitable explosion. Staying in that bed, willing myself to be calm and serene, was the toughest thing I'd ever done.

Somehow, I managed. Dr. Stevens arranged for me to have a scheduled C-section instead of the natural labor I wanted, explaining to us that the risk of stroke would be too great under the stress of contractions. On that momentous day as they wheeled me into the operating room, I heaved a sigh of relief; everything was going to be fine and the worst was over. All the tests showed our baby was perfectly healthy and once I gave birth, I'd be fine, as well.

I didn't find out how wrong I was until I woke up in the recovery room. The delivery itself went well and the baby was fine, Dr. Stevens told me the first time I held Sindi in my arms. This was the only good news she had for me.

The bad news—which followed shortly—knocked the wind out of my lungs. It turned out that it was highly unlikely that my blood pressure would ever return to normal—that I would have to take the medication I'd been taking, most likely for the rest of my life. But the worst news was that there were complications during the C-section. I hemorrhaged and Dr. Stevens was left with no other option but to perform an emergency hysterectomy. Jerry and I would never have another child.

Oh, I was grateful to be holding my perfectly healthy little girl in my arms. But I couldn't stop the tears that ran down my cheeks as I took in the reality that that precious little girl was the only baby I'd ever have.

"How was Daddy?" I asked Sindi as she skipped into the kitchen, where I was busy with the pancake batter.

"Great! He said he'd bring the ice cream, too." She stood on tiptoe beside me to try to get a peek at the griddle. "Are they done yet? Mrs. Murphy is very hungry." She held up Mrs. Murphy so she, too, could check the progress of the pancakes.

"Almost. Why don't you get the syrup out of the refrigerator?" I flipped the pancakes onto a plate, trying my best not to give in to the all-too-tempting temptation of having several myself.

I set the plate in front of Sindi at the table and grabbed a bowl from the cupboard for my own meager breakfast of no-fat, high-fiber cereal. As I poured the flakes, I wondered why if the box reads "No Fat," it's pretty much guaranteed that what's inside will taste like shredded cardboard. Is fat the only thing in this world that has any flavor?

Sindi's pancakes looked tastier by the second.

"What else did Daddy say, baby?"

Sindi swallowed a large bite of fluffy pancake smeared with butter and dripping with gooey maple syrup. My stomach growled and I sternly reminded myself of the ten remaining pounds I needed to lose.

"Daddy said he's proud of me cuz I can use the phone all by myself, like a big girl!" She beamed a big, gooey, sticky-looking smile before taking another bite.

I was proud of her, too. She was a very smart little girl and she'd done lots of things way ahead of schedule, like holding her own bottle at just a few months of age and talking well by eighteen months. Currently, she was learning numbers and reading simple children's books. Oh, dear—she was growing up so fast!

"I'm proud, too. You're a very smart little lady, indeed, Sindi. Finish up those pancakes and then we'll get started with the balloons, okay?" I stood and went to the sink to rinse out my bowl, ignoring the fact that my stomach was still rumbling with hunger.

"Okay, Mommy. Only two more bites to go!"

"I'm going to run upstairs and get the bag of balloons we bought." I turned to leave the kitchen; it'd become imperative for me to put some distance between myself and those fat-filled, syrup-dripping, delectable-smelling pancakes. "Don't rush. I won't start decorating without you," I added as Sindi tried to wolf down the last two bites of pancake in one big mouthful.

I got over the worst of my post-partum depression by throwing myself into mothering Sindi. I didn't go back to work—not even when I was given the green light to return to normal living after my Cesarean. I wanted to savor every moment of her childhood, especially since she's the only baby I'll ever have.

And for the last four years that's exactly what I did. I loved every minute of every day I spent with our beautiful daughter. I cherished every little smile and every single burp, and I celebrated every milestone of babyhood as she reached it. As Dr. Stevens predicted, my blood pressure still needed to be regulated with medication, but I'd found it was really no big deal to take a pill every day and keep my doctor's appointments, and I'd faithfully done both things since the day Sindi was born. I never missed a pill or an appointment.

Except for your appointment this month, my guilty conscience quickly reminded. I'd missed my appointment because the car broke down the week before and with all of the excitement surrounding Sindi's upcoming fourth birthday, I'd forgotten to reschedule with Dr. Stevens. And I'd run out of pills three days ago. I made a quick mental note to give the doctor's office a call right after we finished with the party decorations.

I got the bag of balloons from our closet upstairs and took a quick peek at the gift we'd bought for Sindi—the grandest dollhouse I've ever seen, complete with all the miniature furnishings, wallpaper in every room, and tiny working lights. Sindi's eyes had lit up like stars when she spied it in Clayton's Toy Store the week before. I called Jerry at work and he'd dropped by later that evening and bought it on his way home from the office. Later that night after Sindi was asleep we sneaked it into the house and hid it in our closet. Now I grinned, just thinking about how surprised she'd be when Jerry brought it downstairs later that night.

Sindi's wild about dolls, stuffed animals, and everything to do with them, hence—the theme we picked out for her party that evening. We'd gone to the party store and Sindi picked out paper plates, cups, and napkins with little pink bears on them. We also found pink and white crepe paper and teddy bear cutouts for decorating the dining room and, of course—pink and white balloons. I found the best thing when Sindi wasn't looking—a cake pan in the shape of a teddy bear. I couldn't wait to see the expression on her face when she saw the cake I'd stayed up late last night decorating; I knew she'd be thrilled.

Suddenly, though, I felt very lightheaded—and then it was hard to breathe. I sat down on the bed as white spots danced in front of my eyes and wondered, What in the world is wrong with me? I'd never felt like that before.

Then another cramp seized my left arm, and it was much more painful than all the others were. I was panting and rubbing my upper arm, trying to work out the cramp, when I realized with startling clarity what was happening to me.

How could I be so stupid? I wondered in growing dismay. My arm isn't sore because I overdid it with the exercise. It's a warning sign!

All at once I slid from the edge of the bed onto the floor, trying to concentrate on breathing deeply and properly even though it suddenly felt like there were a hundred cinderblocks resting on my chest. Moments later I was lying on my side, still trying desperately to breathe normally, when the pain shot through my chest and lingered in my left arm. My chest hurt as though it'd been hit with a battering ram.

My God, what am I going to do? I thought, panicking, feeling like I would cry if I had the breath to do it. I was alone in my house save for my four-year-old daughter and I was having a heart attack!

I made an effort to crawl to the phone sitting on our nightstand. But it was no use—I couldn't even move that far. And I could hear Sindi skipping up the stairs, merrily chatting away to Mrs. Murphy.

Oh, God—no! Don't let my little girl find me like this! Useless tears ran down my cheeks as I thought of what seeing me like that would do to my precious little Sindi.

Then all at once, she was standing in the doorway to our bedroom.

"Mommy? Are you okay?" She ran to my side with Mrs. Murphy firmly in hand.

"Mommy . . . doesn't . . . feel . . . well," I panted. I could see the concern in her small features—the sheer terror welling up in her eyes—and that frightened me even more than the pain in my chest and arm. The room was spinning and my sight was beginning to fade as she knelt down beside me and started to cry.

"Mommy!" she shrieked.

"Call for help . . . sweetheart," I whispered, feeling the pull of the waiting darkness.

My last thought was a silent prayer to God: Please don't let me die in front of my little girl on her birthday. Please. . . .

I was dreaming a very pleasant dream when I realized that something was tickling my nose. Something very fuzzy. I slowly opened my eyes and looked around.

I blinked heavy eyelids several times, trying to focus on the room. Everything was white—very white, and very clean. I slowly realized I was lying in a hospital bed. I briefly wondered about just how I'd come to be there, and then I remembered—

I had a heart attack.

I turned my head and felt that odd tickle again. Mrs. Murphy, Sindi's stuffed tabby cat, was tucked under the plain, white, starched sheet with me. That's when I noticed that I wasn't alone in the room; Jerry was sitting in the room's only chair with Sindi on his lap. They were both asleep and they looked so peaceful together. But one glance at Jerry's wrinkled clothes and Sindi's clashing outfit told me their peacefulness was an illusion. They'd been at my bedside for heaven only knew how long and they were doubtlessly worried sick. Tears sprang to my eyes as I thought of what a horrible ordeal it must've been for Sindi. No child should ever have to see such a thing.

I saw her eyes slowly open and then a wide grin appeared on her face. "Mommy! You're awake!" She leapt from Jerry's lap and ran to the bed, clambering up beside me.

"Hi, sweetie. How's my baby?" I put my arms around her, resting my chin on top of her head, cherishing the lingering scent of baby shampoo and trying not to tangle what seemed like a dozen tubes all hooked up to my body in some way or another.

Jerry, now also awake, came to the side of the bed and took my hand. "How do you feel, baby? Julia, honey—oh, gosh—I was so scared." There were tears in his eyes as he kissed my hands.

"I'm okay," I lied. The truth is I felt like I'd been run over by a truck. But I really didn't care; all that mattered was that I was alive and my family was with me.

A tall man wearing a white lab coat entered the small room. "Good morning, Mrs. White. I'm Dr. Jameson." He picked up the clipboard hanging off the end of my bed and studied the paperwork and charts inside of it.

"What happened?" I asked him, realizing I needed official confirmation of what I strongly suspected from a doctor.

"You had a heart attack. But thankfully, it was a very minor one. You should make a full recovery."

I smiled, gripped Jerry's hand even tighter, and kissed the top of

Sindi's head. Still, I was curious. "What caused it?"

"Actually, I feel there were several causes. First, your blood pressure seems to have soared out of control and this is most likely the primary cause. Your husband explained that you'd let your medication lapse the last few days, which of course would be the culprit behind your pressure shooting up. But I also feel that I need to warn you that this very stringent diet you've been on is probably a contributing factor, as well."

"But isn't losing weight good for the heart?" I asked, dumbfounded.

"It is. But since you do have a preexisting condition, it's very risky for you to start a diet without first consulting with your doctor."

I felt very foolish, indeed. I had no idea that missing three little pills could cause such a thing. And I never gave a thought to consulting a doctor when I decided to lose weight. All in all, it was a very costly lesson to learn, but I definitely learned it well.

Dr. Jameson smiled. "I'll have the nurse bring in a breakfast tray. If you keep doing as well as you have been we'll be able to let you go home in just a couple of days." He walked to the doorway and then turned back to us. "That is one brave little girl you have there, by the way. I know adults who aren't as calm in a crisis."

"What was he talking about?" I asked Jerry after Dr. Jameson made his exit.

Jerry smiled, reaching over me to ruffle Sindi's curls. "Our little girl saved your life. She called 911 and told them that her mommy was on the floor—that she couldn't wake her up and to come quick. She even remembered our address correctly when the emergency dispatcher asked her for it."

I was stunned. "My goodness, Sindi! How did you know to do all that, baby?"

All at once she was positively radiant with pride. "Daddy told me 'bout 911 when I learned the telephone."

Jerry grinned; I've never seen a father so proud of his daughter. "Believe me—I had no idea when I taught her just how important it would be."

"I'm glad I be-membered, Mommy."

"Me, too, baby," I said, hugging her and Jerry close as the tears streamed down my cheeks, "me, too."

THE END

168

ABOUT A SON
A True Story Mom's loving tribute of pride and devotion in the face of unimaginable heartbreak

My son was thirty-one years old when he died, a victim of AIDS. He left us just as winter came to the North Country, the snow falling to make a soft, white blanket, our breath hovering before our faces, biting us with its frosty teeth.

It was a time that brought our family to one pivotal point: the death of a loved one.

Betrayals of the universal plan—the child dying before the parent—the cycle of life's expectation that the young will bury the old, in reverse.

Terry went to the doctor for the last time shortly before he died. He needed medical attention for the stubborn infectious agent so deep in his lungs. He had a deep, racking cough and a high fever that refused to subside—a continuous cycle of physical and mental changes taking him gradually away from us. Each day that went by, it was more difficult to help him.

In the end, comfort became his pillow. The bed, his closure. We needed to find a new level of human consciousness to communicate with Terry. It was forged from the hope that we could bring him to a safe and secure meeting place with us, a nesting place with the intuitive power to speak to him without words, for he could not always hear us. The connection, then, must come through the spirit—a spirit with light for his inner man; the light for his journey to another place. Our bond of love would share the message.

A soul's exchange of life for death.

I remember the day we took him to the doctor for the last time. It was with much effort that my daughter and I loaded him into the car. The twelve-mile trip seemed to take forever. Arriving within the hour, my daughter parked the car. Then we transferred Terry from the backseat into a wheelchair. My daughter pushed him ahead as I shielded him from the wind with my body, even though it took us only seconds to reach the front door. A man with a kindly face held the giant glass door open for us as we laboriously moved him inside.

Terry was our precious human cargo, the young man with the infectious smile and never-ending vitality, now near death. We could give him only the inner commune of our combined love. We were there for him and we wanted him to know it. I am certain now that our wish was granted. His many bodily responses told us so.

Terry was diagnosed with a form of bronchitis that eventually turned into pneumonia. His breathing was labored, his heart rate rapid, the precise balance of his immune system in lethal disassembly. His T cells, the soldiers of infection, could not rally, so it was to be the hospital for Terry. Prescriptions were given to contain the pain and make him more comfortable, but we knew then that his time was short. There was a challenge to his will to live, the slow surrender of his life on earth, and we did not ask that a war be waged. We prayed only for an end to his suffering; it moved us forward on feet of clay. Terry was at the threshold of his journey.

Looking back to the beginning of his time, I remember the day when Terry came home to share his secret with me.

That day started out like any other day. I was washing dishes, looking out the kitchen window. He drove into our yard and stopped the car and got out, his relaxed, casual manner so familiar to me. A pair of jeans and the bright splash of color for a shirt; they were his trademark.

"Hi," I said, opening the door, stopping long enough to dry my hands on the dishtowel. "How're things?"

"Okay," Terry answered, his face serious. There seemed to be a vulnerability in his manner, or was it just my imagination?

"Come on in," I said, and we sat down together at the kitchen table.

"I brought you something," Terry told me. "Here," he said, handing me a box wrapped in brown paper. "Open it."

"For me?" I exclaimed, taking the gift. The paper was rough to my hands; in retrospect, every little thing is remembered.

I opened the gift; a very special picture lay before me: a little clown with greasepaint, all decked out in his outlandish Sunday best. The little clown stared up at me, his most pronounced feature a minute trail of tears falling down his comic little face, splashing onto his clothes.

"Like it?" Terry asked me.

I smiled at him. "Of course I do."

"It's my clown, Mom . . . just for you. The tears are mine."

"I shall treasure it always," I quickly retorted, hiding my reaction to the impact of his words. A shadow had passed between us; I felt fear.

"I hope so," he said, his voice like that of the little boy who once lived in my house.

We became very quiet, neither of us knowing what the other needed to say. It was my first indication that something was very wrong.

Finally, rising from his chair, Terry came to me, a strange and faraway look in his eyes—an answer, or maybe a question to the mettle of life that lies between mother and child.

"I brought you this picture to tell you something, Mom."

The words—direct, cold—sent a chill clear through me.

"Something good?" I questioned weakly, almost hopefully.

"Not this time," Terry answered.

I stared at him. "What, then?"

"AIDS," he told me, looking away. "I'm HIV-positive, Mom," he said, pausing. "It's the infection that comes before AIDS. It's a life-threatening disease, Mom."

"My God," I finally managed, totally unprepared and without any real knowledge of the disease which would take my son's life.

"I've got maybe five or six years to live."

"No," I said, suddenly aware that my whole body felt wooden, the wound too deep to bear. "You seem so well."

"I still have time, Mom," he said gently.

I shook my head firmly. "I don't want to believe you," I told him. "I love you too much to lose you."

"It's true, Mom."

There are no words to say what I felt.

"Nothing can change it. There's medication, but there is no cure."

"But—why?"

"I'm a homosexual, Mom. It's an epidemic for us." His words continued, giving a very personal qualification of it being a sexually transmitted disease. It was as if he were asking me if I had a moral judgment to pass.

"I love you, Terry . . . for just who you are," I told him. "You're my son."

We lingered there together, the delivered ultimatum of fate a powerful blow.

The prophecy of medical fact came true for my son. The year was 1989. There was no cure for AIDS.

He remained well for a number of years, leading a normal life. He had the comfort of his companion to help. Eventually, though, he got very sick. There were sweats, sore throats, fevers, and above all, the weakness. The pile of records he carried to his night job became too heavy for him to handle; he was a DJ and it broke his heart to have his passion come to an end.

There were signs of change for those who loved him, too—gradual change ringing the warning bell. His usually round, almost chubby face became alarmingly thin and drawn, but it was the deep, intense sadness in his eyes that spoke to us. I had never known such sadness.

Eventually Terry became very sick and needed help with his care. A depression patient myself, I quietly questioned my ability to care for him, but in the end I was firm in my resolve to be with him—another part to factor into the universal plan: a mother's love.

171

There were daily rituals for Terry's physical care. I attended to those needs, said his prayers, and shared his tears; once again, it was like caring for him as I had when he was my newborn son. I stayed close to his side in the effort that became my total existence, responding completely to his every need. The extent of the care was new to me; I learned my way through every need that came before me.

The medicine that might've helped Terry was too toxic for him to take. There was no medical treatment for his AIDS. Each day brought its duties, such as the daily changing of his bed linens. I was careful to keep wrinkles from touching his body, afraid that I might be the one to hurt him somehow, in some tiny, unforeseeable way. Sometimes Terry would open his eyes very slowly as I worked, only to close them again. Most of the time, he remained in a very deep sleep. At times, though, his arms would reach out involuntarily toward something that might sustain him.

I sat vigil at his bedside. It was the final resolution between mother and child, the empathy of our shared time resolute. There was a trial to be endured, a great kindness in the drugs that insulated him from the pain. Fear was caught up in it all. Somehow, though, I found my own way to accept what must be. I would hold my precious son close and ask God to be good to him.

Maybe He heard me.

In the end, Terry's immune system lost the fight. Terry was to slip away to another place.

"I love you, Terry, and I'll always be with you," were the last words I ever said to him.

His was the God-given comfort of a deep sleep, only the echo of my words for over the rainbow. It had taken about six years for him to die. That was Terry's time.

I hope that our story might help one who must walk the same path. May it bring to you the things to be shared. And the things to be endured alone.

Terry Washer died of AIDS at Elliott Hospital in Manchester, New Hampshire on November 28, 1990.

Good-bye, Terry Lee.

THE END

PLEASE, SAVE
MY UNBORN BABY

I sat at the table sobbing. I was terrified, paralyzed by fear. This should have been a happy time for me. Having a baby and being pregnant was something to celebrate. Yet, I couldn't. The what-ifs plagued my mind.

I wanted to feel calmer, but I couldn't. This pregnancy could change everything—for my family and for me. I loved everything that we had, and I didn't want it to change.

"Our baby is not going to be deformed!" Timothy shouted at me in frustration. His angry tone brought tears to my eyes.

"I didn't say that he would be!" I defended myself. "What I said was, that after reading a magazine article on inherited birth defects, that I was scared he might be. Is that some kind of a crime, Timothy?"

"Yesterday you were on top of the world, and now you're scared because of some article? I can't believe you're being so stupid!"

"That's the meanest thing you've said to me in the six years of our marriage!" I collapsed onto the sofa in tears. Timothy immediately softened his tone.

"I'm sorry, Ariel, but you're making a mountain out of a molehill. Why worry about a problem that we probably won't ever have? When the pregnancy test was positive, honey, you were on cloud nine. Today, you're crying. That just doesn't make any sense to me." Timothy gave me a gentle pat on the shoulder, but I pulled away from him.

"It makes perfect sense if you'd only listen to what I was saying," I said in a nasty tone.

"All I know is that you wanted another baby! Cried, begged, and pleaded for another baby! You even prayed for another baby every Sunday with your friend, Amanda. And now you're saying you're not sure? Suddenly, you're scared to have another child? I'm sorry, but that just doesn't make sense, Ariel!"

The way he put it made me sound like a crazy person, and I hated that. I reached into my pocket for a tissue, and the only one I found was wrapped around a half-eaten cherry-flavored safety pop that our four-year-old, Glen, had handed me earlier. I had walked him over to a neighbor's house for a play date so that Timothy and I could talk privately.

I wiped my tears on the back of my hand, and then onto the leg of my jeans. Why couldn't Timothy try to understand how I felt? I tried, once again, to explain the terror that I was suddenly feeling.

"I'm only trying to tell you about my fears, but you won't listen to me. It's not like I'm planning on exchanging the baby." I took a deep breath, searching for the right words. "You know that I'm adopted and have no information at all about my birth parents."

Timothy glared at me, so I decided to study my worn bunny slippers instead of his angry face.

"So?" he said.

"So what if I'm carrying some sort of weird gene like I read about that causes problems? The article listed several. Doesn't that worry you?" A tear slid down my cheek.

"But, honey, you've always known that you were adopted. You knew it when you got pregnant with Glen." He smiled fondly just thinking about our son. "And he couldn't have turned out more perfect."

"That's the whole point! Maybe we're pushing our luck." My voice fell to a whisper. "What if the new baby isn't perfect like our precious Glen? What if he or she is . . . is. . . ." I swallowed hard. "Different," I finished lamely.

"That's not going to happen!" Timothy threw down the newspaper he was holding and reached for the remote control to the TV. "I don't want to hear any more of this gloomy garbage! Put those bad thoughts out of your mind and be happy." He switched on a sitcom that we both usually enjoyed. But tonight, I wasn't in the mood to watch it.

I scowled at my husband in frustration and thought about walking to the set and switching off the noisy laughter. Instead, I yelled at Timothy.

"If I can't unburden myself to my own husband, then who am I supposed to talk to?" I jumped up from our sofa, ran into the bedroom, and threw myself down on our new pillow-topped mattress that we were both so proud of.

Our bed was really special to both of us. We'd shopped a long time to find the perfect nest for our lovemaking. Both Timothy and I enjoyed a wild and enthusiastic sex life, and we wanted a special place to create our own private excitement. We had gone from store to store, trying out each mattress and giggling at our private joke. Glen had even giggled with us because when we were happy, he always laughed, too.

The mattress had cost a lot more than we had figured, but we both agreed to skip our weekly movie and dinner out in order to be able to make the payments. And believe me, the sacrifice had been worth every penny.

We made our new baby on that bed during one of our wild encounters. "Love fests," we called those special times when we were both in the mood and as hot for each other as we had been during the excitement of our dating days. I knew exactly when I became pregnant. Timothy laughed at me when I snuggled against him and said that we'd just made a baby. Then I bought the pregnancy kit and proved to him that I was right.

But now, everything was spoiled. I was terrified that my baby would be imperfect in some way. Even the billowy softness of the bed didn't comfort me.

I longed to tell someone who would understand how I felt; I longed to discuss the article that had scared me so. The article had caused a sort of sickness to enter my soul. I wished, now, that I had never picked up that miserable magazine at the supermarket. But of course, it was too late. Every word seemed etched into my brain.

I knew that I couldn't tell any of it to my mother, even though I loved her dearly. She'd be in as big a panic as I was, and knowing Mom, she would find some way to blame herself for the problem.

Anyway, I had already broken Mom's cardinal rule by blurting out my fears to Timothy. Shortly after our marriage, Mom gave me some advice:

"Don't blab everything that happens to your husband," Mom had said. "Men just don't understand a woman's feelings. Instead of just listening and sympathizing, they immediately start trying to solve the problem. It's enough to make you crazy, so just keep your mouth shut about stuff."

At the time, I had thought her advice was old-fashioned and silly. But I soon learned that in some instances it was better not to tell everything. Like the time I bought a couple of pounds of bacon because it was a dollar cheaper if you bought two. Then one pack grew moldy before I got around to cooking it.

That day I ran directly to Timothy with the ruined meat expecting sympathy. Instead, he said, "Well, you didn't save very much, did you? Next time freeze the extra package." I'd felt as if he'd thrown a bucket of ice water in my face, so after that, I just hid the evidence of whatever went wrong and kept my own counsel.

But that was with little things.

When it came to important things—things of consequence—earth-shattering things, I'd always shared with my sweet, loving husband. And in the past he'd always been there for me, willing to comfort me and make me feel better about whatever had happened. Timothy was the perfect mate, wonderful and kind and understanding. Until now.

During the last year, when I had so longed for a second baby and we couldn't seem to become pregnant, Timothy had been a tower of strength. He'd even offered to take tests to make sure his sperm count was okay. I'd thought that was really sweet. Not many of my friends' husbands would have offered to do that. It would have been too much of a threat to their manhood.

Take my very best friend, Amanda, for example. Like me, she wanted a baby more than anything. The poor thing had never had even one child, and she and Adam had been married for seven years. Poor Amanda suffered through all of those miserable infertility tests a woman must take, and she told me some of them were painful. Then her husband wouldn't even consider taking a test to check his sperm count. And, from what I understand, that test might even be pleasurable. A little embarrassing, maybe, but pleasurable nonetheless.

Amanda and I had spent many a Sunday afternoon talking babies and playing with Glen while the guys were watching football. We'd always end by having a prayer asking God for us both to get pregnant.

My prayer had been granted. Yesterday I had bought my test kit, breathed a little prayer, and then checked the stick. When a blue line appeared, I shouted: "Hallelujah!" so loud that Timothy ran into the bathroom to see what had happened.

Then today I read that awful article and my joy disappeared, leaving me filled with dread. Scary thoughts immediately attacked me.

I took Glen next door so he wouldn't hear our conversation, and then paced the floor waiting for my husband.

When Timothy walked into the door, tired and ready to relax after a ten-hour shift, I threw myself into his arms and began sobbing my heart out, scaring him half to death.

"Ariel, sweetheart." He pulled me close, trying to comfort me. "What's wrong? Is your mother sick?"

"I'm worried about our baby." I sobbed.

"Is Glen sick?" His face creased with concern.

"Not Glen. I'm worried about the new baby." I put a protective hand over my stomach.

"Are you spotting blood?" He sounded as scared as I felt.

"No, nothing like that. I'm worried about . . . possible problems." Then I told him about the magazine article I had read.

Timothy rolled his eyes. "Nothing is going to be wrong with our baby." He sat down and picked up the evening paper, found the sports section, and began reading. I smacked him lightly on the shoulder to get his attention back.

"Timothy? You're not listening to me. I said I was worried. I want to talk about it."

He shot me a pained look. "You don't smoke or drink. You exercise regularly and take care of yourself. Everything will be fine, just quit worrying."

"You don't seem to understand that I'm talking about inherited diseases," I said. "Listen to me; I'm scared!"

Timothy laughed. "Why, sweetheart, you're just having what your mom would call a 'sinking spell.' It's probably your hormones all mixed up because of the baby." He reached over, pulled me onto his lap, and then nuzzled my neck. "After a good night's sleep, you'll be your old self again."

But I couldn't believe him. And that night, for the first time ever, I turned away from Timothy when he wanted to make love.

"I'm too worried about the baby. I'd better ask the doctor if it's okay to have sex."

"It wasn't a problem the last time!" Timothy snapped. Then he turned away from me, and I felt even worse. It was a long time before I could drop off to sleep.

The next morning I woke up with an even greater sense of dread. A spirit of foreboding permeated my whole body, settling into my bones. But I didn't tell Timothy. I knew he'd just get mad and we'd have another fight.

If only I could talk about my fears to Amanda. Then a new worry crept through my heart. When I told Amanda about becoming pregnant, it would probably make her feel bad. There I was, with one child already, and I was going to have another. Amanda didn't have any. How could I ever explain to her my doubts about my pregnancy? She'd probably hate me and I really wouldn't blame her.

I went about my usual tasks of making breakfast, showering, dressing, and then getting Glen ready for preschool. I put on a brave smile and faked not being worried. Timothy had a smug "I told you so" expression on his face that made me want to smack him, but in order to keep peace and get everyone on their way, I gritted my teeth and ignored him.

In the car Glen chattered away. He was eager to see his teacher, and excited about another day at school. I answered his questions automatically. I was glad that my job as a claims clerk for an insurance agent forced me to keep busy.

I decided not to tell my boss about my pregnancy just yet. My due date was a while away. Then I also decided not to tell Amanda, either. That hurt my conscience a bit, because I knew that when she eventually learned, she'd be hurt. Still, I didn't think that I could tell her about my doubts without spilling the beans.

More important, I wouldn't let Timothy tell Glen. He was pretty angry about that, but I claimed that nine months would seem like a long time to a small child so Timothy finally agreed.

Of course, it changed my Sunday afternoon prayers a bit. Amanda seemed puzzled, but I shrugged and said that we should just concentrate on praying for her and she seemed okay with that.

The worst thing was that my dynamite sex life was ruined. I

couldn't even stand the thought of Timothy touching me, so I lied and told him that the doctor felt it would better for us not to have sex during the pregnancy.

Timothy was worried, knowing that this was unusual. He wanted to have a conference with the doctor, but I wouldn't allow it. I didn't even tell him when I had my ultrasound and discovered that the baby would be a girl because I was afraid Timothy would learn that I was lying about the no-sex thing. I just showed him the picture and said it had been a spur-of-the-moment thing.

Time flew by and suddenly my clothes were starting to get too tight. I bought some baggy blouses and some of those dresses that hang loose, the ones that women with weight problems sometimes wear because they hide your figure. Amanda was too polite to say anything about my weight gain, but a few other people mentioned it. I just shrugged and ignored them.

One afternoon the preschool called me at the office and said that Glen was running a fever, so I left work and picked him up. I called his pediatrician on my cell phone, explained the symptoms, and was told that he needed rest, plenty of fluids, and something for the fever. I only needed to bring him in if the fever lasted more than three days.

After I got Glen into his super hero pajamas and found a stack of his books, we settled into the rocking chair, Glen snuggling against me on my lap.

"Read my new book first," Glen begged. "The one I got at Sunday school for being the best listener."

"Sure, sweetie." I sorted through the books and found the one he wanted. I opened the bright cover and began to read.

"God made everything beautiful." I showed Glen the illustration of a beautiful garden.

Glen grinned up at me with a smile that lights up my world. I turned a page and he looked at a picture showing several children of different ages and races standing and holding hands.

"God filled his world with people of all colors and sizes." Glen patted the picture, smiled. Then he turned the page, his face bright with anticipation.

My heart seemed to stop beating. This page showed various lesser able-bodied children. Three were in wheelchairs, one wore a hearing aid, and another had thick glasses that looked like the bottom of a pop bottle. But all of the children were smiling and looking happy. A bright sun radiated golden rays of color over the figures. It was a minute before I could speak.

"What does it say, Mommy?" Glen prodded. I cleared my throat.

"God made everyone special." My voice broke as I read the caption.

"Mommy, are those kids sick like me?" Glen asked, his face rapt with attention.

I thought about giving him a glib answer, assuring him that the children were fine. Then I looked at his honest little face and knew that it would be very wrong not to tell him as much of the truth as he could bear. I took a deep breath, trying to find exactly the right words.

"Some of the ones in the wheelchairs might be very sick. It could be that they can actually walk, but are too weak to stand for long," I answered honestly.

"Some of the kids need a wheelchair because they're sick?" Glen asked in his sweet little-boy voice. He thought a minute. "I'm sick. Do you think that I might need a wheelchair, too?" His voice sounded hopeful and I smiled.

"No, sweetheart, you're not that sick, and you'll soon be well. You won't need a wheelchair." I hastened on to explain about the children. "Most of the kids in the wheelchairs are probably disabled and can't walk at all." I so hated having to tell him that sad fact of life.

"Not ever?"

"Not ever." My heart was heavy with sorrow. What if our new baby was disabled and could never walk?

"I don't know any kids who ride in a wheelchair," Glen said. "But if I did, do you think they'd let me ride with them? It looks big enough for two."

I laughed. "Well, I don't know. Maybe they would." I looked at my little boy carefully. "Would you mind having a friend who couldn't walk?"

"No. He could give me rides in his chair, and I could carry things to him when he needed them."

My heart swelled with pride at my kindhearted little boy and tears stung my eyes again. I could hardly speak, but it didn't really matter because Glen had already turned the page and we looked at all of the different children playing together. The healthy children were interacting with the less healthy ones.

"See?" Glen said. "That's the kind of friend I'd be. What do the words say?"

I cleared the frog out of my throat so I could speak. "Love one another."

Glen smiled and turned to the last page. It showed a huge sunrise bursting through heavy clouds.

"Because God loves you!" I finished the book.

Glen loved the story and asked me to reread it over and over until he had memorized it and was able to recite the entire story to me.

As I listened to his sweet, serious voice speaking the sentences, the words somehow became alive and real to me. My heart beat faster, and I began to feel hopeful for the first time in months.

Glen triumphantly read the last page. "God loves you!"

Then without warning the most incredible thing happened. A feeling of comfort and love swept through me. A truly unbelievable phenomenon! It seemed almost as if God, Himself, were comforting me.

A rush of well-being swept through my entire body like warm oil. For the first time in months, I wasn't under a dark cloud. My soul took wing with a joy I couldn't even begin to explain.

Suddenly I knew that everything was going to be all right, no matter what happened. Even if the worst thing in the world occurred and our baby was born with some sort of defect or disability, I knew that things would still be all right.

Knowledge entered my heart that God would give Timothy and me the strength to find joy even in our troubles. Like the picture in the book, our healthy child and our ill child would play and laugh and share together.

Tears of joy rolled down my cheeks and I brushed them away before my little boy could notice.

Hearing Glen read the words, "God loves you!" in his sweet, childish voice somehow imprinted them into my heart and made them real to me. The terror that had haunted me for months lifted.

The front door opened and Timothy walked into the living room. He watched the two of us for a minute with a tender look on his face.

"How's my best girl and guy?" he asked in a voice husky with emotion, walking toward us.

"I came home sick, and we've been reading my new book," Glen said.

"I called the doctor and he said it's probably a virus that's going around," I said in answer to Timothy's suddenly worried look.

"But I'm not going to need a wheelchair," Glen informed his dad.

"Well, I'm certainly glad to hear that." Timothy squatted beside us and gave Glen a mock-serious look.

"The book is about disabled children and how God made everything and everyone beautiful," I explained.

A frown swept across Timothy's forehead. He lifted Glen up into his arms and cuddled him against his broad chest.

"Maybe this isn't the best book for Mommy to be reading right now, little buddy," he said.

"You're wrong," I hastened to say. The warm happy feeling God had given to me still flowed through my body. I couldn't explain it. I knew I didn't deserve such kindness. The peace I felt was a wonderful, unearned, undeserved gift from God. "It was the perfect book." My heart was almost singing.

"Let's all sit on the sofa together. Mommy and Daddy have a little surprise to tell you about, Glen." I stood up and walked across the room.

A big grin spread across Timothy's face as he realized what I was talking about.

"We certainly do," he said, "and it's long past due."

The three of us settled on the sofa. Timothy and I snuggled as close as we could get and Glen perched half on Timothy's lap and half on mine.

"Tell me," Glen said. "Tell me about the surprise! Am I going to get a puppy?"

"It's better than a puppy," I said with a laugh.

"Better than a puppy?" Glen thought for awhile, and then a big grin spread over his little face. "Am I going to get a brother?" He clapped his hands.

"How about a sister?" his dad said with an even bigger grin. "A little girl who's as pretty as her mother."

Glen had to think about that for awhile; then he decided it might be all right.

The evening took on a festive air, almost like a holiday. Timothy insisted on cooking dinner so I could rest. He thawed chicken breasts in the microwave and boiled one to make soup for Glen. The others he sliced and diced with veggies into a stir-fry.

My heart was filled with pure joy. It seemed as if a boulder had been lifted from my shoulders. I suddenly realized that the responsibility of caring for my children wasn't Timothy's and mine alone. God would help us. We could trust Him to enable us face anything that happened.

That night after we'd turned off the lights and slipped between freshly laundered sheets, I was the one to turn toward Timothy. I pressed myself into his arms and gave him a long, wet, sexy kiss. His breathing quickened and he ran his hands down my body, caressing parts that had been untouched for too long. Fire leapt through my body and I wanted him inside of me. I touched his body in places I had neglected the past months. He groaned loudly.

"Make love to me," I whispered.

"I want to more than anything, but we can't, sweetheart. The doctor said not to."

I was caught in my own deceit! I bit my lip, dreading what I had to tell. It was a minute before I could speak.

"I lied about what the doctor said; I'm so sorry. Can you forgive me?" I was so ashamed that my voice was barely a whisper.

Timothy was silent for a long minute. He stopped caressing my body. I missed his touch, and my heart pounded waiting for his answer. Would he be able to forgive me?

"I can't believe you lied to me, Ariel. I thought we always told each

181

other the truth, no matter what." His voice sounded so hurt.

"It was horrible of me, and I'm so terribly sorry." I swallowed hard. "I've never lied to you before, but it's as if I became a crazy woman after I read that article. I'll never lie to you again. I promise. Please say that you'll forgive me."

Tears streamed down my cheeks as I lay beside Timothy in the dark. How could I have made such a terrible mistake? Had I ruined my perfect marriage?

Then Timothy reached down and wiped my tears away with tender fingers.

"Don't cry, sweetheart. Of course I'll forgive you." He kissed me gently.

I pressed myself against him with all of the intensity that burned in my heart and slipped my tongue into the velvet of his mouth. Timothy growled deep in his throat.

Our lovemaking was wonderful. The depth of our passion was reflected in tenderness and gentleness and mutual need. All I could think of was pleasuring Timothy, and by doing that, my own needs were fulfilled.

The next day at work I told my boss about the baby, then I called Amanda. I confessed the entire truth without sparing myself. I figured she'd hate me, that she would never understand what I had experienced. But I was surprised.

"Oh, Ariel! I'm so glad that you told me all of this. You've been acting so strangely that I thought I had done something to offend you. I thought that you were tired of my always whining about not having a baby. I was afraid you didn't like me anymore." I assured her that I loved her as if she were my very own sister and would keep on praying that she would soon be become a mother.

We have prayed that prayer for months without results, but we will never give up. Prayers get answered.

My own baby is due any minute now. I trained a temp to cover my job while I'm on maternity leave. My suitcase is packed and ready to take to the hospital.

Nadine Lee will be our baby's name, after both of our mothers. Timothy and I pray every night that she will be healthy and whole and perfect with all ten fingers and all ten toes. And we have every confidence that this will be the case. But even if she isn't, she will be ours and we will love her with all of our hearts, and we will also teach her to love herself. God doesn't create any babies who aren't beautiful and special, in their own way.

THE END

I'LL NEVER SMILE ON MOTHER'S DAY AGAIN

Craig and I got married with the intention of filling our home with babies. We both loved children and we believed that we'd make wonderful parents.

At the age of twenty-seven, I figured that I had plenty of time to have at least three or four kids, and maybe even as many as six. He thought it was funny that I'd wanted so many kids, especially since I'd grown up an only child. I told him that it was the very reason why I wanted a big family.

"Big families seem to have so much fun," I explained.

Nodding, he agreed. "Most of the time, they do, but there are other times when I was growing up when I wished that I didn't have to share my things, especially with my little brothers. They always tore things up." He had two older sisters and three younger brothers. But, he still loved the idea of having a large family.

"There are more good points to it than bad," he admitted. "We were very close and protective toward each other. And, there was never a lack of someone to play with."

Since both of us had good jobs, we decided that I'd continue working after we got married, at least until our first child was born. We'd figured that we'd save as much money as we could and then, we'd buy a house big enough to accommodate the children that we wanted so badly.

I didn't get pregnant right away, so when I was offered a promotion, I took it. It involved quite a bit of travel in the beginning, but my boss assured me that the hectic pace would slow down eventually. However, I found myself out of town more than I was home during the first few years.

"We'll never have kids at this rate, Holly," Craig told me. "In case you don't remember, it takes the two of us being together to make babies."

I grinned. "Yeah, I know. At least, times have changed and women can still give birth to healthy children after they turn thirty."

"It's a good thing," he said as he glanced at the calendar, "because your birthday is coming up in a few weeks."

Craig and I discussed our plans, and we both decided that I needed to take a step down from my position so that we could concentrate on our family goals. We had a huge savings account, and we'd put a large-enough chunk of money down on our house that our monthly mortgage payments would be manageable, even with my lower salary.

"Are you sure that you want do this?" my boss asked, when I told him.

I nodded. "Absolutely." And, I had no doubt in my mind. The most important thing to me was to get pregnant and to start increasing the size of our family.

My boss understood and offered me a slightly lower position in order to keep me with the company.

"You're an excellent employee, Holly, and I'd hate to lose you," he told me.

As soon as I was settled into my new position, I became obsessed with babies. They seemed to be everywhere I looked. That was fine in the beginning, but soon, I became irritated that I didn't already have a child of my own.

Whenever I saw a toddler with his mother or a pretty little baby in a carriage at the park, my heart ached to have a child of my own. In fact, there were several occasions when I had to leave certain places so that I could cry in private. Craig felt the same way, but he didn't cry. He just gritted his teeth and told me that he knew exactly how I felt.

We even talked about the possibility that something might be wrong with one of us. "Let's see a specialist," he suggested. "We're long overdue."

"I agree," I said. "We should have done this years ago."

The problem in the past had been that I'd been too busy with work to worry too much about it. But, eventually, we'd both become obsessed. Even Craig liked to lie in bed and talk about how great it would be to have a little one around the house.

After the first round of tests, nothing showed up that would have prevented us from having a child.

"I'm referring you to another clinic," the doctor told me, "where they can run further in-depth tests. I can see that the two of you would make wonderful parents."

We thanked him and took the referral. At the second clinic, they told us that there was nothing wrong with either of us—except anxiety. Craig looked at me, then back at the counselor.

"Is there anything we can do?" Craig asked.

She nodded. "Even though we can't find anything wrong, we'll still consider helping you along. There are medications that you can take to increase the likelihood of a pregnancy."

"Let's do it," I said.

Craig squirmed in his seat but didn't say a word. I could tell that he wanted more information.

The counselor told us about some of the success stories, as well as about some cases where even the medicine couldn't help. There would be no guarantees, she explained, and the procedures were quite expensive. I still didn't budge in my desire. We had plenty of money saved, and I was willing to do whatever it took to get pregnant.

"You do understand that the possibility of having multiple births is much greater," the counselor told us. "There's a much higher rate of twins, triplets, or even more babies being conceived."

"That would be fine," I said. "In fact, I like the idea of having more than one at a time, since I'm not getting any younger."

We had to attend more counseling sessions. Craig and I learned more than we ever dreamed we would, about all the methods that could be used to help couples like us. Finally, after several months, he nodded his assent.

"Yes, I think it sounds good," he told me. "It would be a shame for us to not take advantage of something like this." We began our journey toward parenthood immediately.

First, I had a series of shots to increase my fertility. Craig teased me about wanting him all the time. I tried to laugh it off, but he was right. I was so desperate for children that I literally chased him around the house when I felt like it might be a good time for me to conceive.

By the end of the year, I was pregnant. Since we'd been through every step of the way together, Craig was with me when I found out.

We immediately jumped up and wrapped our arms around each other in glee.

"Now, our dream will finally come true," he whispered into my hair. "We're going be parents."

"Let's hope that there's not more than one or two," the doctor told us. "Three at the most."

"What's the problem?" I asked.

"The larger the number of babies, the greater the risk of survival," he explained. "We'll know something soon."

A month later, we learned that I was carrying twins.

"Perfect!" the doctor exclaimed while Craig and I stared at him in joyous disbelief.

We went home and called our families. It only took me a few minutes, since I just had to inform my parents and my aunt. Craig had to call all his brothers and sisters, who were almost as happy as we were because they knew how long we'd wanted children.

"You're going to be grandparents again," I heard him tell his mom and dad. Then, he held the phone out from his ear while his mother squealed. I laughed.

That night, we celebrated with sparkling cider. "No alcohol for you for the next several months," he told me. "And, it's probably a good idea for me to stay away from it, too. We're in this together."

I can't remember ever being so happy. Craig was the perfect, doting husband, and I let him do things for me because it brought both of us so much joy. We never imagined that anything could go wrong, once I was finally pregnant.

Everything was fine until my fifth month. I was in the doctor's office for a routine ultrasound, a procedure that they insisted upon doing every month, when the technician frowned at something that she saw on the screen.

"What's wrong?" I asked.

She shook her head. "Let me get the doctor," she said.

When the doctor came back, he looked at the screen, frowned, and then looked at me. "We need to talk after the ultrasound."

My hands began to shake and my stomach churned. Something was obviously wrong.

Please God, I prayed, don't let anything harm my babies.

Craig and I waited nervously for the doctor to get the pictures from the ultrasound scan. Finally, he brought one into the office and put it up on the board.

I glanced over at Craig, who was chewing his nails, something that I knew he only did when he was nervous. I fidgeted with the hem of my maternity blouse.

The doctor explained that one baby was doing extremely well, and I let out a sigh of relief.

"But," he went on, "the other one isn't growing properly."

"What does that mean?" Craig asked anxiously.

"It means that one baby is getting all the nutrients and the other is getting virtually none. We need to monitor the situation very closely."

I nodded. Since our babies were so important to us, I vowed that we'd do whatever it took to ensure a healthy delivery. I'd already fallen in love with the babies inside of me, and I was willing to lay my life on the line for them.

Over the next few weeks, I went to the doctor's office every day, so that they could take pictures, take blood, and do all sorts of things to my body. I always got a detailed report of what they'd found, and it didn't look good for the baby who wasn't growing.

"I'd like to recommend that we do a partial cesarean," the doctor said. "What we don't want is to jeopardize the healthy baby, and at this rate, infection is a very real possibility."

"Are there risks to the healthy baby if you take the other one?" I asked.

The doctor nodded. "With surgery, there's always a risk."

Craig and I exchanged glances. Then he turned to the doctor and asked. "What would you do if this were your baby?"

"I'd have the surgery and pray for the healthy child," he answered sympathetically.

That's exactly what we did. It was a very tense operation, and Craig never left my side. Having a baby had never meant more to us than it did then.

Immediately after the surgery, while I was still in the recovery room, the doctor came in and spoke to us. I was a little woozy from the anesthetic, but I could still hear what they discussed.

"The remaining baby seems fine so far. We'll still need to watch the baby's progress carefully." The doctor turned to leave, but stopped. "Would you like to know the sex of your child?"

Craig turned and looked at me for an answer. I nodded.

"You're having a little girl," he said. "We'll do everything we can to make sure that she's healthy and born close to her due date."

After he left the room, Craig came over and hugged me. "A girl," he whispered. "I hope she looks just like you."

"I don't care what she looks like," I told him, through my tears. "I just want her to make it long enough to be born healthy."

"Me, too," Craig said as he kissed my forehead. "Get some rest."

He sat down in the chair by the window while I slept. I went home the next day with the order to remain in bed for the next week.

Craig took some time off work so he could take care of me. I went on disability leave from my job so that I could concentrate on my pregnancy. Taking care of myself was more important than it had ever been. Sure, our income was cut in half, but I figured that it didn't matter. After all, that's why we'd saved.

After Craig went back to work, he made arrangements with his sisters and our mothers to stop by every day and make sure that everything was okay. I wasn't supposed to stay on my feet for very long, so they helped me with some of the cleaning and cooking. On the weekends, Craig not only cleaned the house, but also catered to my every whim. I felt very blessed that I had such a wonderful husband. I knew that not all women were so fortunate.

We had a few scares during the pregnancy with spotting and cramps that I thought might have been contractions, but I managed to carry Joy to full term. She came out pink and noisy, which made everyone in the delivery room laugh.

The whole medical team was there, cheering for me, and I was grateful to have everyone with me. They all knew just what Craig and I had been through. After Joy was born, they'd stayed behind to hold her and to offer wonderful words of encouragement.

Joy was passed around the room, from one nurse to another. Even the anesthesiologist took a turn holding her.

"She's so beautiful," he said with misty eyes.

Craig thanked everyone for taking so much time with us and for being such a wonderful source of encouragement when we'd needed

187

it. "We're having a party next month, and I'd like for all of you to come," he told them.

"I wouldn't miss it for anything in the world," the doctor said.

Baby Joy cried through the night and slept all day for the first week.

"It's a good thing that you're staying home, or I'd never be able to go to work," Craig said after his vacation time was over. He'd stayed home for two weeks after Joy was born, but he'd run out of time, and any other days that he took would be unpaid. Since we depended on his income for survival, we couldn't afford for him to take any more time.

Everyone came to the party, and most of them brought gifts for Joy. My life couldn't have been better. The happiness of having a baby in the house couldn't be matched.

Although I'd never have traded our experience for anything, we did have new worries. We'd used all of our savings for the fertility specialist. Insurance didn't cover any of the procedures that weren't standard, so we were flat broke and could barely cover our basic bills.

Craig didn't want me to go back to work, but after a couple months of barely making ends meet, I insisted.

"There's a wonderful day-care center near my office," I told him. "We can bring the baby there, and I can visit her during lunch."

"I don't know, honey," he said. "If you have to go back to work, maybe we can get our mothers and my sisters to help out."

I shook my head. "No, I don't want to ask them for so much. They're all busy with their own lives. We can put her in the day-care center, and she'll do fine. She'll be in the car with me every morning, I'll see her during lunch, and then she'll ride home with me in the afternoon. Besides, Joy loves riding in the car."

Finally, he agreed because we were so broke. It was the first time during our marriage when we didn't have excess funds, and it was pretty miserable, not to mention frightening. What if Joy needed something that we couldn't afford?

Joy didn't seem to mind going to the day-care center at all. In fact, because of her sunny disposition, she thrived there. I was the one who was miserable, after I'd left her every morning.

It took a long time before we were able to save a dime from my job. Our credit card bills had grown so high that we used most of the money to pay those. Once they'd been paid, I put the same amount that we'd been paying our creditors into our savings account.

"I'm glad we finally have breathing room again," Craig said. "It's a good thing we had our savings to begin with, or we would have been in dire straits."

"I know this is a bad time to bring this up," I said one day, after we'd had a really nice afternoon at the park with Joy, "but I was thinking that we might want to have another child soon. We're not getting any younger, you know."

He scratched his head. "I'm not sure, Holly. Look at all we went through to have Joy. It wouldn't be the end of the world if she was our only child."

"I don't want her to be an only child. She needs a sister or brother," I protested.

"Let's think about it before we do anything," he said as he backed away from me.

Every day that passed brought my desire to have another child to a new level. I craved having another baby. Joy was so wonderful that I'd been able to forget all the things we'd had to endure so that she could come into the world.

There were times when I grieved for the baby that we'd lost, but the doctor told me that such feelings were normal.

"You saw yourself as being the mother of two children, and it was a hard reality when he didn't survive," he said consolingly.

"He?" I asked. "The baby was a boy?"

The doctor nodded. "Yes, Joy's twin was a boy."

Knowing that only made my desire stronger. And, the doctor had been right about the fact that I saw myself as the mother of two children. Although I'd once wanted a large family, I knew that two would be enough.

"We just don't have the money, Holly," Craig argued. "What if we need it for Joy?"

"We'll find a way," I insisted. "When I was little, my parents didn't have much money, but I was just as happy as any other kid."

"That was a long time ago, Holly. Things are different now. People's needs have changed."

Craig and I hadn't argued much during our marriage, but we'd begun having heated discussions about the issue of another child. For the first time since we'd said our vows, we were on extremely opposite sides concerning what we wanted for our family. He wanted one child and financial security, while I wanted another baby, and wasn't concerned about the money.

My mom called one night, after I'd been crying. "What's wrong, Holly, honey?" she asked.

In spite of my not wanting to share anything negative about my husband with my mother, I told her about the arguments that we'd been having over the issue of how many children Craig and I wanted. And, to my dismay, she agreed with him.

"It's not the end of the world to have only one child, Holly," she said. "We only had you, and that was enough for us."

"Why didn't you have more?" I asked. "I know that you've always loved children. You would have been a perfect mom for a whole bunch of kids."

She got quiet for a few seconds. "We tried for years, but I kept having miscarriages. It wasn't meant to be."

"Oh, Mom," I said, "I'm so sorry. I had no idea."

"Sometimes you have to accept what you've been given and be happy with it," she added. "And, your father and I didn't want to burden you with our disappointments. We were afraid that you'd think we weren't happy with just you. We were thrilled to have you for our daughter. In fact, we still are."

"Yes, I know that." After what I'd learned about my mom, I suddenly had a lot of thinking to do.

After I got off the phone with her, I asked Craig to sit down and talk with me. We put Joy to bed, then went into the kitchen where she wouldn't hear our voices.

I began by telling him what my mother had revealed. He sat there and listened until I was finished. Then, he took my hands in his and kissed my wrists while I waited to hear what he had to say. I knew that was what he liked to do before he told me something that he believed I really needed to hear.

"Holly, your mom and I may agree right now, but I'm not saying that I won't change my mind later. It's just that I don't want the time we now have with Joy to be overshadowed by looking too far into the future."

Those were words that I knew he'd considered carefully. And, I had to admit that Craig was right. We needed to focus on what we had, not on what we didn't. I was happy with my baby, and I saw that I needed to allow myself the time to enjoy her more, without the extra pressure of worrying about having another baby.

"Okay, we stop discussing the idea of having another baby for now," I agreed. "But, maybe we can think about it in a year or two?"

He stood up and grinned. "Sounds good to me. By then, maybe our financial situation will look brighter, and we won't have to worry about how we're going to pay for another child."

After we'd cleared the air, I had to admit that I felt much better about life. Joy continued to develop and to amuse us with her adorable ways. When she smiled, the whole room lit up. And, when she cried, she had both Craig and me there to tend to her needs. My family truly was the most special thing in the world to me.

All that we'd had to endure in order to have our precious child made her all the more special. No one had ever wanted a baby more than I wanted her. She was positively the light of my life. I realized that my desire to have another child was due, in part, to the fact that

I was so happy with her. Because of my wonderful little girl, I was hooked on babies. Plus, there might have been some sort of hormonal thing going on. Whatever the case, motherhood certainly did agree with me. I loved every minute of being a mom.

Craig treated me like a queen, and Joy looked up at me with adoring eyes. I'd never felt so on top of the world before. I was positively giddy with happiness.

Because of all we'd been through, Craig told me that he wanted to do something really special for me on my first Mother's Day. I told him that wasn't necessary, but he insisted.

He called my boss and asked him if I could have off the Friday before Mother's Day, so that I could use the gift certificate to the spa that he'd given me. There, I'd get pampered with a massage, a facial, and a mud bath. That was something that I'd always wanted, and Craig wanted to treat me to it. My boss was wonderful and agreed.

"I'll take Joy to the day-care center and pick her up on the way home so you won't have to worry about it. You can just relax and have a good time," he told me. "And, on Sunday she and I will take you to Chadwick's for brunch."

Chadwick's was my favorite restaurant, one that specialized in steak and seafood dishes. My husband really was pampering me, and I was enjoying it thoroughly.

That Friday morning, I kissed my husband and baby good-bye before they left. Joy reached out for a hug. I touched her nose with my finger and told her that I loved her. She giggled and patted my cheek with her chubby little hand. My heart turned over with love.

Craig winked and told me to have a wonderful day. "I wish I could drive you there, but I have a presentation this morning, and I have to rush as it is."

"I understand," I told him. "I don't mind driving myself. I'll see you tonight."

"Oh, and don't bother cooking when you get home," he added. "I'll order pizza. This year, Mother's Day will last the whole weekend."

After they left, I felt so happy that I could have burst. My love for my husband had kept growing through the years, and I felt like the luckiest mother in the world to have a baby as precious as Joy. I didn't know anyone who was happier than I was at the moment. And, my husband was the most wonderful man I knew.

I got ready for the spa in complete silence. Normally, I listened to the radio, but I just wanted to enjoy a few private thoughts about my family as I took my shower and got dressed.

When I arrived, I checked in at the registration desk. Several people were talking about a terrible accident, involving a train and a car that had taken place that morning.

"I saw the news this morning," one of the women was saying, "and it looks like the people in the car got hurt pretty badly."

"That's awful," I said as I turned to follow the hostess down the hall to the room to begin my day of pampering.

"You can say that again," she replied. "It'll be a miracle if anyone survived, from the looks of that mangled heap of metal."

I only thought about that for a minute, until the massage therapist came into the room. She immediately put on some soothing music, and before I knew it, I was totally relaxed and in my own little world. It was truly what I'd needed. I'd been so tense from all the stress of the past few years that my muscles had tightened.

She kneaded my shoulders until they felt like jelly. After an hour, she told me to relax until she could take me to the bath area where I'd have my facial and mud bath. I just lay there and dozed until she came back into the room.

Finally, in a soft voice, she told me that it was time. Gently taking my arm, she helped me up. It was hard to stand with my muscles so relaxed. I giggled as I tried to walk.

"I'm acting like I've had too much to drink," I told her.

"Everyone does after they get their massage. You were tighter than most, so you'll feel it more," she said.

Everything about that day was absolutely wonderful. I was served lunch in a room filled with lush, tropical plants and flowers. The platter was filled with shrimp, vegetables, and various exotic fruits. I enjoyed every single bite.

That afternoon, I had more treatments—to my face, my feet, and my hands. I knew that my husband must really love me, to want to pamper me so. A smile crossed my face as I thought about how I'd reward him for giving me such a generous Mother's Day gift.

When the day was over, I felt rested and ready to go home to my family. A warm feeling flooded my body as I thought about a quiet Friday night at home with Craig and Joy.

I wasn't prepared for what I saw when I pulled up the street to my house. There were police cars parked outside, and people milling around in my yard. Something must have happened!

As I got closer, I saw my mother sitting on the porch, dabbing at her eyes with a tissue. My front door was standing open. Where were Craig and Joy? I glanced at my watch and realized that it wasn't quite time for them to be home yet, so I let out a sigh of relief. At least, I didn't have to worry about them having been home when whatever it was had happened.

My mother quickly glanced up when she saw my car. She stood unsteadily, then she walked down the porch steps toward me. I turned off the ignition just as she got to the edge of my driveway.

192

"Mom?" I asked as her knees buckled beneath her.

I noticed that my dad had run out of the house. He was right behind Mom. "Holly, have you heard?" he asked.

"No," I replied frantically. "What were you doing in my house? Was there a fire or something?"

My dad cleared his throat and shook his head. We'd been joined by a couple of the uniformed policemen.

Suddenly, I felt a deep pain in my chest. Something had happened to my husband and baby—I could just feel it.

"Where are Craig and Joy?" I screamed, trying to break away from the group so that I could find them.

"Let's all go inside together, Holly. We have something to tell you," my father said as he took my arm.

I wanted to cry, although I didn't know why. If something had happened to the two loves of my life, I knew that I couldn't survive. My heart would surely break in two.

"Holly, honey—" my dad began before he choked on his words. He had to take a step back and steady himself.

One of the cops looked at him, then at my mom. "Would you like for me to tell her?" he asked gently.

Shaking her head, my mother pushed him away. She knelt down at my feet and took my hand. As she did that, I knew it must have been the worst news possible since they were having such a hard time telling me.

"Where are they?" I asked, my voice sounding strange to my ears. My body was going through the motions, but I felt more like a robot than a person.

"They were on their way to the day-care center, and the train—" my mother began. She had to stop because she was sobbing.

"Apparently, Craig tried to beat the train at the railroad crossing," my dad continued for her. "The train got there right when they did. The conductor said that there was no way that he could stop the train."

My entire body went numb. "Where are they?" I repeated. "Where are my husband and baby?"

"They didn't make it, Holly, honey," my father said, crying. "Our son-in-law and granddaughter didn't survive."

As the world began to swirl around me, my ears rang. The voices that I heard sounded like surreal. In fact, nothing seemed real. I opened my mouth to talk, but I wasn't sure if any words came out. My entire body felt cold and clammy.

"She's in shock," some voice behind me said.

Nothing I did to try and function seemed to work. An ambulance had arrived, and soon, I was on a stretcher looking up at a sea of unfamiliar faces. Why was I there? Everything was distorted.

I awoke in a hospital room with my parents by my side, the morning sun shining through the window behind them. My mother rang for a nurse as soon as she saw that I was awake. Her eyes were puffy and red from crying, and so were my father's. Although I felt warmer, I still wasn't sure if I was awake. Had I dreamed what had happened at my house when I'd come home from the spa?

"Sweetheart, we wanted to be here with you when you woke up," my mother told me. "There are some people who need to talk to you, but we told them that they couldn't, not until you felt better." A tear slipped down her cheek as she took my hand. "Oh, Holly, honey, I'm so sorry. I wish that there was something I could do to change things."

My dad pulled her toward him. "We can't change anything, but we can be here for our little girl."

That's when I knew for certain that it hadn't been a dream. There I was, in a real hospital, facing the reality of losing my loving husband and precious baby daughter. And, I was feeling all-too-real pain, deep inside. How could something so terrible have happened, when life had been so wonderful? Was I being punished for something? Was it wrong for me to have been so happy?

All throughout the day, people came and went from my hospital room. People from my office stopped by to offer their condolences. I thanked them and tried to act like myself. But I couldn't, because I wasn't myself anymore.

Just the day before, I had been part of a wonderful family of three. Only a day later, I was a widow and the grieving mother of a child who died before she'd had a chance to live her life. Joy would never know what it was like to play on the beach. She'd never experience tasting a glass of lemonade on a hot summer day. She'd never know what it was like to grow into a teenager who longed for her first kiss. And, I'd never be able to hold that precious child in my arms again.

Craig, the love of my life, wouldn't be there to comfort me at night after a long day at work. He wouldn't be there to talk with about our dreams for the future. My whole life had been taken away from me in one horrifying second.

All the things that I'd lived for since I'd married Craig had vanished in one instant. My future had changed in the blink of an eye.

I was released from the hospital the next day, which was Mother's Day—the day that was supposed to be a celebration.

"You're coming home with us," my mother told me, leaving me no room for argument. "I'll go to your house later next week and sort through things so that you won't have to."

"No, Mom," I told her. "That's something I need to do alone."

"Are you sure?" she asked. "Won't it upset you too much to have to go through all of Joy's and Craig's things?"

"I have to do it. I want to do it," I told her.

"Okay," she said slowly, "if you're sure about that."

All day that Sunday, I sat and stared out the window of my parents' living room, replaying the same thing over and over in my mind. It was Mother's Day, the day when we'd planned to go out for a wonderful meal and celebrate the fact that I was a mother. Joy had made all of that possible. I'd never be able to experience such happiness again. It would have been my first Mother's Day celebration with her, and in an instant, it had all been taken away from me.

Over the course of the week, we had a double funeral for Craig and Joy. People came from all over, including many people that I'd never even seen before. Craig's boss gave me a hug and told me that if there was anything he could do, just to call him. My own boss was very sympathetic.

"When Craig called and asked for the day off for you so that you could go to the spa, I should have turned him down," he said. "This never would have happened if I had."

I shook my head, trying to hold back the tears. "Don't blame yourself," I told him. "It's not your fault."

I understood what was going through his mind, though. I'd been thinking the same kinds of thoughts—that if I'd done something different, I'd still have Craig and Joy. I should have insisted on taking Joy to the day-care center since Craig had been running late for his meeting. But, it was too late. There was absolutely nothing that could be done, and those thoughts were futile.

It took me a couple of months before I could go back to work. Craig had left enough life insurance so that I'd never have to work again if I didn't want to. But, I needed a diversion. Staying home all day only intensified the pain.

People walked on eggshells around me for a long time before things got back to normal. I was relieved when someone finally cracked a joke during a business meeting. At first, everyone looked at me to see what my reaction would be. When I laughed, there was a collective sigh, and then everyone relaxed. Although I'd had to force myself to be cheerful, I did it more to bring normalcy to the situation than for any other reason. I still felt sick inside.

As the months passed, I began to feel more normal. Although the deaths of my husband and baby never made sense, I could get into a car without having to gasp for air. Seeing babies still bothered me, but I was finally able to breathe around them without feeling as though I'd lose my mind.

I never actually got over losing my family, but I did begin to heal, after several months had passed. I'd thought that I'd be able to remain in the house we'd bought when we'd decided to have a family, but it was too difficult, so I sold it and moved into a new apartment. My parents encouraged me to move close to them, so I did. It was nice having them nearby, for those times when I couldn't handle being alone.

Nearly a year has gone by since that awful day in May. Mother's Day cards are in all the shops, and I see commercials advertising restaurants and gifts that are perfect for "that special woman in your life." Every time I see something that reminds me of what I've loved and lost, I cry. My parents have assured me that my feelings are normal.

"I don't know if it'll ever go away," my mother told me, in her infinite wisdom. "But, you're still a wonderful person, with a full life ahead of you. Remember that there are still people here who love you."

I nodded as tears trickled down my cheeks. And, I know that I have to continue celebrating the love that I feel for my own mother on her special day.

"You don't have to do this, you know," she said when I told her that I wanted to take her out to dinner on Mother's Day.

"Yes, I know," I said. "But, I want to. You and Dad are all I have left."

On Mother's Day, no matter how much it hurts, I'm going to have dinner in a restaurant with my parents, and I'm going to force myself to remind her how much I appreciate her. After losing my own daughter, I understand how my mother feels and why she was willing to make so many sacrifices for me. I love her very much. She knows it already, but there are times when we need to tell the ones we love how much we care. You never know when they'll be gone forever, and I'd hate to have regrets.

THE END

MOM VS. MEDICINE
I challenged a doctor and saved my baby's life

"My life is perfect." Had I really said that just a few short months ago? At the time, I was convinced that I was blessed beyond measure. Not many people would've argued with me.

"You know, Donna, I should hate you," my best friend, Maggie, said as she helped me pack up all the gifts from the baby shower she had just thrown for me. "You have it all. You and Gabe are more in love than any two people have a right to be. You just moved into that beautiful house in Plainview, your promotion was announced last week, and I know you'll have the cutest baby in the world. Until I have one someday, of course. If I have one someday."

Pausing to stretch the kink out of my aching back, I couldn't help but smile at her. Tall and gorgeous, she had an air of elegance that could be intimidating. That persona served her well as a high-powered corporate attorney at the firm where we both hoped to make partner someday, but I knew her better than that. The real Maggie was the one who threw this shower together at the last minute, forgetting to order the cake, and mixing her themes so the room was decorated in a combination of Valentine hearts and football paraphernalia.

"Got it covered either way," she announced as the guests entered the room with quizzical looks on their faces. "Hearts for a girl, footballs if it's a boy. Or maybe vice versa. Who knows these days?" She grinned.

"Now, Maggie, dear, we know perfectly well that Donna is having a boy. And what is that outfit you're wearing supposed to be?" my mother asked.

I winced at Mom's imperious tone of voice. It was one she often used with my friend.

Her eyes sparkling with merriment, Maggie winked in my direction and turned to respond. "I was hoping someone would ask." She laughed. "I'm the Godmother, of course." Beaming with pride, she modeled her outfit–a brash display consisting of a pinstripe suit, spats, and a fedora. Sprouting from the back of the suit was a pair of sparkling fairy wings.

Not sure what to do or say next, Mother stalked into the living room and commandeered the large overstuffed chair that was reserved for me.

Somehow in the midst of party chaos, and with brownies instead of cake, Maggie pulled off a successful shower. Everyone seemed to enjoy themselves, and I got quite a stash of clothes and gadgets for the nursery.

"Donna, sit down. I'll get this stuff gathered up and Gabe can carry it all out to the car when he gets here. He can do his part in all this, too. Other than the part he already enjoyed, that is."

Easing myself into the chair abandoned by my mother, I slipped off my shoes. "Oh, that feels good," I said, massaging my swollen ankles. "I hope Gabe gets here soon. I'm ready for a nap. You'd think I was the one who did all the work here today but all I did was sit, open presents, and listen to all that conflicting advice. So tell me, what do you do for colic, anyway? Is it a hot water bottle to warm the tummy or more burping? Or is it changing the formula, or maybe it's going for a ride in the car so the automobile's vibration can have a soothing effect?"

"Well, personally, I'd opt for an apple martini and a backrub if I wanted a soothing effect, but everyone is different, I suppose," Maggie quipped.

"Make it a cold beer and a foot rub if you're talking about me," Gabe called out as he made his way into the room, almost tripping over a rapidly deflating balloon, its curly ribbon tail dragging along the floor.

"All right you two, very funny," I said. "But this is serious. Suddenly, I'm scared. I'm not ready to be anyone's mom. I don't know what to do if the baby gets sick, or even how to tell if he's sick or just wet or hungry. This baby is getting ready to be born and he has no idea what a bad mom he's going to be stuck with." My eyes filled with unexpected tears.

"Oh no, mother-to-be meltdown. Prepare to offer loving support," Gabe said as he moved to put his arms around me. "Babe, you're going to be the best mom in the whole world. You're loving and smart and funny and you work hard to be the best at everything you do. You have more experience than you give yourself credit for. Just look at how much more civilized I am these days. I put my dirty clothes in the hamper now, and I almost never burp in public anymore."

"Do you really think so?" I sniffed, wiping away a tear.

"Have you heard me burp today?"

"You know what I mean," I couldn't help snapping. "Do you think I can be a good mother?"

"I know you can," my husband assured me.

"Me, too," Maggie chimed in. "Don't get spooked now. This is the best time of all. This kid is going to adore you. You're going to be the best, the smartest, and the prettiest mom in the world. Right up to the time he hits thirteen. Then you'll be the biggest geek in the world and he'll be embarrassed to admit he knows you. That's when he'll turn to me for help. He'll tell me how hopelessly old-fashioned you both are and how lucky he is that I'm still cool. Because I will be, you know. And besides that, your kid isn't going to have colic. He's going to be perfect in every way."

Maggie was a wonderful friend, but she had absolutely no future as a fortune-teller.

Jacob G. Allen was born three days later. He was everything I hoped for. Gabe and I marveled over the perfection of his tiny hands and feet. We were awed by the responsibility we had just accepted, and we promised to keep him safe and happy forever.

"Oh, my, it's good to be home." I sighed, snuggling into Gabe's arms after our first full day alone with our baby.

"It's more than wonderful to have you both home. I missed you like crazy even if it was only a couple of days. This house seemed cold and very empty without you. Don't go away anymore," my husband whispered, planting a kiss on the end of my nose.

"I won't," I promised. "Both my guys are here. Where else would I want to be?"

"How are things with the new mom?" Maggie phoned the next morning. "I stayed away yesterday to give you guys a little time to yourselves, but I'm coming over later to hold my godson, and I'm bringing dinner, so don't cook."

"I think we're doing okay, but the little rascal was up most of the night. That's normal, I guess, and I'll be able to catch up on my sleep when he goes to college. Thanks for bringing dinner. I don't think I can find time for cooking in my schedule for a day or two."

"Problem?" Maggie asked.

"Jacob spits up a lot," I explained.

"All babies spit up."

"I know. But he spits up all the time. It worries me."

"What do you mean, all the time? He's only been home a day."

"I know, and I hate to sound like a whiner but he isn't eating right so he's hungry all the time and then when he does eat, he spits it up."

"He's not eating right?"

"He has a hard time latching onto my nipple and he doesn't get much nourishment."

"How can you tell how much he's getting?"

"Maggie, I know he's hungry. He cries until he's exhausted. I'm not doing it right, but I can't figure out what I'm doing wrong."

"Honey, this is all new to you and to him. Relax a little and give it some time. Talk to your pediatrician. It'll get easier once you get used to each other."

"I hope so. I've been around other babies and I've seen them spit up a bit from time to time. This is different."

"What does Gabe say?"

"He says the same things you do. He thinks I'm overreacting and worrying over nothing. He's wrong, and so are you."

The conversation was cut short by a plaintive wail, announcing that baby Jacob was awake and hungry.

"I have to go. I'll see you later, and thanks again for making dinner."

Dinner that evening was tense. No one could relax with the baby crying most of the time. I kept trying to feed him, only to watch him spit it right back up.

Maggie gave me a hug as she prepared to leave. "Call the doctor in the morning, get this checked out."

"I will, but I hate to come across as an over-anxious new mom."

"The best advice I can give you is to listen to your instincts. You're smart and capable, and you're this baby's mother. You know best. Call the doctor. I'll call tomorrow night to find out what she had to say."

"Thank you." I hugged her back. "I'm convinced this isn't normal, and it helps that you believe me."

"I believe in you, kiddo. Trust yourself."

"It's probably just a touch of colic," the doctor assured me. "But I am a little concerned about his weight loss. Most babies lose a little bit in the first few days, but we need to keep an eye on this. He should gain it back, plus some more. If he doesn't we may need to supplement the nursing with some formula."

"So you don't think I'm worrying over nothing?" I asked the pediatrician.

"I never think mothers worry over nothing," she said. "If a parent is concerned there is usually a reason for it. Very often it's not as serious as we tend to imagine, but usually there's something to it. Don't ever hesitate to let me know of your concerns. That's why I became a pediatrician."

"The doctor thinks it's a touch of colic," I reported to Gabe and to Maggie later that day.

"I guess that's not surprising," Gabe added. "My mother tells me I screamed almost non-stop for two months when I was a baby. She swears she could hear my cries echoing off the walls long after I finally exhausted myself, and her, too."

"I believe it," I told him. "It's so hard to hear your baby cry and not be able to do anything to help."

As if on cue, Jacob woke and began to wail.

"Here we go again," I told them.

"Here, let me hold him," Maggie offered. "Maybe I can soothe him a little and you can have a bit of a rest."

"I'll take you up on that offer. You can give him some water. See if that will stay down. I hope it's not my milk that's making him sick. I may have to put him on a bottle. I always wanted to nurse my babies, though. It seems more natural and cozy."

"Bottle feeding can be just as right and just as cozy when the one holding the bottle loves the baby as much as you do. Everything will okay, you'll see," Maggie tried to reassure me.

I wondered how she got to be so smart about all of this, and I had to hide a pang of jealousy as I watched my baby drift off to sleep in my friend's arms. He looked more peaceful and content than he ever did with me. Soon after that, Maggie put Jacob in his crib and whispered good-bye to us.

Gabe took me in his arms, holding me close. "Alone at last. Listen, do you hear that?"

"What?"

"The quiet. The baby is sleeping; the visitors are gone. It's just you and me."

"Feeling a bit neglected these days?" I asked him.

"Not exactly neglected, I'd say more kiss-deprived than anything. And hug-deprived, too. I'm really quite pitiful, and people are beginning to notice."

"They are? You poor man. I guess we better take this time to get you caught up. I think I'm feeling a little kiss-deprived myself now that you mention it."

It felt good to flirt with my husband again, and I vowed to do more of it in the days ahead.

"The formula isn't working," I told the doctor two weeks later. "Jacob is spitting up as much as he did before. Even more, I think, and he's lost more weight."

"We may have to try another formula. Sometimes it takes a bit of time to find the right one for a finicky baby."

"Finicky? My child is not finicky. He's hungry and he's tired and he's losing weight. You have to do something. You have to find out what's wrong. Run some tests or something."

"Now, let's not get too stressed out here. It's not good for you and it's not good for him. I've had good success with this brand of formula," she said as she handed me a sample can. "I'll give you these samples so you can get him started on it right away. Give me a call if you have any questions. I promise you, Donna, he's going to be fine. Sometimes colic can be hard to cope with, but it does go away eventually."

"Eventually," I fumed as I drove out of the office's parking lot and into the afternoon traffic. "I don't want it to go away eventually. I want it to go away now!"

Jacob began to cry again just as I pulled into our driveway. I felt my own tears mingling with his as I lifted him out of his carrier and held him close to me.

"I'll find out what's wrong with you, I promise," I whispered, kissing his tiny head and taking in the sweet smell of hair. "Mommy's here. Hush, sweet baby. Mommy and Daddy will take care of you."

Over the next few weeks we tried more formulas and followed every suggestion offered by well-meaning friends and family. Nothing helped and the spitting up turned to vomiting.

"Whoa!" Maggie exclaimed one evening as we sat in the den. Gabe had just finished feeding the baby when he let loose once again. "That must have gone six feet across the room! Is this baby possessed?"

"We've joked about that ourselves," Gabe replied. "But frankly we're scared. This isn't normal. This can't be colic. But what can it be?"

"Beats me. Have you considered changing doctors or getting a second opinion?" Maggie asked us.

"That's our next step," I told her. "We have an appointment tomorrow with Jacob's doctor. If we don't get any more advice than to change the formula again, I'm going to insist on tests. If she refuses, we move on to a doctor who will run them."

"Good for you. I admit that at first I thought it was new mother anxiety and things would settle down once you got more comfortable, but this has gone on too long. Promise you'll call me and let me know how it goes."

"I will, although I may not have to. You might hear me screaming all the way to your office if that's what it takes to get someone to listen to me."

Once again Jacob's doctor tried to reassure us that our son had a very stubborn case of colic, or maybe even reflux.

"As long as he's spitting up white stuff it's not likely to be anything serious. If it were green it would indicate bile is present. That would be a sign of a serious, even dangerous problem, such as a twisted or blocked bowel. I just don't see that here. Let's try one more formula change."

"No!"

"What do you mean, no?"

"I mean that I am not going to do this again. No more formula changes. No more let's wait and see. Today we either agree to run some tests or we get another doctor. I have to do this, I insist."

"Very well. I'll set it up. I want you to feel comfortable that your baby is getting proper care. Give me a few moments to make a call. We'll do an upper GI series. Then we can plan what to do next."

When the doctor returned to the examining room, she announced, "Good news, there's an opening at two o'clock at the radiology center right here in this building. You guys go get some lunch and then go right on up. They'll be expecting you."

We drove to the nearest diner. But neither Gabe nor I could eat; all we managed to do was push some food around on our plates and sip a bit of water.

"Let's just go there. Maybe they can take us a little early if we're sitting there in the waiting room," Gabe said, laying enough money on the table to cover the bill and a generous tip.

We actually had to wait until two-thirty before we were called into the examining room. Jacob would have to be fed a bottle of formula mixed with barium, which shows up on an X-ray. That way the doctor could see how the formula passed through his system.

"I want to watch," I told him.

"We both do," Gabe agreed, taking my hand.

Together we watched the formula go down through Jacob's stomach and hit the valve between his stomach and small intestine, where it stopped. Within mere seconds it came pushing back up and out, shooting across the room.

"This is no simple colic," the technician told us. "Wait right here."

Before we knew it, a radiologist had entered the room and Jacob's pediatrician had joined us.

"I just got the call," his doctor explained. "Jacob is very sick. You have to take him to the hospital immediately. He's going to need surgery."

"What is it? What's wrong with him?" I asked her.

"He has a condition called hypertrophic pyloric stenosis and we need to get him to the hospital. I'll explain more once we get there and the surgeon is with him."

As we raced to the hospital with our sick baby, we couldn't help but feel that we may have been able to avoid the urgency of this surgery if our child's doctor had only listened to us sooner.

I held my baby in my arms as we sped through traffic. I knew Jacob should be in the safety of his carrier, but I was too frightened to let go of him. While I sat in the backseat, Gabe drove through the lunch hour traffic, both of us praying that our baby would be all right.

The surgeon had been notified that we were coming and met us as soon as we checked in. He explained to us that Jacob would need surgery, but before we could proceed some tests had to be run. If Jacob proved to be dehydrated he would need some fluids before the operation.

A short time later Jacob was admitted onto the pediatric unit. A nurse was already hooking up his IV.

"He's dangerously dehydrated. It's a good thing you got him in here. Look how thin he is." She cast a disapproving look in our direction.

I wanted to tell her that we tried to get someone to listen long before this, but it really didn't matter what she thought. I had enough to worry about without concerning myself with her.

Knowing that worried parents never want to be too far from their sick child, the hospital provided a cot for us. Gabe and I alternated trying to sleep while the other watched over our son.

In the morning, both of Jacob's grandmothers and his godmother joined us to hear an explanation of the procedure that would be performed. It would finally allow our son to get the nutrition he needed to live and grow normally.

"Between the stomach and the small intestine is an area called the pyloric muscle," the surgeon began. "When it works right, this muscle opens and closes to help empty the stomach into the small intestine. In some babies, the muscle enlarges and gets thick. The middle part gets narrower and narrower, it may even close completely. When that happens, any food the baby swallows has nowhere to go and it gets pushed back out, pretty forcefully at times."

"We know all about that," I assured the doctor.

"I'm sure you do." He smiled. "What I'm going to do is a procedure called pyloromyotomy. I'm going to make an incision in Jacob's belly button and cut the thickened pyloric muscle. I'm going to split it partway through. Then I'm going to separate the split muscle, leaving the inner lining intact, and making room for food to pass through to the small intestine where it can be processed as it should be."

"How dangerous is this procedure?" Gabe asked, the fear in his voice echoing my own.

"I know that you two are going to worry no matter what I tell you. There is some danger, just as there is in any surgery, but this is a safe and relatively easy procedure. There can be complications, such as accidental perforation of the stomach or small intestine, but they are very rare. Now that we have the laparoscopic technique available, we make a tiny incision in his belly button."

"How long will he be in surgery, Doctor"?

The doctor cast a quizzical look first at my mother and then at me before answering.

"It's okay," I explained to him. "This is my mother."

I proceeded to introduce the doctor to Gabe's mother and to Maggie.

"It will take between half an hour and forty-five minutes," the doctor explained. "I love doing this operation," he told us. "Hey, don't look at me like that," he joked. "It's not that I like to see sick babies, no one likes that. But I do like fixing them. In these cases, a critically ill baby is wheeled into the operating room, and in about thirty minutes he's completely cured. How great is that? Jacob will be able to eat within a few hours, and he can go home in a day or two."

"And then what?" Maggie asked.

The doctor looked at her a moment. "What do you mean?"

"Will he be on a restricted diet? Or some kind of special formula? Will he be able to eat hot dogs and popcorn and stuff like that when he gets bigger and I take him to the ballgame?"

"His digestion will be completely normal within a few days. He may spit up a bit from time to time, but he won't have the vomiting problem anymore. No special formula, no special diet. As for the hot dogs and popcorn, peanuts and candy, I'll defer to his mom on that. It sounds pretty good to me, though."

The hardest thing I'd ever done in my life was to hand my precious baby over to the nurse to be wheeled into the operating room.

"He's going to be okay, isn't he, Gabe?"

"He's going to be better than okay," my husband assured me. "He's going to be perfect, just like we always knew he would be."

"I wonder what caused it? Maybe I did something I shouldn't have when I was carrying him. Or didn't do something I should've. What if it happens again? What if we have more children and it happens to them, too!"

"Hold on, don't go getting carried away," Gabe's mother spoke up as she entered the waiting area. "I was on the Internet last night to see if I could find anything on this condition and there is a lot of information out there. Here, take a look at this." She handed me a sheaf of papers she'd printed quoting a pediatric surgeon at another hospital.

"It says here that they see as many as thirty cases of this a year. Usually in boys. In fact, it is most common in first-born males."

"Do you think Matthew might have had it?" Gabe asked his mom.

Matthew was Gabe's oldest brother; he died tragically of SIDS when he was only a few weeks old.

"Maybe," his mother answered. "We'll never know. He did spit up a lot and he had colic. But then again, so did you."

"There appears to be some indication that it can be passed on from one generation to the next," I read aloud. "It also says that some doctors think that if a nursing mother uses some types of antibiotics they might pass through the breast milk to the baby, making the child more at risk for stenosis. It mentions erythromycin here as one of them. But I haven't been taking anything at all."

"Nope, she hasn't," Maggie added. "I couldn't even tempt her with an aspirin when she had a headache. I wonder if it can come back again. Does that paper say anything about reoccurrence after surgery?"

"Yes, it says it's very rare. It also says that most cases of this disease are mistaken for colic or an allergy to formula. It takes a while for the muscle to thicken, so the onset is gradual, from spitting up to throwing up and then projectile vomiting. Everything that happened to Jacob, right down the line."

"And he's going to recover fully, too, just as it says here," my mom predicted.

She was right. He was in his recovery room within two hours. Shortly after that he was pink and cooing at us. Almost as if to say, "I'm fine now; when's lunch going to be here?"

Gabe and I took turns sleeping and watching over him through the night, but this time it was easier. Jacob was thriving. We took him home three days later.

Over the next few weeks, he continued to improve. He gained weight and began to sleep through the night. His smile came much more often than his cry. It was a real miracle, one I would be grateful for the rest of my life.

"Now our life really is perfect," I whispered as Gabe and I watched our baby sleep. "Can you believe it? He's had a full bottle three times today and not so much as a hiccup. A burp or two, but no hiccup."

"Better yet, no belly blaster across the room." Gabe grinned. "Now, how about some dinner for us? I'd love to take you to a fancy restaurant to enjoy some wine and some candlelight. I think I know where I can find a sitter on short notice. One with a pinstriped suit and glittery wings. What's Maggie's number again?" he asked.

THE END